THE GIFT

KATE ANSLINGER

LIGHTHOUSE PEN, LLC

THE GIFT

BY KATE ANSLINGER

For my mother, the lover of twists and turns

GRACE

I always knew I was different. My mother said that while other babies enter the world screaming, I was presented to her with a smile on my face and a look of calm in my dark, ocean-blue eyes. That was before they turned green and before I knew that I had a gift. Mom said that when she first held me, I looked up at the ceiling as if I was staring at something that made me unbelievably happy. Within minutes of being born, my tiny hands reached toward the light in the delivery room as a look of contentment swept across my face. The peace in my eyes was like nothing that she had ever seen before and because of that, she asked the nurses if I was healthy.

"Why isn't she crying?" she shouted at the nurses in a panic as she looked down at me with her own frightened green eyes. The nurses confirmed that I was fine and that all my physical tests and response times were average, if not above. They told her that some babies just don't cry at first.

They assured my mother that, one day, I would find my voice.

CHAPTER ONE

GRACE MCKENNA WAS ONLY THREE YEARS OLD WHEN THE FIRST VISION catapulted her into what her mother assumed was a really bad tantrum. They had been walking down Main Street in Wentworth, a small Massachusetts town that boasted the best holiday shopping. It was almost Christmas, and Grace had been mesmerized by the colossal Christmas tree on display at the center of the bustling ice skating rink.

"Wait right there, Grace. Don't move," her mother said, as she turned toward the clerk at one of the stands selling homemade Christmas ornaments. Her mother kept one eye on her and one eye on the clerk as her hand navigated through her tattered faux leather fringe purse to retrieve her last five-dollar bill to purchase the glittery ornament. Money was low as it always had been, but Ellen McKenna did her best with what she had and was determined to make Christmas special for her daughter. The small, artificial Charlie Brown tree that they had at home had been swiped from a dumpster after the holidays last year, and Ellen used what few ornaments had been handed down to her. She couldn't leave the rest of the tree bare, so she hung silver measuring spoons from the scrawny branches, showing her daughter that they didn't need to spend a fortune to add some shine and sparkle to their lives.

"Mama! Look!" Grace yelled, pointing to a little girl who was twirling effortlessly in the center of the skating rink in a short pale-blue skirt, shimmery tights and a sparkly turtleneck sweater.

"I'll be right there, sweetie," Ellen said as she watched the clerk wrap the ice skater figurine ornament, complete with tissue paper and a sparkly red bow. Grace fell in love with watching the skaters glide across the ice, their ribbons trailing from their heads like the dolls she thought they were. Her eyes followed the skater in the blue skirt as she used a toned leg to push off the icy surface and accelerate across the rink and into the arms of a boy who skated with as much finesse as she did. She positioned herself in front of him, their arms linking as they soared across the ice arm in arm, creating a dance to the background music of Sinatra's voice bellowing "I'll be home for Christmas."

"Do you want to be an ice skater someday?" A man's voice pulled Grace from the trance. Startled, she dug her hands deeper into the pockets of her red hand-me-down pea coat. One of the big black buttons on the pocket dangled by a thread, partly from her habit of twirling them when she was nervous and partly from the wear and tear of a winter coat worn by several children before her.

As a little girl, Grace was painfully shy. Had her mom been within a few feet, she would've darted to her and maneuvered her way between her legs, using them as a security blanket in which she could wrap herself to get away from the stranger. Instead, she slowly looked up at the man, the owner of the deep scruffy voice that interrupted her concentration on the dancing skaters. She parted her lips to speak; the few sentences that she could put together at her young age mashed together and clogged her thoughts. Her wide-set green eyes, innocent until that moment, widened and latched onto his as if being pulled into a tunnel. Their eyes locked like two forces of opposite energies, hers pure and green, and his bloodshot, brown, and filled with corruption.

Maybe her first vision was the worst simply because it was the first, and it transformed the clarity of her innocence into a murky mess, having wiped her clean of any natural thoughts she had yet to form. Or maybe it really was the worst. It started with the body of a fair-skinned woman being dragged across muddied earth, the kind that is usually the result of a rainy spring day. Bursts of the woman's placid face flashed in and out like a blinking light. Grace was only three years old, but she was old enough to have the innate ability to know wrong from right; something about these images left a sick feeling in her stomach. A flash of red hair splayed across the woman's emaciated face, chunks of crusty mud cemented into the corners of her mouth and deep into the hollows of her eyes. Dried blood left a line of color down the woman's ashen body, starting at the neck and dipping between her breasts, ending at a jutting hipbone. A flash of the woman's face, displaying a pair of terrified eyes just seconds before a knife ran the length of her neck, leaving a neat slice for a pool of blood to spill out and onto her sharp collar bone. The images didn't come in order, but rather in short bursts of disarray.

The vision made Grace emit a high-pitched scream.

"Grace!" Ellen looked up from her interaction with the clerk and ran over. The freshly wrapped ornament fell to the ground, landing on a bed of fake cotton snow that enveloped the outside of the skating rink. Completely unaware of the man, she ran right past him, nearly jabbing his burly body with an elbow. By the time Ellen reached Grace, the little girl was lying on the ground flailing her limbs in protest, as if someone was holding her down against her will.

"Grace! Grace, honey, what's the matter?" Ellen's voice escalated.

As a crowd started to gather around the scene, the man meandered away, hidden by the puffy winter coats and hats of the audience.

The visions kept coming, flashes of crime that infiltrated Grace's mind. The red-haired woman's naked body being pulled and dropped into a pool of murky water. Her red hair fanning out above the smooth black pool, making her look like a mystical mermaid. Her eyes were closed, a look of peace masking a face that had just witnessed her own murder. And then a flash of her sinking.

"Grace! Please, honey, what happened? Did something happen?"

Ellen looked up at the audience, seeking witnesses who saw the start of her daughter's breakdown. "I just looked away for a second!" she shouted, feeling the need to defend herself. "Grace! Baby, what happened?" She cradled Grace's little body in her arms, pulling the peacoat closed where it had been torn open from the jerking movements of her daughter's arms and legs.

"The man." Grace pointed a delicate finger toward the crowd, as heads swiveled in search of a mystery man. When no one came forward as a witness, the crowd opened up and dispersed, going back to their Christmas shopping.

"Maybe you should pay more attention to your child," a heavyset woman said as she waddled by. Her eyes were so small, they looked like two raisins pushed into her head.

"Dude, that was weird," said a teenage boy to his friend. "Maybe she's like that chick in *Poltergeist*. She looked possessed."

"That man is bad, mommy," Grace said between bouts of shaky sniffles.

"What man, honey? Which man is bad?" Ellen asked, shaking off the comment of another passerby who accused Grace of seeing ghosts.

"He's gone. I don't see him anymore." Grace craned her neck, looking beyond the elegant skaters who hadn't missed a step in their routine. They soared across the ice like figurines in the center of a snow globe, far from the world Grace had just witnessed.

"Baby, are you sure you saw a man? What did he look like?" Ellen asked, trying her hardest to push out any doubt that had surfaced. Grace had a tendency to be a creative little girl, often having tea parties with invisible friends, but she'd never gone to extremes like this, especially in such a public place. She was painfully shy and did anything she could to divert attention from herself. "Honey, was the man one of your invisible friends?"

"No, mommy. The man is bad. He hurt the girl." Grace's voice was still slightly heightened by her adrenaline.

"Honey, let's go home." Ellen had reached her limit. Now there was a girl, too. Surely Grace was making this one up. She turned, remembering the ornament she had dropped, but there was no trace of the shiny red package.

After the incident at the ice skating rink, Ellen put every earned penny toward psychologists, behavioral specialists and psychics on a mission to find out what her daughter was seeing and if her behavior was normal. Nearly every shrink said that Grace was lonely and using her imagination to build worlds inside her head. The behavior specialists claimed that Grace's "visions" were normal and it just meant that she was searching for more attention. "This behavior is quite common in single-parent homes," one specialist told her. The psychics went to the opposite extreme, saying that Grace had powers from the other side and for ten more dollars they could tell her what her daughter should do next to protect herself from the visions and evil that were headed her way. Ellen became fed up that no one was taking her seriously; she was determined to keep at it, believing the girl and standing by her when everyone else thought she was a freak.

While not a religious person, Ellen had a childhood friend who went on to become a priest at a church in Boston. As a last resort, Ellen brought five-year-old Grace to Father Burke, begging him to see her and give her an explanation. His response had been the most simple and straightforward: "Grace has been chosen as the recipient of a special gift. She was created by God to see visions of sinners. There are people of all backgrounds who have used meditation and hypnotic tools to receive the gift that Grace has naturally been given." Father Burke said the words calmly, as if he were talking to a friend about the weather. He was the first person to treat them with respect.

He told Ellen that Grace's visions were called "pictures," and that based on his experience, these pictures would contain one scene and usually appear in a flash without prior notice. "It happens very quickly," he said, "and the images will remain just long enough for Grace to notice them before they vanish." Ellen nodded. "When God gives you a gift, you are to use it and share it with the world—to help others. So, my advice to you is to take these visions and piece them together to bring down the sinners. I know it's not the easiest thing to do, but I'm sure Grace will find a way."

Father Burke passed away from a heart attack only two years after their initial meeting. With Grace too young to understand, Ellen saved his words of advice and gently nudged Grace throughout her life, pushing her daughter to get involved in the world of law enforcement where she could use her gift to help people.

CHAPTER TWO

GRACE TRAVELED THE WINDING ROADS TO WORK, FAMILIAR BUMPS AND dips paving her way through the colorful fall Massachusetts' country-side. The tree limbs reached for the road, creating a tunnel of red, yellow and orange, a clear sign that it was fall, with winter just around the corner. She never got bored on her route to work. The trees always greeted her like old friends, cheering her on at the sidelines of a race. She wrapped her hand around the stick shift like a bird-claw grasping its prey, the smoothness of the leather calming the inevitable nerves she experienced before starting every shift at the police station.

When Grace was in college, a psychology teacher taught the class about a neurological phenomenon called Synesthesia. The teacher stood in front of the class and passionately described the phenomenon as being a stimulation of one sensory or cognitive pathway that leads to involuntary experiences of another sensory or cognitive pathway. It wasn't until this class that Grace realized she possessed the phenomenon.

For as long as she could remember, the feel of leather always made her revert to a place of calm. She first discovered the sensation when she sat on her mother's black leather couch in one of the many apartments they lived in outside of Boston. It was the nineties, when frumpy leather couches were considered modern and hip. She had only been about fifteen years old when her mother told her who her biological father was. As Ellen told the story about how she was the product of a violent rape, Grace pressed her sweaty palms into the couch, and gripped the black leather so tightly that she was afraid her hot-pink nails would tear the material. She had sensed a simultaneous calm, which she would later discover as the result of contact with the leather. She had sat quietly, trying to breathe, her rigid teenage body perched on the edge of the couch, leaning forward and staring at the mauve carpet. Tears slowly appeared at the corner of her eyes, though she tried her best to refrain from crying.

Her mother had always been her role model, providing a mold that she had so badly wanted to contort her own world to fit into. Ellen McKenna had been a bit of a free spirit, straying from a straight line, while Grace lived her life more rigid, thriving in the presence of rules and direction, but that didn't stop the two women from forming a rare bond of opposites. Straight-laced Grace McKenna was the product of a violent and tragic crime, but her mother had assured her that she was still the best thing that ever happened to her. While she had hid the truth for the first fifteen years of her daughter's life, Ellen felt that Grace, who was always far more mature than her age, was old enough to know.

For years, Grace had asked why there was never a man around to take out the trash, guide her in a daddy-daughter dance or be a master griller in the summer months. Ellen would always come back at her with a well-thought-out response. She had claimed that she only knew him that one night for about thirty minutes before they engaged in a heated romance that lasted only until the next morning at dawn. Knowing the carefree persona of her mother, Grace didn't find the story anything but believable. Every time her mother told this story, she would have a faraway look in her eyes, the white around her pale green irises transforming to a shade of red, tears coming to life in the corners. Grace had assumed it was her mother's heightened emotion, Ellen having always been a firm believer in showing authenticity with one's feelings.

When Grace was greeted by the usual surge of emotions in her pre-teen years, Ellen had been sure to educate her on the importance of owning one's feelings.

"Gracie, are you sad today?" Ellen had asked through the partly cracked door to her daughter's room one Saturday afternoon. Grace had been paralyzed by a broken heart, refusing to do anything but lie in bed listening to Sinead O'Connor on repeat as she sulked about being dumped by a seventh-grade bad boy.

"Leave me alone, mom," Grace said, maintaining a sullen stare on the pale blue wall in front of her bed.

"Grace Hope McKenna, what I'm about to say to you is going to help you get through the rest of your life, so listen up." Ellen eased her way into the room, and folded her tall form into a sitting position at the end of the bed. "Emotions can be uncomfortable—debilitating, even. And there is nothing wrong with any particular emotion. But one thing that you need to do is accept them. You are not flawed because Bobby whatshisname dumped you. It's not your problem, it's his. Stop blaming yourself for other people's cruelty." Ellen regurgitated the words like a trained psychologist as she gripped Grace's foot, a lump in the pastel quilt her daughter was swaddled in.

As if a firecracker was set off in her head, Grace's eyes darted to her mother's, making a connection that she would take with her for the rest of her life. From that moment, Grace learned how to accept and understand her emotions before separating herself from them. Not long after that, Ellen told her about her father and how for years, while she was traumatized by the event, she had learned that she was not responsible for other people's actions, and when possible, to make the best out of every situation.

Learning that her father was a rapist was like being told that she was infected with a contagious disease. She felt dirty. And, for the first time, Grace looked at her mother as broken, instead of the fun-loving, quirky woman who had always danced while cleaning and dropped Grace off at school within seconds of the bell ringing. While she never had an activity calendar posted with highlighted events, and almost always sent Grace to parties and school with store-bought treats instead of homemade, Ellen knew how to love her daughter and she did so with every fiber of her being. Ellen hadn't missed a single one of Grace's sporting events, recitals or school plays. While she may look disheveled and typically trickled in at the last minute when there was standing room only, Grace could always count on her mother to be standing in the back of the auditorium or gym in her post office uniform. Her shirt would be un-tucked, her arms wrapped around a small gift that would inevitably be wrapped in leftover postal packaging.

According to her mother, Grace's father never got caught, at least publicly, and Ellen never saw the man again. Like a ghost, he was without a face and name; almost as quickly as he tore apart Ellen's life, he was gone. For years, Ellen had checked with the police officer on duty who had taken her report the night of the rape. Fresh on the force at the time, Adam Mullen was a rookie who was dead set on finding the rapist. He was determined to make his career notable. After a year, he moved on to other cases, but he still kept in touch with Ellen, usually to relay the same information—the description that she gave to the police never showed up in the police blotter of Clayton, Massachusetts. Clayton was the town where she had been the night of the rape. She was attending an evening theater arts class at the local community college down the street from her parents' house. Not more than five minutes before the attack, she had said good night to her acting partner and current flame. She walked to her car alone in the dark, toward the lot that was designated for part-time students. Her attacker didn't even try to sneak up on her. He had just walked up to her and grabbed her like he was staking his claim.

It wasn't hard for him to have his way with her; although she was feisty, she was a tiny little thing, much like she was as a middle-aged woman—birdlike and frail. Ellen didn't know for certain, but from the way he forced himself upon her body, tackling it like she was his prey, she was pretty sure that he had raped several women. It was obvious that he didn't have his heart set on her, like he was thirsty for only this body. She just happened to be the weak and unaware college student who was walking through the parking lot on that specific night.

While Ellen endured nightmares and mental trauma for years, she said that it was a blessing in disguise because she ended up with a beautiful baby girl who she could mold and teach about the good in the world. At the time, Ellen had been working at the local pub and attending her acting classes with the hope of becoming a Hollywood actress. She had been somewhat of a hippy and believed in things happening for a reason, which is why she kept and raised Grace on her own. Every now and then, Grace could see that faraway look in her eyes. It spread across her face in only a matter of seconds, and left a glaze that stayed behind long after. Before Grace discovered that she was the product of a violent act, she had attributed the look in her mother's eyes to her aloof, oftentimes spacey personality.

Gripping the leather on the stick shift on her commute to work calmed Grace the same way that it did on that day in 1996. Grace molded her hand around the stick shift, her wheels hugging the sides of the worn sidewalks that flanked the streets of Cabotville, where she lived. The town was far enough away from the police department to not run into locals when she went to the grocery store in her pajamas, yet close enough to avoid the traffic that is commonplace for anyone who lives within ten miles of Boston.

Grace worked in Bridgeton, a small beach town, and lived in Cabotville, an even smaller town on the opposite side of the tracks. With only one small city between work and home, Cabotville contained all the staples she needed to survive, including the Cabotville House of Pizza, where she got a free slice nearly every week for filling up her punch card. As if the town were designed solely for Grace, it contained a posh pet parlor, a coffee shop that offered up the strongest cup of espresso, and a quirky little second-hand shop that her mother frequented. On occasion, Ellen volunteered at the shop, providing her expertise on various tchotchkes to the locals.

Cabotville was exactly where Grace wanted to be when she slept, ate and went about her quiet life.

DIRT AND ROCKS crunched and hissed beneath the tires of her silver Jeep Cherokee, a gift Grace gave herself for getting promoted to detective two years ago. She swerved to avoid the memorized potholes on the road that intersected with the street the Bridgeton Police Department resided on. As she rested her hand on the lid of her travel coffee mug, a drop of hot liquid splashed up, hitting her palm. She took a deep breath and looked in the rearview mirror as she watched the tree-lined roads behind her disappear, then looked up ahead to the cement wall that carved out the sandy outline of the beach and the colorful clusters of houses that made a crease in the landscape. Small storefronts started to come to life, as lights flickered on like little bursts of sunlight on a cloudy day. Gus Wiley waved from his donut shop as he turned the sign on the front door from "Closed" to "Open." As Grace merged onto Main Street, she jerked the car to steer clear of two construction cones glowing against the early morning darkness. An unfamiliar green pickup truck pulled out from one of the narrow side streets that meets Main Street, cutting her off. The truck carved its own path in front of her, elevating her heart rate and waking her up faster than the coffee.

"What the hell!" She swerved to the right, gripping the steering wheel with both hands, her right hand slick with wet coffee, the cup tipped on its side on the floor from the sharp jerk and twist of the Jeep. Before she could catch her breath, the green truck was gone, as if she had imagined the whole thing. She pulled off to the side of the road, up against the beach wall to catch her breath. Her nerves were jumpy from the flash of fear that surged through her body. Had Grace been in a police car, she would've started a chase, but she'd already been reprimanded a handful of times for working off duty. The need to protect ran rampantly through her blood—there was no off switch, no removing the thoughts that swam through her mind splashing around the why's and how's of criminal psychology. She inhaled deeply, holding it in for a solid five seconds before she released her breath, slow and controlled, creating a fog on the windshield. She pressed her hand against the cold glass and softened away the blur.

"Let's try this again," she said to herself as she used a shaking hand to adjust the rearview mirror.

CHAPTER THREE

Grace hoisted her bulky bag across her chest, headed across the parking lot and swiped her fob to gain access to the station, her second home.

"Good morning Barb." She held up a messy coffee cup in a wave to the station's veteran receptionist. Barbara O'Connor had been at the station for over forty years—or as she put it, since before she lost her virginity. While Barb wasn't the classiest gal around, she was proficient as hell and knew the town inside and out. Not only was she good with directions, but she knew all of the little nooks and crannies when it came to the best dive-restaurants and pubs. The officers relied on her for tidbits of information that weren't common knowledge. She loved to surprise outsiders with juicy tales of town gossip and the town's history that seemed to forever live on in her heart. Barb had been born and raised in South Boston, so her knowledge extended beyond the small town of Bridgeton and well into the depths of the city, involving anything from old school crimes to up and coming city socialites.

"Good morning, Princess." Her head remained down, enthralled in a newspaper article. Frizz coiled off of her curly red bob. Her fingers danced on the desk, long red fake nails drumming the old metal desktop. A gold chain dipped from both ends of her black-rimmed glasses, keeping them adhered to her at all times.

"Can you believe this? They're getting rid of Bruce's Market down on Franklin Street! I've been going there since I was five. My mother used to send me there for milk and eggs. You know back in my day, it was okay to send your kid to the store for a few groceries. Didn't have to worry about all of these child abductions and weirdos stealing kids. Where am I gonna get my baked goods now?" She continued to look down intently on the paper while rambling on. "You know, I tell ya, this city is going down the shitter. I wouldn't be surprised if they decided to put some drug-infested night club there in its place."

By the time Barb looked up from the newspaper, Grace had already logged into her computer and was sitting comfortably in her chair with the office door wide open so she could still listen to Barb's rants. Her office was not far from the control room and Barb's desk, which was basically the hub of the station.

Barb spun around in her chair and faced Grace's office door. "We did drugs in my day, but it wasn't like today where these kids are overdosing and girls are making out with other girls." She shook her head in disgust. "At least in my day, we had some class about it. We got dressed up, made a real night out of it, ya know?" She looked off into space as if caught in a dream.

"When are you going to bring in those pictures of you in 'your day' that you promised? I'm dying to see you in action, Barb." Grace's words snapped her out of her trance.

"Hey, did you have any hot dates this weekend, Princess?" Barb asked, jumping to a different subject. The good thing about Barb was that she would never get stuck on one topic for too long. The woman bounced from subject to subject as if she were a ball being paddled in a game of Ping-Pong.

"Nope. Just some late night pizza with Brody." The words shot out of Grace, practiced and rehearsed. These were the same words she said to Barb every Monday morning. Brody was her eight-year-old Newfoundland. He was also her boyfriend, as far as most of the people she worked with were concerned. When she rescued him four years earlier, she had decided to give him a human name so people would think that she was spending time with a man, and she would have little explaining to do when it came to her lack of love life. Barb caught on quickly, though. The woman was smarter than she looked. She always had one ear on the job, with the other ear opened to the gossip and drama in the station.

Not only had Barb been at the station for eons, but she was a master at keeping secrets. Over the years, she had built up the trust of the officers and somehow became the resident counselor. Often, she could be found at an officer's desk, nodding intently with a furrowed brow and arms across her chest or hands planted on her plump hips. She knew more about the staff than the mice that frequented the crevices of the building. But she was brimming with loyalty, which was why she never told even the deepest, darkest secrets the officers shared. She kept her lips sealed as tight as a cork in a brand new bottle of wine.

"Oh Princess, when are you going to take advantage of your youth and get out there and meet a man?" She strutted toward Grace's office door, welcomed herself in and plopped herself down on the desk calendar, cheeks spilling over the edge of the desk. "I mean really—get the gettin' while the gettin's good, if ya know what I mean." She lowered her glasses, and the metal chain swung them side-to-side until they settled on her bosom. She gave Grace a wink, hopped up off the desk and gave a double pump with her fists while thrusting her pelvis.

"I don't need any *gettin*, Barb. I've got Brody as my companion." Grace picked up the small square frame from her desk and showed her the smiling, slobbery Newfoundland staring back, his pink tongue nearly touching the bib hung across his neck. "See, the perfect man— he's happy, he doesn't talk and he snuggles for endless hours at a time."

"Oh for the love of Pete!" Barb pried the frame out of Grace's hand, gripping it with her stubby, turquoise-ringed fingers. "This is ridiculous! Did you make this frame?" She flicked the back of her hand toward the photo and used her nail to pick at the fluorescent puffy paint that said "Brody" in messy cursive scrawl.

"What? I was doing a craft project with my little sister!" Grace defended herself.

"Wait a minute, I thought you were an only child?" Barb put the frame back down on the desk and rested her arms across her chest like two beefy sausages.

"I *am* an only child. I'm a volunteer with Big Brothers Big Sisters." Grace reached into the top drawer of her desk and plucked a small rectangular photo out of the compartment that held pens and pencils. "This is Sasha, my little sister." She used her fingers to accentuate the quote around sister. "I meet with her twice a month. Take her on little dates to the movies, out to lunch. Stuff like that." Barb held the school photo in front of them, Sasha's half smile and squinty brown eyes look back as if pleading for a friend. Her brown hair was pulled back into a messy half-ponytail, and uneven, overgrown bangs settled across her forehead. The purple-beaded necklace they'd made on one of their dates rested on her tattered hand-me-down sweater.

"Well, well, why am I not surprised that you volunteer your time to help a kid? You're a good duck, Princess, you know that?" She handed the photo back and slid herself off the desk, her clogs making a smacking sound as they hit the linoleum floor.

"I try my best, Barb."

"For real though, will you please just go on one measly date with my nephew, Eric? He's a good kid. Hard worker. Works for that big construction company that's working on those new condos over by Faneuil Hall. I'm not a huge fan of the fact that they're destroying my favorite little businesses so yuppies can move in from the Midwest pretending they're all Boston and whatnot but—"

"Fine, Barb. I'll go on a date with your nephew," Grace broke into her babbling. Maybe if she went on one date, it would get Barb and everyone else out of her hair. The kid was related to Barb, so he must have some good in him.

"Well, I'll be damned!" Barb did a double take, before slapping her hand on the metal desk and nearly falling over in her chair. "The angels in heaven must be singing, our very own Grace McKenna is going on a date—with a man!"

"Slow down . . . I'll only meet him for coffee. No cocktails. The last time I did that, I ended up having to drive the guy home and tuck him into bed. That was after he told me he loved me after I'd only known him for three hours," Grace said.

"Well, I can assure you that Eric won't be pre-gaming before the date or drinking during. You see, he's got a bit of a problem, but he's been sober for four years. Really been hitting up those AA meetings for youngsters."

"Barb!" Grace said to the back of the woman's red head as she turned away to tend to some files. "What else do you need to warn me about?" She jumped up from her desk, marched to Barb's cube and tugged at her arms so they were face to face.

"Nothing. He's a good kid. It's just . . . well, he has a couple kids of his own, too." Her hazel eyes darted side-to-side, looking for any place other than Grace to settle on. "Just two. They're around five or maybe ten, I'm not sure. I'm so bad with ages . . . and kids." She locked her eyes on Grace's. "Listen, can you just give the kid a chance? He's had a rough go of it. First the drinking thing, now his ex is trying to gain full custody of those kids and I know how much he loves those girls. Two beautiful daughters that he adores. Just one date. If anything, it'll boost his self esteem."

"Okay, fine. One date," Grace said, having succumbed to Barb's nagging. Barb was a good woman and has done her fair share of helping Grace with cases. She went above and beyond her job to help, always ready to do some fact-checking or criminal research.

As always before meeting someone for the first time, Grace was enveloped in fear that she would have a vision when she met the guy. Her visions tended to be more of a problem than a gift, which is why she lived life like a hermit, staying confined to the privacy of work and surrounding herself with people she knew didn't have a secret crime-filled past. For the longest time, her mother had used her gift to filter through her long line of gentleman callers. She would have Grace come over to her house for their arrival, acting as the daughter who just happened to stop by. Grace's only job was to shake their hands, make eye contact and, if nothing bad flashed before her eyes upon these gestures, her mother was free to continue with her night on the town.

Only once did her gift intervene in a bad date. Grace hadn't even had to shake the guy's hand to know that he was bad news. As soon as he walked through the threshold of her mother's house, she could feel the negative vibes wafting off of him. They had been so strong that if she could actually see the bad aura, she imagined him to be encased in a black cloud that followed him around everywhere. She didn't want to shake his hand, let alone make eye contact, but she had made a promise that she'd use her gift on her mother's man-finding project, a project that she herself had been the original backer of. As soon as she gripped his hand and sealed her eyes onto his, she was enveloped in visions of violence.

From what Grace could gather, the guy had beaten every girlfriend he ever had. A vision of him choking a blonde woman presented itself to Grace as she looked into his hooded brown eyes. His eyes were prettier than one could imagine for a criminal, dark and long-lashed in a way that could easily entice women. He could charm the pants off any woman he encountered, which is why when the vision came through, it came in the form of numerous flashes, like a camera taking a burst of action shots. The longer Grace stared into his eyes, the more of his history rose to the surface like a diver coming up for air. He slapped a red-haired woman across the face so many times that her pale skin matched the pigment of her long, flowing mane. A brunette with sad brown eyes seemed to be the victim of the worst abuse. He clocked her in the head with a gun, and she fell to the ground unconscious. That was all that Grace saw before her mother sidled up beside her and asked her if she was having Rizzo's for dinner. Rizzo's was the local restaurant that Grace ordered from far too much. If Grace answered "yes," then her mother could be sure that her date was free from a seedy past and go about her business. If Grace responded with "no, not tonight," then Ellen would suddenly come down with an illness. This man was the only one who she had to fake an ailment for, and it was rather awkward, but it may have saved her mother's life.

Ellen thought that her daughter had a gift, but at times it could be a curse. Grace didn't want to see the painful things that people did or be pulled into a past of violence, all the while seeing the person walk through life lying to everyone with ease and charm. This was the reason Grace didn't go on her own dates; it's the reason why, when she was off duty, she secluded herself. It was also one of the many reasons why she became a cop. Ellen had guided her to the career path, steadfast in her belief that her daughter had been given the gift for a reason and that she should use it to help people.

Grace dived into the pile of files on her desk, making calls and searching for updates on pending cases. She didn't necessarily have the urge to throw someone behind bars, but a good newsworthy case was certainly something that kept her up at night. Instead, she flipped through shoplifters, ticket-dodgers and files that were too minimal to spike her adrenaline. Just as she was about to get up for another cup of coffee, her desk phone rang. The red light designated for Chief Welch blinked rapidly.

"Good morning, Chief." Even though she had already been there for three hours, it was still early morning for some people and the station was just starting to get busy.

"Detective McKenna. How are you this morning?" Her boss's steady voice came through the receiver.

"I'm good. How are you?" Grace went along with his small talk, eager to hear what he had to say. It could be the most time-sensitive matter, but he made it a point to always establish a proper greeting, appearing calm and collected at all times. Jimmy Welch had been the chief for nearly ten years, on the force himself for at least twenty, and not many of the officers could say they had once seen him raise his voice or show a hint of anger. He could be completely calm while reprimanding an officer, as if there were no distinction between doing something wrong and having a conversation about the weather. The time that he reprimanded Grace for working off duty, one would've thought he was inviting her over for dinner, his eyes always making direct contact and his words as even and soft-spoken as a hypnotist's. Chief Welch had four daughters and one son, all under sixteen years old. Grace guessed that his wife was the loud and feisty one, because too much calm in one home couldn't be good.

"I'm good, I'm good. I know you're always eager for a new case and something just came in that I think is right for you. Do you have a moment to chat now?"

"Yes. Yes, of course." Grace tried to tone down her excitement.

"Okay, great. Why don't you come by my office in ten minutes? I just have to fix myself another cup of coffee."

"Great! See you then." Grace hung up, embarrassed for sounding so eager. She'd always been cautious of the other officers thinking she was a suck-up, as she tended to go a little overboard when it came to pleasing authority. Admittedly, it was one of her downfalls. She was a hardcore rule follower and thrived on routine. Some would say she even had a touch of obsessive-compulsive disorder. If her routine got thrown off by even a few minutes, she felt completely out of sorts. Grace wasn't proud of it and had a pile of half-finished self-help books on her nightstand, but nothing seemed to change her natural ways. As her mother always said, "You are God's special gift to me, and I love all of your little quirks and idiosyncrasies." Even though Grace was a grown woman, Ellen McKenna still made sure that her daughter knew that she was the best thing that had ever happened to her.

CHAPTER FOUR

Chief Welch's office was all smooth edges and clear surfaces. Police officers were always taught to keep their family and work life separate, and Chief Welch had taken this rule seriously. One would never know this man was a father of five by stepping into his office. His desk was free of clutter; a lonely calendar sprawled across the gray metal surface with a few notes scribbled on some of the dates. The only evidence that he was a family man was the empty juice box sitting on his desk and a partially unpacked lunch sack. Single men didn't take their lunch to work. Single men went out to lunch at the local delis and pubs that lined the streets outside of the station. There were plenty of single male officers at the station, and Grace had never seen one of them carry a lunch sack into work. A group of them left for lunch at the same time every day, a giant blue cloud walking into a sandwich joint. They took advantage of the uniform and wore it out in public any chance they got in hopes of scoring a date or two.

"Take a seat, Detective McKenna." Chief Welch didn't look up as he fumbled through his lunch sack. Grace slid into the cold metal chair and looked around the room, hoping there was something she could start a conversation about to ease her nerves. At thirty-six years old, Grace still got nervous around anyone who had authority over her.

"You would think I was in kindergarten by the way my wife packs my lunches." He giggled as he pulled out a fruit rollup. "It's never too early to eat one of these things, right?" He motioned to the clock, its arms resting on eight-thirty.

"You've got that right!" She instantly scolded herself for her enthusiasm. Grace was fully aware it made her sound young and naïve, and as a female in this business, she needed as much respect as she could get.

"Okay, okay let's get to business here." He pulled out his file drawer as a loud squeak pierced the silent air. The police stations were always the last to be funded for new furniture.

"First of all, how are you, Detective McKenna?" He smoothed his hand over a manila file folder.

"I'm good. How are you?" She returned the greeting, trying to get the spotlight off of herself.

"Good. I've got three teenagers at home who are driving me crazy, but other than that, I can't complain." A smile reached across his face, displaying a perfect set of teeth. Based on the age of his children and his time on the force, Grace estimated he was around fifty, but he looked great for his age. A broad chest kept him sitting upright and was proof that his days at the gym had not been wasted. His salt-and-pepper hair molded to his head in all the right places, a chiseled jawline peaked out behind slightly aging skin. Every time Grace locked eyes with him, she was relieved not to be transported into a past of violence or corrupt activity, and not overcome with visions of murder, theft or lies. He held his smile for too long, making her want to force a comment or a question to break the awkward pause.

"Which is harder—teenage boys, or teenage girls?"

He took a deep breath, paused and tilted his head to the side. "Ha! Depends on the day." He cleared his throat, taking his time to respond. "I gotta say, the boys are the ones who are getting on my nerves the most these days. I think my wife would disagree, though—she always ends up taking the wrath of Amelia, our teenage daughter. You see, teenage girls always like their dads. Come to them when they need something, confide in them when mom just doesn't understand. I'm sure you know how that goes, though."

Grace nodded, hoping that he didn't ask about her father. After all these years, she had still miraculously managed to avoid discussing a father figure in her life. The only close encounter was when one of the other officers made a comment about her following in daddy's footsteps, assuming that was why she became a cop. If they only knew.

"Anyways, speaking of teenage girls. . ." He used his pinky finger to flip open the file. There was a picture of a young girl stapled to the inside of the file, dirty blonde hair clinging to the side of her fair skinned face. A gold M dangled from a chain on her neck. A couple of teenage blemishes peeked out from behind a thick layer of foundation. "We have a missing person report. Mackenzie Waterford, seventeen years old. Athlete. Up for valedictorian of Bridgeton High. Her parents called this morning."

Chief Welch took a sip of water from a personalized bottle that resembled a canteen. A black and white photo of his family was tucked behind the plastic and the words "We love you daddy" hugged the cylinder bottle in a fancy font, probably the only thing that alluded to him having a family. Grace imagined that every Father's Day, his family gathered around him to present him with breakfast in bed and homemade gifts and cards.

"She was supposed to be sleeping over a friend's house the night before and never returned the next morning. Been gone since Saturday morning. Now that it's Monday morning, we're definitely cleared to call this a missing person report. But here's the kicker—this isn't the first time they've called in a report on the girl. I'm guessing she's a repeat offender of making her parents worry." He used his index fingers to smooth out his dark eyebrows. "The parents are frantic, same as they were the last time she went MIA. I need you to go to the house and question them, then contact any friends who may have been in her path leading up to the call. The parents may be challenging, but I feel like you're up to this case."

"Absolutely." Grace tried her hardest not to sympathize for the girl, not to say anything like, "Oh my gosh, that's terrible." She was supposed to be a cop in this situation, not a friend or an innocent bystander reading about the incident in the newspaper.

Chief Welch steepled his fingers and held them to his lips. Grace could tell that he was trying not to get attached to the case, trying not to think about his own teenage daughter at home. While missing person cases often turned out to be a miscommunication between parent and child, there was always that chance that it could be the one that ends up on billboards and milk cartons. "Do you have any questions?" He smiled kindly as he asked; his blue eyes breaking into two slits, revealing a display of crow's feet.

"Yes, sir. Actually, I do." Grace cracked her knuckles, a nervous habit. "Who called, the mother or father?"

"Good question, McKenna. This is why I trust you; you're always thinking about the little details that could lead to big answers." He nodded his head in approval and Grace couldn't help but feel like a first-grader receiving a gold star. "The mother called it in. She said that she contacted all of Mackenzie's friends that she knew of, including the girl whose house she was staying over. It sounds like a game of *I tell my mom and you tell your mom*, if you ask me. But, you never know."

Grace wondered if Chief Welch's teenagers ever tried to pull the wool over his eyes like that.

"Okay, I think I'll start by familiarizing myself with the file," Grace said as she took the folder from him. She forced herself to make assertive eye contact, even though on the inside she was on edge. While she'd had several missing person cases in her career, all of them had ended up being false alarms: a wife who was out on a two-day shopping binge; a teenage boy who ran away with his girlfriend for a couple of days, threatening that they were going to get married. The closest one to an actual missing person was when a little boy had been playing in the woods and got caught up in a game of cops and robbers, taking his role as cop so seriously that he refused to leave the fort that he had built and used as a hideaway.

"Remember, time is of the essence with missing persons. I have faith that you will do wonders." He leaned back in his chair and took a bite of the fruit rollup. "There is nothing better than chewy sugar first thing in the morning. I can already hear my dentist scolding me." He winked as he read the ingredients on the package.

"Thanks, Chief. I'll keep you posted." Grace said as she closed his door quietly, much more subtle than the way most of the male officers exited a room.

The station was now bustling with noise. Officer Jeffries had a man pinned against the wall by the reception area. His ruthless effort in the gym had served as a means to make up for his lack of height, but he still looked foolish with arms that looked like slabs of meat, and the way he angled his body between furniture, as if he was too muscular to fit. Anger surged through his Irish skin, making the color rise up and surpass the red shade of the man he was strangling. Grace slid into her office, eager to get to work on the Mackenzie Waterford case, while keeping an open eye on the activity in the lobby. She loved the location of her office because she always had easy access to Barb for speedy fact-checking, and she was only a few feet away from the main entrance for quick escapes. When she needed privacy and quiet, she simply shut her door on the chaos.

"Listen, asshole, I'm not asking you again! Why were you in such a rush?" Jeffries's words were sprinkled with a Boston accent, even though he was born and raised in rural Connecticut.

"Hey hey hey!" Sergeant Connolly emerged from his desk in the corner. "Jeffries, back off. You know the protocol," he said as he used his stature to tower over Jeffries and pull him off the man in one fluid motion.

"He's talking back to me. I don't like it when people don't respect the law," Officer Jefferies said, anger rattling his words and contorting his syllables into sharp hisses. Barb tried her best to muffle a laugh from the receptionist desk. Curtis Jeffries was born a privileged kid in an upper-class neighborhood in Hartford, Connecticut. His father was a highly paid criminal defense attorney. He was the middle child, with an older and younger brother who went on to become equally successful lawyers in New York City. Jeffries had attended private schools before he moved to Boston for college and, for reasons that most likely had to do with the need for power, decided to become a police officer. Even though he had been on the force for at least ten years, he still showed all the signs typical of a rookie cop—cocky, overbearing and loud. The bodybuilding frame was just an added bonus to the arrogant persona he walked around with every day. It was widely acknowledged throughout the station that Curtis Jeffries only had the job because of an uncle who happened to have a connection to some Boston politician who hailed from Bridgeton.

"Jeffries, sit down." Sergeant Connolly squashed Jeffries' confidence with only a few words. He sunk into his metal chair, his easy anger making a vein carve its way down the right side of his forehead. Ever since Jeffries tried to hit on Grace and was denied, he had been exceptionally surly to her, often throwing sexist comments her way. It was particularly satisfying for Grace to see him get knocked down a few pegs. His foot tapped the floor and banged against the desk in rapid motion, a nervous habit he'd had for years. "What's the problem?" Sergeant Connolly faced the man, dropping his hands low on his hips and taking the wide signature stance that comes second nature to police officers.

"This asshole, in his green pickup truck."

"Enough Jeffries! I'm asking *him*. Now, why did Officer Jeffries pull you into the station? I can only imagine what lovely crime our fine Officer Jeffries is accusing you of." Connolly rightfully blamed Jeffries for a false accusation. Over the past several months, Jeffries had brought innocent victims into the police station, accusing them of crimes, when really all they did was talk back to him. He had earned himself quite the reputation for concocting ridiculous stories in an attempt to feel some sort of power. Just last week, he had been off duty and out at a bar. Shortly after midnight, after a few drinks, he stumbled into the station with some innocent college boy that he had handcuffed and verbally abused, all because the kid made a pass at Jeffries's friend. On several occasions, he had been warned about using his stature as a police officer to hold power over others. It was only a matter of time before he really messed with the wrong person.

"I-I was just pulling into the right lane. I accidentally cut him off.

You see, I've been having this issue with my rearview mirror. I-I promise I'll get it fixed." The words came out of the man's mouth, mashed together and tripping over one another. His body was thin with a set of shoulders that hunched over so much it looked like he would fall forward any minute. Deep lines carved out a map on his face, showing either a hard life or too much time spent in the sun. Greasy salt-and-pepper hair was pushed back on his head, revealing a forehead that looked far too big for his small deep-set dark eyes. "I just been so busy workin' . . . I ain't had a chance to get my mirror fixed." He raked a shaky hand through his hair and tilted his head, like a puppy begging for a treat.

"Where do you work, sir?" Connolly asked.

"Price Chopper over in Greensdale. I was in a rush to get to work. They lowered my hours, so I need all the time I can get—that's why I was in a rush." His hands couldn't stay still and darted from his chin to his pockets to his forehead in rapid succession. "I been at the store for years. Started out as a bagger and worked my way up." Greensdale was another town over, known for its abundance of heroin users and rundown businesses. Price Chopper was one of the only businesses still thriving in the small, shoddy city. Most people didn't pass through Greensdale unless they absolutely had to.

"Alright. Well, why don't you get to work. And do us a favor and get that mirror fixed, okay? It's not going to do you any good to be driving around with a botched mirror. I've seen people get killed all because of something as minor as a little crack in a rearview reflector." Connolly planted his arms across his chest, revealing two athletic forearms. He had a perfect jawline, jutting out just far enough to look masculine, but giving way to a cleft in his chin that gave women something to talk about. His lips protruded enough to be considered full and his almond-shaped hazel eyes appeared to hold secrets. If he didn't always have the slightest sprinkling of stubble on his face and hair that was forever messy, he'd look like a pretty boy. But Mark Connolly was too nice, too modest and far too quiet to be considered anything but a good old Boston boy. Grace had often wondered about his past. She had heard from Barb that, like her, he kept to himself on and off duty.

"Yes sir." The man jabbed his hands in jean pockets, finally caging his nerves.

"But—" Jeffries's voice slipped out in a high-pitched chirp, as if he were going to explode from the silence during the entire interaction.

"Enough, Jeffries! Find a real case to work on." Connolly waved a hand toward the door, motioning to the man that he was free.

"Never a dull moment," Barb said between small puffs of laughter.

CHAPTER FIVE

THE MOMENT THAT GRACE LOOKED UP FROM THE WATERFORD FILE, SHE was filled with regret. The man who Jeffries had been verbally assaulting slithered by her office. He gave her a nod and a curt smile and, without realizing, he gifted her with flashes of his past. It was too late to look away, too late for Grace to unsee the images of the little blonde girl letting out a deafening scream as she ran through the woods, her sneakers lighting up the path for her kidnapper. The last vision that seared through Grace was a set of frightened green eyes on a bed of fiery red and orange leaves.

"Hey Princess, here's a picture of Eric." Barb interrupted the vision and like a flash of lightening the man was gone, leaving his trail of his crime imprinted on her. Barb angled her monitor so that Grace couldn't miss the giant face that took up the screen across from her office. The image had been cropped, allowing him to use it as a profile picture for a dating site. "Not so bad on the eyes, huh?" She gave a wink and clicked her tongue.

Grace's eyes followed the evil man as he walked out the door. It took everything in her power to keep herself pinned to her chair, to hold herself back from jumping up and demanding the man be questioned. This wasn't the first time she had found herself torn between right and wrong, nor the first time a criminal has made his way out of the station undetected, tugging at her morals. Reality haunted her, pulling her in different directions. Should she risk her career and invite the possibility of being admitted into a mental hospital, or let the vision slide past and bury it with all the others that had built up over the years? These questions had turned themselves over in Grace's mind since the first day she attached the holster to her hips and secured the cuffs to her belt loop. It was hard enough prior to her life as an officer, as she had to slide the puzzle pieces of her visions together to form a picture of a scene. The pictures would then transform into a story, one that would always turn out bad. Her visions never revealed saints, or those who strived to better the world with their bleeding hearts, but instead narrowed down the bad like the target at the end of a sniper's rifle.

"Earth to Grace!" Barb's voice interjected itself into the battle going on in her head.

"Barb, he's on dating sites?" Grace asked as she launched herself up from her desk and peered over Barb's shoulder at the screen, hoping not to be caught in a mental pause. The man's face was kind, with eyes that seemed to greet his wide smile with open arms. Grace could tell he came from the same blood as Barb by the small hints of red that glistened amongst his thick brown hair, proof of their Irish descent. Barb had lost her shine to some dull strands of gray over the years, but like Barb, Eric had a smattering of freckles that danced on his upturned nose. He looked like the type of guy who liked to laugh and had an invisible bag full of go-to jokes that he pulled out to get a conversation going.

"He's on *a* dating site." Barb held up a chubby finger. "As in, ONE. I know, because I'm the one who convinced him to set up a profile," she said as she puffed out her chest.

"You know how I feel about dating sites, Barb." Grace slid back into her chair, defeated and already regretting her promise to go on a date with the guy.

"Listen, Princess, can't you see . . . he is so much like you already! He didn't want to go on a dating site, either. But good ol' Auntie Barb convinced him." She retrieved a container of Coffee-Mate powdered creamer from her bottom drawer and shook the container onto her Dunkin Donuts coffee until it turned into a mound on top of the brown liquid.

"Fine." Grace looked at Eric's photo one last time and rationalized that at least maybe she could learn a few good jokes from the guy. "And, why don't you just have them put the creamer in when you order it at Dunkins?"

"Princess, if I've learned one thing in life, it's that the high turnover at Dunkin Donuts makes for poor customer service and incorrect orders," Barb said as if she was doling out the most useful piece of advice. "Mama has learned to take matters into her own hands. I order it black, and dress it up the way *I* want."

"Whatever you say, Barb."

"Hey, McKenna," Connolly said as he sidled up to Barb's desk. "Got a minute?"

"Yeah, sure. What's up?" Grace wasn't sure why, but there was something about the man that made her nervous.

"Sorry to interrupt." He rested his hands on his hips.

"Oh, you're not interrupting anything here, Marky," said Barb as she swiveled around in her chair to get back to work. "She's all yours."

"Thanks." He turned and met Grace's eyes. "I just wanted to let you know that if you need any help with the Waterford case, give me a shout."

"Oh, thanks." Had it been any other officer offering help, she would jump on the defense and assume they were doubting her abilities, but Mark Connolly was different. "But, you know how missing person cases go—there's a good chance she'll turn up after a wild night out or something."

"Yeah." He shook his head as a shy smile peeled across his lips. "I got a little sister about that age, so just wanna keep an eye out."

"Oh . . . yeah. Of course. Totally understand," Grace said, kicking herself for minimalizing the case.

"Thanks. Hey, here's my cell, in case you need me when I'm off duty." Mark slid a pen out from his front pocket and plucked a Post-it from Barb's overstuffed plastic desk organizer. Grace knew that she could easily get his cell from the officer directory list, but kept quiet as he wrote down his phone number with his left hand. It had seemed so old fashioned to see a man write down his number, in the age when people were able to share contact information by tapping their phones. He gave a tight-lipped smile and stood there awkwardly for a moment.

"Okay, thanks. I'll definitely keep you posted."

"Thanks." He started to turn on a heel. "I really appreciate that," he said before walking back toward his desk, leaving a slight piney scent behind.

"What was THAT?" Barb swiveled in her desk like a schoolgirl.

"Turn around." Grace tried her best not to let Barb get all fired up about something that meant nothing.

"Come on, Princess—he knows you can find his digits in the directory. YET, he felt the need to personally write them out for you, like you're his little schoolboy crush. I'm just callin' it like I see it. And what I see is a boy who wants a girl to contact him *after* hours," Barb said, the words coming out in muffled whispers.

"Hush, Barb. The guy is just concerned about his sister."

"You know what they say about protective big brothers."

"Actually, no I don't. What do they say about protective big brothers?" Grace said, trying to humor the woman.

"They make for sensational lovers."

"Ew, gross! Enough! Connelly is my colleague and I'm not even remotely attracted to him," Grace lied.

"Tsss." Grace could see the laugh ripple its way through Barb's body. "I question my sexuality, I'm ready to give men up altogether, and even I can't help but get my panties in a bunch when he walks by." She let out another clicking sound with her tongue. "Maybe it's that delicious piney cologne he wears."

"He doesn't wear cologne. He's far too modest for that. It's deodorant." The words spilled out of Grace's mouth before she could stop herself.

"Ha!" Barb slammed a hand on the desk and turned around. "Well

well, looks like our little Princess here has got herself a crush." Barb's eyebrows danced on her forehead as she threw a few seductive jumps and rolls into her shoulders. "Doesn't mean you can bail on your date with my nephew, though." She pointed a warning finger at Grace.

"Whatever, you don't have to worry about that because I don't have a crush and even if I did, I would NEVER date a colleague, so keep your dirty thoughts to yourself," Grace said before she passed the threshold into her office, her safe haven. She picked up the phone and dialed the number to the Waterford residence.

"Hello." The urgent voice came across the line halfway through the first ring.

"Hello, may I please speak to Mr. or Mrs. Waterford." Grace always dreaded the first interaction with worried parents. She never knew if they were going to be angry and take out their aggression on her, or be so saddened that they couldn't even answer simple questions. The potential and possibility of emotions on the other end could be anywhere on the broad spectrum of human nature.

"This is . . . ah . . . Mrs. Waterford." A meek voice came through the line.

"Hello, Mrs. Waterford. This is Detective McKenna from the Bridgeton Police Department. I'm calling in reference to the missing person report you filed this morning."

"Um . . . you better talk to my husband." Before Grace could object, some high-pitched voices passed through the phone, then a deep cough, followed by a masculine voice.

"Hello, this is Anthony Waterford."

"Hi Mr. Waterford. As I was telling your wife, I'm Detective McKenna from the police department."

"Yes, I figured. Hi Detective McKenna. Thank you so much for calling. It's been one heck of a morning around here." His syllables were enhanced, making his words sound like they were coming from the lips of a newscaster.

"Yes, I can imagine," Grace said, trained to sound compassionate, yet authoritative. It had been a hard voice to perfect, so contradicting. Right when you were sure that you had shown an ounce of your heart to prove you were the right fit to lead a case, you had to put your foot down and cut off the emotions that had a tendency to attach themselves to the family of the missing person, or the abused wife, or the neglected child. Although, Grace didn't have children, so she had yet to know the undying love that goes along with being a parent. It had been easier for her to sleep at night after leaving a case like that. She could put those emotions away and close the drawer and not worry about a little one of her own sleeping across the hall under the same roof. While Grace had witnessed parents go wild for their children, unable to see their own erratic behavior, she couldn't yet claim that feeling of love for herself.

"Mr. Waterford, I'd like to come by and meet with you and your wife. Get to know a bit about Mackenzie's home life." Demanding to visit a family's home had always been one of Grace's weaknesses, as she never knew if they would get defensive and try to refuse her visit. People were odd about their homes. Opening the door to someone's house was another way to see into their life, to uncover more of who they truly were. Although in Grace's case, all she had to do was seal the deal with eye contact.

"Please, Detective McKenna—call me Anthony."

"Anthony, I'm sorry. I don't think I caught your wife's name," Grace said, as she thought about the awkward exchange between her and the woman who answered the phone.

"Oh, I'm sorry, Beth is a bit out of sorts right now. I'm not sure she knows her own name. Kenzie's disappearance has come as a shock to us all. It's very unlike her to leave without telling us, and for such a long time. We've contacted all of her friends, but no one seems to know where our little girl is." Grace could hear the desperation building in Anthony's voice.

"Well, I am going to do everything I can to help you find her," Grace said, as her eyes were drawn to the other side of the station. She followed Officer Jeffries' stalky frame as it marched toward Mark's desk, his face the shade of an angry red. She watched as he threw his arms in the air and words flew out of his mouth, escalating with each syllable. All Grace could make out was *I just don't understand why. . .*

35

"Thank you, thank you so much, detective."

"Your address is 109 Perkins Drive, correct?"

"That's right. Will you be over soon?" A touch of urgency coated his question.

"Yes, sir. I'm on my way."

Grace carefully slid the file into her navy blue canvas bag, threw the leather strap across her chest and marched out of her office. "Barb, I'm heading out for an interview. Call me if you need anything, or if Chief Welch needs me."

"Yes, dear." Barb continued staring straight ahead at her computer screen, intent on punching some numbers into a database. "And what did I tell you about sucking up? It's not flattering. You're playing in a man's world here, you need to start acting like one." Barb had always given Grace a hard time about how she always brown-nosed Chief Welch. Grace couldn't help it—the job was her world. She wanted to leave her mark on the police world and pave the way for female officers everywhere; if it meant sucking up a little bit to get good cases, then so be it.

"Bye, Barb."

She hustled past the row of clunky metal desks and pushed her small frame through the double glass doors. The cold winter air nearly knocked her down, its grip raw and stealing the breath from her.

"Be careful. It's icy out there." The voice startled her.

"Thanks, Mark." She turned back briefly to see a gloved hand wrapped around a small Dunkin Donuts cup.

"I'd give this to you to warm you up, but . . ." He held up the cup in an offering, before looking down into the Styrofoam, like he was looking down into a tunnel searching for answers. Something tickled at Grace's insides when she was in the presence of the man, and she couldn't help but think about his impeccably trained body. Every morning before his shift started, he would hit the punching bag and press and pull weights in the on-site gym. She had seen his well-developed back muscles through his sweat-drenched T-shirt when he walked by her desk to the showers. Tendons and veins carved their way down his forearms, and all it took was one glimpse for her to realize that he had a taut and toned ass to go with the package. She had seen him hit the bag so effortlessly and with the determination of a man on a mission, it made Grace wonder what exactly he was thinking about when he was throwing punches.

"No worries. I got one." Grace held up her silver travel coffee mug. She felt his eyes penetrating the back of her head as she walked toward her Jeep.

She tossed her bag on the passenger seat and slid behind the wheel, giving Mark one more glance in the rearview mirror before gliding out of the lot.

CHAPTER SIX

THE NEIGHBORHOOD WHERE THE WATERFORDS LIVED WAS WHAT GRACE imagined the Stepford wives to inhabit. A group of mothers talked animatedly as they pushed strollers on the freshly cemented sidewalks. Unlike the New England that Grace knew, this section of town was brand new, each house pristine and complete with top-of-the-line fixtures and landscaping. All the houses were brick, as opposed to the multi-layered paint on the other homes so common in the rest of the town.

Grace remembered reading about this development in the Boston Globe when it was first built, *Modern homes with old New England charm, Bridgeton is the future of small town living with a big city feel,* the article had boasted. It was unlike Bridgeton to be featured in the Globe, but the new development had caused an uproar between the old townies and the new yuppies. The townies didn't want the yuppies tearing down the old classics that their parents' parents' parents had built, and the yuppies didn't have the patience to renovate one room at a time. Small towns, especially small beach towns, didn't typically have the luxury of big yards and freshly built houses, but Bridgeton prided themselves on being the first along the east coast.

One of the three streets that was affected by the controversial development was Perkins Drive. Grace read the street numbers on the mailboxes, all in identical flowing gold font plastered on the black boxes at the end of the driveways. The driveways were massive, designed to hold the minivans and SUVs of today's parents. Basketball hoops stood proudly on the side of nearly every driveway, flanked by sprawled out bikes. Where Grace had grown up, the residents knew better than to leave bikes out and unlocked. Anything that was left in the open had been up for grabs. Here, in this neighborhood, it was the middle of the day and surely kids were inside eating lunch or playing on their tablets, yet they left their belongings out like they were unsuspecting missionaries.

The summers here were probably bustling with family-fun activities. Grace pictured apron-clad dads at their grills bumping beer bottles and talking about sports and moms discussing the various activities offered at their local rec center. Rec centers didn't exist in the rest of Massachusetts; old sweaty gyms that offered moldy steam rooms were the closest thing to a community center. The Waterford residence was at the foot of a cul-de-sac. While nearly identical to the other houses in the neighborhood, it lacked the seasonal décor that seemed to be planned out so the lights and ornamentation were uniform from house to house. From what Grace could tell, and from what she assumed the rest of the neighborhood felt, the Waterford family was slacking.

Three slow, deep breaths was tradition for Grace before she confirmed she had her lucky pen in the front pocket of her uniform and her grandmother's gold cross dangling from her neck. Some would call her superstitious, but after thirty-six years of living with a "gift," as her mother called it, she never knew when she would look into the wrong set of eyes and be pulled into a world of horror. While the visions showed her only brief flashes of time, those images burned themselves into her memory forever. It didn't take much effort on her part to recollect the first image she saw back when she was three. The red-haired woman had essentially gone through life with her, making herself at home in Grace's mind.

She stepped out of her car, her boot grinding into the salt on the pavement. The forecast called for snow, so naturally everyone in the area was preparing for the storm of the century. A man in a blue maintenance uniform looked up briefly as he maneuvered a bag of salt. His eyes darted from Grace to the Waterford house and back down as he went to work sprinkling the salt onto the pavement, creating an even coverage. The bag looked like it outweighed him by at least ten pounds. He hunched over and used his whole body to shake the contents out, making it look like he was a junior high student dancing with a girl for the first time, his eyes on the ground, his body full of awkward movements. A little girl on a bike with pink streamers and a purple basket came darting toward Grace from nowhere. She made a sharp turn into the Waterford driveway and came to a halting stop right beside her.

"Are you here to talk to my parents?" she asked, adjusting a ribbon of pale blonde hair that was sticking out of her helmet and plastered to her cheek.

"Well, that depends. Are your parents Mr. and Mrs. Waterford?" Grace gripped the strap of her bag and lowered herself so that she was eye level with the girl.

"Yesssss."

"Well then, yes, I am here to see your parents. And what is your name?"

"My name is Penelope. But, my friends call me Penny. And my daddy calls me Penny Bear. What are all those ribbons on your shirt?" Penny pointed to the colorful line of ribbons that peaked out from behind Grace's navy blue jacket.

Before Grace had a chance to explain, Penny pointed to the scar that was a straight line through Grace's right eyebrow. "What's that? Did you get in a fight?" she asked.

"Not really. This is a scar." Grace pulled the gloves off her hands and took her pinky finger out to exhibit the small scar.

"Cooooool! I think I wanna be a police woman when I grow up," Penny said, her eyes wide, her lips pink and chapped from the cold. Grace was surprised the little girl was allowed to be out in the cold,

although she wasn't much different as a child, always outside partici-
pating in her solo outdoor adventures.

"Well, I think you can be anything you want, Penny." Grace giggled
at herself on the inside, sounding like she was some kind of Girl Scout
leader. "Maybe you can take me to meet your parents. How does that
sound?"

"Sure! Does that mean I can be, like, your assistant?" Penny hopped
off her bike and pulled on Grace's free hand, leading her to the front
door.

"Yep, I think that means you can be my assistant," Grace said, as
she allowed herself to be pulled to the door. She made a mental note
to take Chief Welch up on his offer for her to talk to elementary
school students about safety. There was something so real about being
around children, and she didn't have to worry about seeing horrifying
pictures when she looked into a child's eyes; instead she was greeted
with the innocent wonder. Typically, Grace liked to make her own
entrance at the front door, but she was already smitten by little Penny
and couldn't deny an opportunity to mold a little girl's career dreams.

"Daddy! Mommy! A police officer is here and she's a girl!" Penny
wiggled her way out of the pink ski jacket she was wearing and
dropped it on the bench that sat underneath a row of hangers holding
clumps of winter jackets.

"Hello, Detective McKenna. Thank you so much for coming." Mr.
Waterford marched up to the door, pulled Penny to his side and
extended a hand for Grace to shake. "And it looks like you made it in
record time." He looked at the thick silver watch that hugged his
wrist.

"Pleasure to meet you, Mr. Waterford." Grace leaned in and gave
her practiced handshake and eye contact. A pair of kind blue eyes
smiled back at her. *Score one. The father is clean.* Grace cheered on the
inside.

"Please, call me Anthony." He motioned for Grace to go ahead of
him as they made their way into the living room before he crouched
down to address his daughter. "Penny Bear, can you go upstairs and

start working on that project we talked about earlier?" he asked in a secretive tone.

"You mean . . ." Penny leaned in and finished her sentence in his ear.

"Yes! That's exactly it!" A bright white smile spread across Anthony's tan face. "Now, when I'm done talking to Detective McKenna here, I'll come up and help you finish it, okay?" There was no denying Anthony was her father, the two were like mirror images of each other.

"Okay!" Penny ran out of the living room, slid across the hardwood floor landing and raced up the stairs.

"She's only seven. I don't want to tell her that her sister is missing just yet." He turned toward Grace. "As you can imagine, Penny really looks up to her big sister. I don't want to say anything to worry her until we find out more details, you know?"

"I understand."

"Have a seat." Anthony waved his hand toward the living room. Grace's boot sunk into the plush white carpet, surely leaving an imprint behind. She scanned the photos on the dark wooden entertainment center, various sets of eyes stared back at her. A family photo with Anthony at the center, his arms gathered around the three women in his life. A photo of Penny looking up at Mackenzie, as she proudly holds up an award, her blue dress opposing her clear rich brown eyes. Mackenzie as a young girl, a sobering look imprinted on her face as she looked down at baby Penny swaddled in a pink hospital blanket.

Grace slowly dropped down into an accent chair opposite a love seat covered in paisley pale blue upholstery. Anthony sat on the love seat gently, his body erect as his hands smoothed over his pressed khaki pants. A dark coffee table sat between them, magazines fanned out to perfection like they were in a doctor's office waiting room.

"Mr. Waterford— I mean, Anthony." Grace pulled out her notebook, rested it on the table and plucked a pen from her front pocket. "Will your wife be joining us?" Grace concealed the surprise in her voice. Usually it was the mothers who were frantic and firing off a million questions and willingly displaying the missing child's belong-ings. She leaned back in the chair and angled the notebook toward herself, trying to disguise any alerts that she may write down. *Wife: out of vision upon arrival.*

"Yes, of course. This has been so hard on her. Kenzie has only been gone for two days, and to be honest, I'm guessing she'll come back and she's just being a typical teenage girl. But, her mother . . . well, mothers are always a bit more dramatic." He lowered his voice slightly. Grace couldn't help but feel a little sting when he said *girl,* as if girls were the only ones who acted up and played games; as if they went missing because they were simply silly girls. Anthony's true side seemed to be revealing itself.

"Yes, I understand." Grace had to force the words out. "But with all due respect, Anthony, I think it will be very beneficial for Mrs. Water-ford to be present during this meeting. After all, mothers have a way with knowing their daughters right?" She reversed the sting, hoping he would feel the twinge. All too often, Grace had to go out of her way to ensure that men knew that she could be just as fierce as her male colleagues. It was a constant battle, one that her mother had warned her about.

Without another word, Anthony slowly rose from his chair, adjusted his cardigan sweater that could've easily been stolen from Mr. Roger's closet, and walked to the bottom of the staircase.

"Of course. Anything to make sure our girl is okay." He offered a warm smile and eyes that were aimed directly at Grace, confirming the initial good feelings she had about him. "Beth, honey, can you come down here? Detective McKenna would like to speak with us." He stood at the bottom of the stairs as if he was anxiously awaiting his bride.

Beth's slight frame skittered down the stairs so quietly that for a moment Grace wondered if her feet even touched the stairs with each step. Her body was frail, and when she moved it looked like the branches of a weeping willow blowing in the wind.

"Hello, Mrs. Waterford." Grace walked over to the woman with an extended hand. As she expected, the woman's handshake was like a dead fish, weak and floppy.

"Hi." Beth's eyes darted to Anthony's and back to Grace's. They were a pretty shade of pale brown interrupted by reds and purples from tears or lack of sleep. Brown hair with a crown of frizz greeted her shoulders and a naked hand reached up to tuck a strand behind her ear, a nervous reaction.

"It's okay, honey. Take a seat." Anthony guided her into the living room. "Sorry, she's a bit worried about Kenzie."

"Understandable," Grace said, tipped off by the odd combination that the two made. She hoped to God the woman was just shy and concerned, and that with a little prodding she would open up. Or was she one of those subservient women who was too meek to speak for herself?

While Grace couldn't stand men who treated women as if they were a lower species, it maddened her even more to see a woman who allowed herself to be led around like a puppy on a leash. Men were naturally the violent sex, having the inherent desire to fight, control and dominate. She was over the abusive husbands, the controlling fathers and the rapists. When it came to crime, a man was usually the one to blame. The only exception was a case that was way before Grace's time. A woman from Maine had been arrested on several counts of homicide back in 1984. It turned out she had been taking in new lovers and torturing them before sawing off their extremities. The limbless bodies were discovered in an upscale hotel in downtown Boston. The woman had been a well-known paralegal at a big-time law firm in Boston, and had volunteered on several committees to better the school districts and local parks. *Never judge a book by its cover,* her mother always said.

"So, Mr. and Mrs. Waterford . . . Anthony." Grace would use the formality with Mrs. Waterford until told otherwise. "Let's start from the beginning. When did you last see Mackenzie?" Grace rested a small recorder down on the coffee table and pressed the red button. The wheels crunched and spun to life. She made a mental note to talk to Chief Welch about getting a more updated model, or learn how to use her cell phone for recordings. "I'm sorry, do you mind if I . . . ?" She motioned to the recorder.

"No, no, of course. You're just doing your job. We understand." Anthony pulled Beth into his side. "Don't we, honey?"

"Yes, of course." The words came out of Beth's mouth so low that they were barely audible. Her eyes jerked side to side, as if in a game of dodgeball, before settling on the floor. "Anything to get Kenzie back," she said under her breath.

"We last saw Kenzie on Saturday morning. She was all excited for the big football game later that afternoon." Anthony looked at his watch as if he had a calendar alerting him. "She is very active in school. A lot of her friends are cheerleaders, so she usually gets to the games early with them while they warm up and practice. Kenzie was so busy with soccer, so she never tried out for the squad."

"She plays soccer for the school?"

"Yes, she plays forward. Made varsity her freshman year. It's almost unheard of, so it wasn't surprising when she was practically given the role of captain as soon as her senior year started." Anthony reached for his neck with his left hand and gave a little massage before shaking his head. "Sorry, I'm babbling. I guess I'm just a tad proud of my little girl."

"So, she was around Saturday morning? Did she have any practices or games scheduled for the weekend?"

"No, no. The season is over—ended a few weeks ago. And the last day of school before Christmas break was Friday. Seems like the breaks get longer every year. Anyway, they had a big celebration at the school on Saturday because the team came in first in state. I remember she was so nervous about giving a speech. She had to stand up in front of the entire auditorium, about 500 kids and parents."

"And how was her speech? Did she do a good job?"

"Yeah, flawless execution. In fact, I told her that maybe she should think about becoming one of those motivational speakers." Anthony giggled.

"What time was the celebration?

"It was at 3:00," Anthony said as he smoothed a hand over his face.

"So technically you last saw her Saturday afternoon...not morning?"

"Yes, I guess that's correct," said Anthony, looking as if he'd been caught in a lie.

"Mrs. Waterford, were you at the celebration that night?" Grace asked, trying to bring the woman into the conversation.

"Yes, she did a beautiful job." Beth looked up for an instant, her eyes set on Grace for a long pause, as if she had a brief eruption of confidence. Something about the way her pupils stood out against the brown of her eyes gave Grace an unsettling feeling. She couldn't decide whether she was more intrigued by this woman's burst of assurance, or curious about what was going on in her mind.

"And were you expecting her to be home later that evening, after the game?"

"No, we weren't. She said she was going to be staying over her friend's house."

"It was Taylor Ryder. She was supposed to be staying over Taylor Ryder's house." Beth tucked a piece of hair behind her ear as she said the words.

"Is Taylor a good friend of hers?"

"Yes, they're best friends," Beth said, her contributions short and sweet with a touch of nerves, but much more relevant than Anthony's.

"Kenzie spends the night over her friends' houses quite often. And, like most homes with teenage girls, we tend to have a lot of her friends coming and going and spending the night. It's sometimes hard to keep track of who's staying where," Anthony said, using a hand to push back the bristles of his hair.

"But Taylor is her best friend. She's the one who Kenzie is *always* with," Beth said, slight irritation in her voice.

"Do you know Taylor's parents?"

"Yes, we do," Beth said.

"They are nice people, the Ryders," Anthony said, rubbing his chin again. "In fact, we've done a few family gatherings with them. It's a small town, so everyone kinda knows everyone around here."

"Yes, that tends to be the way it is in these small towns," Grace said. "Are you both from here? Born and raised?"

"Yes—I mean, no. Beth isn't from here. I am. Been here my whole life."

"It's a nice town, you think?"

"Oh yeah, great town. I couldn't imagine raising our girls anywhere else," he said. "The community is so tight, most nights I don't even feel like I need to lock the door." Anthony's eyes fluttered about the room.

"Where are you from, Mrs. Waterford?"

"Beth is from North—"

"Anthony, would you mind letting your wife answer for herself?" Grace put her foot down. She could tell he was trying to help his wife, answering for her when she didn't have the strength to answer, but Grace needed to hear the answers from the person questioned.

"I'm from a small town in North Carolina. Ellis," Beth said, and for the first time Grace could hear the tiny hint of a southern accent trickle into her syllables.

"What brought you to another small town?" Grace asked.

"She came here to go to UMass. That's where we—sorry." Anthony stopped himself. Grace gave him a tight-lipped smile.

"My family was dead-set on me attending school somewhere outside of the South, so I chose Boston. It was really for a silly reason; you see, I was kind of a Kennedy buff back in the day. Haven't seen a Kennedy since I set foot in New England, though." Beth said, starting to come to life a little. Grace could see Anthony out of the corner of her eye, slipping out of his cardigan and folding it on his lap.

"Would you mind if I took a look at Mackenzie's room?"

"Yes, of course." Beth nearly jumped up, excited to divert attention from herself.

"Thank you." Grace pushed herself up from the opulent cushion and slid the recorder into her back pocket.

Following Beth up the stairs, Grace placed her feet in the imprints the small woman had already pressed into the plush white carpet. Beth held onto the rail as if she was going to lose her balance and fall over, similar to the way she shook hands and communicated, as if she was unsure and on edge at all times. Anthony followed closely behind, his wedding ring tapped against the wooden handrail as he glided his palm along the smooth surface.

The landing at the top of the stairs was cozy and welcoming. A small decorative chair sat in the corner opposite a towering chestnut bookcase offering a tidy nook for someone who wanted to take a time out and read. Grace's eyes glazed over the shelves containing an assortment of different reading material, some with worn bindings and others that looked like they had never been touched.

She always made it a point to glimpse at the reading material in the homes where she interviewed. Surprisingly, it had helped her crack cases in the past. Last year, she had credited a bookshelf for helping her pinpoint the suspect in one of the biggest pedophile cases in the area. She'd had visions when she looked into the man's eyes. She had seen the faces of the traumatized children with pleading stares, confusion outlining the edges of their brows as they lay naked in a pile of their own clothes. It was hard enough for Grace to process and make sense of the visions that presented themselves to her, but it was particularly hard when the eyes of an innocent child were staring back at her. The man had been the offspring of a prominent family in town, so it was a shock to the locals when they found out the son of a long line of respectable businessmen had been luring small children into his home, offering them a "story hour" that consisted of studying anatomy. She had seen far too many children's books on his shelf and knew that something was not right.

"This is Kenzie's room." Beth flipped on a light switch, shedding clarity on Mackenzie's world. The white carpet spilled into her room from the hallway, matching the rest of the house's opulent tones. One massive rectangular mirror hung above a cream-colored dresser. Several ribbons and medals hung from hooks on each side of the mirror.

"Soccer?" Grace asked as she cradled one of the gold medals in the palm of her hand.

"Soccer, track, educational achievements. You name it," Anthony said, as he walked toward a shelf that housed several gold trophies and framed certificates that were leaning against the wall in perfect alignment. Each piece looked as if it had been polished and shined with great detail. A spacious cream-colored desk sat along another wall with its drawers closed, gold knobs shining against the ceiling light.

"Does Mackenzie usually do her homework here?" Grace walked toward the desk, surveying the objects placed in perfect precision on the smooth, light wood. A Mason jar sat in the right corner, filled with pens and pencils that were labeled according to purpose. Grace picked up the Mason jar, shook it and plucked out a black ballpoint pen. ENG LIT was inscribed on the clear tape in perfect block lettering.

"Depends. Usually if she's up late cramming for a test, she confines herself to her room. Sometimes, she takes over the kitchen table with her books and papers. Or, she goes to a friend's house." Anthony jabbed his hands deep into his pockets.

"She has a place and a purpose for everything, huh?" Grace stabbed the pen into the tightly filled jar and looked around the rest of the impeccably neat room. "Not really typical of a teenage girl."

"Yeah, she's a bit of a perfectionist." Anthony rested his hands low on his hips, showing off his own perfectly pressed pale-green shirt tucked into khakis, the buttons of the shirt centered and aligned with the fly on his crisp pants. A light cough escaped from Beth's throat, urging Anthony to say more. "If things aren't how they're supposed to be, at least in Kenzie's mind, she tends to get a bit bent out of shape," he continued picking up on the cue.

"How so?"

"Mackenzie strives for perfection. She doesn't settle. I think that's a good thing, especially in today's world of competitive college entrance exams and gosh, the challenges with getting your foot in the door at a company. She has a system for doing her homework. She does pretty much all of her writing for English Lit on her laptop, then she prints it out and uses the pen to mark it up with the changes she needs to make." He walked toward the shelf that housed the awards, and picked up a plaque that read *Mackenzie Waterford, Class President.*

His face was reflected in the gleaming gold plate. "Back in my day, you got into a company and stayed there for years. Nowadays, the competition never ends. These kids bounce around from corporation to corporation, always looking for the next promotion, the next raise."

Beth stepped side to side in a nervous dance, before she caught herself and leaned against the doorframe.

"I gotta say, the tidiness of this room is making me feel like a hoarder." Grace's eyes caught the edge of the quilt, its corners creasing and billowing out evenly on all sides of the bed.

"I'd like to say she gets it from me." Anthony fiddled with some change in his pockets. "My days in the military taught me the importance of having a place for everything and always being prepared."

"You were in the military? What branch?" Grace had learned what questions to ask from hearing her veteran colleagues talk amongst each other. The branch seemed to be the question that could either make or break a bond. She had heard Marines bashing the Air Force for being weak, and Navy guys calling Marines brainwashed; everyone seemed to agree the Army enlisted only those not strong enough to be Marines. Her fellow officers sounded like high school kids on opposing sports teams when they harassed each other about their choice of branch.

"Marine Corps," Anthony said, standing more erect as he said the words.

"Thank you for your service." Grace gave him a tight-lipped smile. The statement always made her feel awkward, as if she was confessing that she herself was not willing to give her life up to the military. And it's not that she didn't think about it. She certainly contemplated enlisting, but being close to her mother was more of a priority. She couldn't bear to leave her mom alone. Anthony smiled back, his fit build still evident from years in the service. "How long were you in?"

"Four years. That was enough for me. No place for a family, and that's all I ever wanted." He cast a sincere smile at Beth.

Grace guided herself back on track. "So, does Mackenzie spend a lot of time with her friends?"

"I guess any time that she has free she spends with them, but

Kenzie is a busy girl. Always has been. I can remember when she was only five or six and she'd have her entire day planned out, each hour allotted for some activity."

"Well, they say busy hands are happy hands, right?" Grace leaned toward the bulletin board, trying to decipher one of the many Post-it notes that stuck to the cork.

"You are right about that, Detective," Anthony said as if they were in the middle of small talk, rather than an interview about his missing daughter.

"And what about you, Beth? Do you know of any friends that Mackenzie spends a lot of time with?"

"Mostly Taylor. She was—is her best friend." Beth stumbled on her words.

"Which one is Taylor?" Grace asked, pointing to the collage of photos stabbed with colorful pins. One side of the board consisted of all soccer photos. Mackenzie on the field in the midst of an aggressive play, Mackenzie with her teammates proudly raising their index fingers after winning a game, Mackenzie and three other girls with faces painted the same shade of blue as their uniforms. The other side of the board held photos of Mackenzie and her friends, but none of the faces seemed to match those of the athletes.

"That's Taylor." Beth stepped forward as if she had been called to the stand. She used a bony finger to point out a brunette wearing a uniform, her cheek smashed up against Mackenzie's as they posed for a selfie. The girl was dark in all the ways that Mackenzie was light. She had dark skin and deep black hair, a set of dark lashes reaching out for her brows. Her hair was gathered into a bun resting on top of her head with a few escaped wisps, softening the sharp angles of her face.

"Do you mind if I take this one for my file?" Grace asked, as she specifically looked at Beth to answer.

"Sure. That's fine."

"Beautiful girl," Grace said, caught off guard by the youthful beauty staring back at her.

"I hate to say it, but all of Mackenzie's friends are pretty. She tends to run in that popular crowd." Anthony sat on the edge of the queen-sized bed, the mattress sinking beneath his frame. "I mean, if you ask me, they all look the same, the girls these days. When Mackenzie has a soccer game, I can never tell which one she is!" He let out a boisterous laugh, the weight of it so loud that Beth's frail body nearly fell over.

"And who are these friends?" Grace said, pointing at the other group of girls, trying to hide from his humor. Again, she looked at Beth for answers.

"Oh, those are the other girls from school." Beth leaned against the doorframe like a wallflower at a school dance. Anthony looked at her, sharing the same confused expression as Grace. "I guess her non-athlete friends. The ones that aren't on the soccer team." She tucked a fallen strand of hair behind her ears. For a moment, Grace could see a resemblance between the photo of Mackenzie and Beth. She couldn't quite put her finger on what was similar—maybe something in the way their eyes were set, although Beth was more hollow around the sockets. Mackenzie's features seemed to fill out the contours of her face just right.

"So, she spends her time on the field with these girls, and her time off the field with this group?" Grace clarified, pointing at both groups of photos like a teacher presenting a lesson to the class.

"Like we said, Mackenzie is a very busy girl. In fact, sometimes we have to tell her to slow down. If anything, the girl works too hard, always chasing perfection. And she has so many friends it's hard to keep track. Always has been a very popular girl," Anthony said, before being interrupted by a cell phone playing an old Aerosmith song. Grace didn't peg him for a rocker type, with his dirty blond hair barely dipping below his ears, short bristles that looked as if they got maintained at a weekly trip to the barbershop. Grace noticed his erect gait, the way he seemed to fall into step as if in military formation.

"Excuse me," he said as he flipped open an outdated phone and shot a look of confusion at the screen. "Hello, this is Anthony Waterford." He pushed himself off the bed and marched out of the room. His voice faded as he walked down the stairs, then quickly escalated.

"Mackenzie! Where are you? What? I can't hear you, honey. Are you okay? Just tell me you're okay."

Grace bolted out of the room, nearly knocking over Beth who was standing like a statue in the doorway.

"Okay, well—Jesus, Kenzie. We have the police looking for you!" Anthony said, showing the first signs of aggression in his voice. "I don't care! That is no excuse!" Anthony made eye contact with Grace, shaking his head. He said goodbye reluctantly before hanging up the phone. "She's at a friend's house. I'm so sorry, Detective McKenna, I'm so sorry. I'm sure you don't have time for this garbage," he said, clearly forgetting they were in one of the smallest towns in the state, where a missing cat was typically the big case of the day.

"She's okay?" Grace asked.

"Oh yeah, she's okay for now. Until she gets home and receives her grounding. Beth!" Anthony called up the stairs. "Come find out where your daughter's been."

Suddenly, Grace was the third wheel, watching the family go through the motions of everyday life.

"What's going on?" Beth appeared at the top of the stairs, her body leaving no trace of her entrance. Beth might have been the most fragile woman Grace had ever seen. Her voice was so low it was as if the words were struggling to reach the surface, drowning in her lack of existence. She walked down the stairs, and joined them in the kitchen.

"Mackenzie was at a *friend's* house. Her 'phone died.'" He threw some air quotes up, to accentuate the death of a teenager's phone.

"Which friend?" Beth asked, seemingly more concerned with the smaller details.

"I don't even know. Carly, Catelyn . . . something like that." Anthony, fuming with frustration, slid his phone across the countertop. It bounced off the stainless steel toaster and slid back across the granite, falling onto the floor with a loud crack. "You've gotta be fuckin—" He stopped himself, suddenly aware of the presence of the stranger in his house. "This is an embarrassment to our family. I'm so sorry, Detective McKenna. I'm so sorry to waste your time like this."

"It's quite alright. But, I will need to speak to Mackenzie. Just to wrap everything up with the case. It's standard procedure."

"That's fine. Serves her right for disappearing and scaring the bejeezus out of her mother." He gathered the shattered pieces of his phone off the floor and dropped them into a plastic baggie. "Guess I'll be busy standing in line at Verizon for the rest of the afternoon. Make yourself comfortable. She'll be home in twenty minutes." He walked over to the coatrack and slid his arms into a brown leather jacket, then slammed the door behind him, leaving an awkward silence between Grace and Beth. Grace heard the gentle opening of a door upstairs and small feet scurrying on the second level. She wondered if Penny had any understanding of what was going on, or if she was as wrapped up in her seven-year-old world the same way Grace was as a child.

"Would you like some coffee?" Beth asked, pulling out the coffee pot and filling it with fresh tap water.

"Sure, that would be great."

"Take a seat." Beth motioned to the barstool pushed into the island in the center of the kitchen. She seemed to have grown since Anthony left the house, her shoulders peeled back and her chin lifted. For the first time, her eyes held steady on Grace's, revealing a confidence that was absent just moments before. "Cream, sugar, skim milk, agave nectar?" she asked, as she turned toward the open refrigerator. "Kenzie is going through a gluten-free, all-natural phase. Not really sure what agave nectar is—you're on your own with that one."

"I'll be safe and stick with the cream and sugar," Grace said, finally feeling a sense of humanity wafting off the woman.

"So, two girls, huh? Must be tough at times." Grace threw the question out there, an attempt to dig up some dirt on the family that appeared to be growing more dysfunctional by the minute. The dynamic alone was off kilter; a prim and proper father who doted on his daughter, a painfully quiet mother who seemed to shrivel in the presence of the father, and a teenage daughter who seemed to be just a tad too perfect. The youngest daughter seemed to be the most stable in the family, or she just wasn't old enough to be tainted by the Waterford characteristics.

"You know, people always say that. They dwell on the drama of the hormonal teen years." Beth poured a fountain of sugar into her coffee cup. A faded image of Mackenzie, Penny and Beth circled the outside of the cup, their three faces so close it looked like they would need to be physically forced apart in order to separate them. "But I love having my girls. And I know—at least I hope, they will always stick around. Be close by."

Beth took a small sip of the coffee and for the first time, Grace saw some allure in her face. She had symmetrical, soft features and nice skin, most likely because she used minimal products. With a touch of makeup, her brown eyes would pop, coming to life against her creamy skin and natural hair.

"You always hear about boys leaving their roots to start a life with their wife. Not my girls. I couldn't imagine life far away from them. But, I don't know. Sometimes I think Kenzie might go far away after college, or change her mind halfway through the discipline she chooses. She gets bored easily, always on the next mission to perfect a new hobby or skill. She has this way about her, it's hard to explain." The words were flowing freely from Beth's mouth, but there was a faraway look in her eyes. "What about you? Any kids?"

"No," Grace said, keeping her answer simple and adept. It wasn't professional and could potentially be dangerous for an officer to impart personal information to victims and suspects. She always wondered how officers in small towns lived in that same small town, where gossip traveled and unraveled itself through a variety of communication means only to get distorted along the way. Her natural reaction was to divert the attention from herself. "Has Mackenzie looked at any colleges yet? I imagine this is a busy time for a girl so involved in extracurricular activities and academics."

One of the benefits of being a female police officer was that women were more trusting and eager to relay information. Grace used this perk to try and delve deeper into Mackenzie's life.

"Yeah, it's been a busy time for sure." Beth nodded in agreement as if they were old friends catching up, but she was still holding back just enough information.

"What schools is she looking at?"

"Harvard is her top choice." Beth tucked a strand of hair behind her ear. "Wow, I never thought I would utter those words." A trace of moisture came to the surface of her eyes, giving way to a slight sparkle against the brown. "It's just, I was such a bad student. I guess I never imagined I could raise a child who excelled in nearly everything she does. I think she gets it all from Anthony." She put her hands up, refusing to accept credit for anything.

"Oh, I'm sure she's got at least one of her good traits from you." Grace imagined that Beth could be an exhausting friend, always needing to be boosted up. Although, there was something about the way her eyes held steady when Anthony was out of the room that made Grace believe that, at some point, maybe this woman did believe in herself.

"I used to play the piano," Beth said, strumming her fingers on the granite island. "Maybe she got my musical talent." She giggled. "Because I know for certain that Anthony doesn't have a musical bone in his body."

"What hobbies does Anthony have?"

"Oh, he's into everything. He's always running out to the hardware store for parts to make things. Last week, he made Penny a balance beam so she could practice gymnastics. Penny doesn't seem to take life as seriously as Kenzie does, though. I don't think she's set foot on the beam since the fresh coat of purple paint dried. She lives life a little more freely. Flies by the seat of her pants."

Grace couldn't help but think of her own mother, always fluttering from one thing to the next. The only thing that remained constant in Ellen McKenna's life was the love that she had for her daughter.

"Do you still play?" Grace was drawn to this woman, longing to know more about the mystery that flooded in and out of her eyes.

"What?" Beth looked up, confused.

"Do you still play the piano?"

"Oh, God no. Haven't played in years. Not since I moved here, I'd say. Would you like some more coffee, or something to eat, Detective McKenna?" Beth ran the conversation off the train tracks, directing it out of oncoming traffic.

"No thanks, I'm good."

"Hello!" The voice of Mackenzie Waterford echoed through the house, followed by a slam of the door, much like her father's had moments earlier. When she walked into the room, it was as if the world had been tilted and started to spin in a different direction. "Sorry mom, I didn't mean to startle you guys. My phone died," the girl said, her voice sounding as pronounced and silky as the dirty blonde hair that cascaded down her shoulders. Highlighted blonde tips reached for a pair of perky breasts that filled out a pale blue shirt. She pulled her brown cardigan tight across her chest, the tones blending with her eyes, the color of milk chocolate rimmed with a deep-pink eye shadow. Mackenzie Waterford was beautiful. Flecks of pale blonde erupted from the backdrop of her natural light brown hair that was parted in the middle and contoured against her cheeks.

"Where were you, Mackenzie?" Beth asked, jumping up from the island to assess her daughter.

"I was at Carly's house. I told Daddy I was staying there yesterday. I was supposed to call, but my phone died and I didn't have my charger, and it just slipped my mind. So, here I am. And I see that you were so startled that you contacted the police again?" Mackenzie set her backpack gently on a kitchen chair, the weight of the bag sending the chair spinning on a swivel.

"Because you were gone and we were worried. Mackenzie, we didn't hear from you for nearly *two days*. How is that supposed to make us feel?" Beth suddenly looked distracted, an urgency settling in her eyes.

"Mom, I was at Carly's house and I forgot. We were caught up in our project. Time just escaped me. I'm seventeen, I think I'm well beyond checking in with my parents every hour." Mackenzie's eyes darted between the floor and her mother.

"For God's sake, Mackenzie, it's been nearly forty-eight hours!

Who is Carly? I know there is no Carly on your soccer team." Beth, proficient in her daughter's friendships, challenged the girl.

"Just some girl I met in drama class. No big deal."

"I'm sorry, this has happened before? Mackenzie has been missing?" Grace interjected herself into the conversation, picking up on the word *again,* her cue to ask what the chief had already prepared her for.

"Well, yes. Mackenzie just kind of gets in these zones where she's focused and she forgets everything that is going on around her . . . which includes notifying her parents of where she is," Beth said, her parental voice shining through.

"Basically, it's my mother being paranoid." Mackenzie walked across the room toward Grace, and with the manners of a polished businesswoman, extended her hand toward her. "Mackenzie Waterford, nice to meet you." She gave Grace a firm, practiced shake and in the moment they locked eyes, Mackenzie Waterford was no longer a beautiful young scholar.

She was a murderer.

CHAPTER SEVEN

BETH

I KNEW SOMETHING WAS OFF THE FIRST DAY WE BROUGHT HER HOME FROM the hospital. Mackenzie was the most beautiful baby I had ever seen, but there was something in the way she stared at me, as if she could see through me and into another world. Prior to even investigating the adoption process, I had researched everything about those first milestones that made every parent giddy with emotion. One of those was eye contact. Babies did not make eye contact until they were at least six weeks old, yet here was this little pink bundle, only two days old, staring at me, or staring at something in or beyond me. In those first days, when she was home and I was walking around in a sleepless haze, I thought her stare was a sign that she was advanced.

As it turned out, Mackenzie was advanced in every single thing she did, never settling for less than a perfect toe-point in ballet at age five, timing her sprints in the backyard when she was conditioning herself for the junior high track team, and reading and re-reading textbooks until she had absorbed the material so much so that she was awarded with perfect test scores.

But, it didn't take me long to realize that it was less about her being advanced and more that she was a neurotic perfectionist. The older she got, the worse it seemed to get. I had never seen Mackenzie come in second or get passed up on a sports team, and it worried me that she would never learn how to appreciate her successes because she never really failed. Anthony was always thrilled about Mackenzie's obsession with perfection, crediting himself for teaching her about the importance of winning and coming out on top. It was something he had learned from being in the Marine Corps. He used to always say, "When you're on a battlefield, you don't have room for mistakes."

Before my surprise pregnancy with Penny, I felt like a third wheel. Anthony and Mackenzie would snub me for not seeking the same thrills they had for competition, and for conquering a challenge and coming in first. It stimulated them much in the way a skydiver gets a thrill from jumping out of a plane at eighteen-thousand five-hundred feet. When we found out that I was pregnant with Penny, it pushed aside my feelings about Mackenzie's neuroses because I had a baby to focus on, someone who was more like me. Anthony had the competitive athlete he had always dreamed of, but I had other ideas about Mackenzie's obsession.

It had always set off an alert in my gut, signaling to me that something was wrong, something was off. When I would bring it up to Anthony, he would say competition is healthy, that was part of today's youth. I don't think Anthony would've gone off the edge if Mackenzie had failed at anything, but I think she would have crumbled and her entire world would have shattered if she was anything less than perfect.

I remember when she was up for class president of the junior class. She had spent weeks putting together all of her well-deserved references from teachers who could confirm that she had the talent to excel in both the classroom and as the leader of her entire class of two hundred students. Her AP teachers signed off without concern, having seen the girl juggle, sports, subjects and a bubbling social life like she was a trained multi-tasker. While Anthony always thought that Mackenzie was a master when it came to divvying up the different portions of her life that made up a whole, I felt it was hazardous for her health; I was petrified that she would influence her carefree and fun-loving little sister.

"Can't you just appreciate that our daughter is a hard-worker, that we will never have to light a match under her ass to get her motivated?" Anthony would say when I was having a particularly worrisome day about Mackenzie's behavior.

"Something just isn't right, the girl should be enjoying her youth. She should be having some fun and learning from her mistakes. How can she

learn when she never ever makes a mistake?" I would say, before he would inevitably accuse me of being jealous of our daughter's successes. It wasn't like this compulsive behavior was something that we taught her; it was more like a result of two types of DNA colliding and turning out a gene that would alter her psyche.

When Mackenzie was toddling around as a two and a half year old, I would try to get together with other moms, hoping to get her used to being around other children before she enrolled in pre-school. There is one instant in my mind that stands out, as it was possibly the only time that I ever saw the girl fail, if only for a brief moment. The other mom and I were holding up flashcards that were colored according to the object. Mackenzie had been having trouble pronouncing R's, so when I held up the red apple card, she was struggling to say the word. When the other little girl proudly bellowed the color and object, pointing her finger at the card and jumping up and down, Mackenzie lost it. Her eyes shrank down to two slits and her breathing grew so heavy, her chest could barely contain its rhythm. I watched as her hands curled into two tight fists, her white knuckles protruding like little teeth trying to eat their way out of her skin. I watched as the color of her face transformed from a healthy glow to a shade that matched the color of the apple. It started at her neck and crawled up her face, filling it in like a red pen. I could see the rage transform her body and her mind and for the first time, I saw the effect it had on her if she wasn't number one. Like an hour-glass filling with sand, I saw the rage make its way through her little body, as she turned toward the other little girl, her fists now open and expanded like two open baseball mitts. With a force fueled by her internal anger, she pushed the little girl down and threw herself on her, unleashing her small limbs and beating the girl in rapid, fearless maneuvers.

The other mother was rightfully disgusted with the ghastly behavior of my daughter and we never saw them again. I imagine she told all the other mothers to steer clear of me and my possessed daughter. Of course, all of the blame was placed on me. They thought I had let Mackenzie run our house and make all the rules, straying away from discipline and normal parental practices. I never bothered trying to defend myself or make amends because I was just as appalled as the other mother. I had felt that we had inherited a daughter who was possessed by the devil and I had found myself researching *adoptions gone wrong, because who really knows what types of things are responsible for nature.*

While the adoption was closed, we were given limited facts about the mother. She had been a teenager who got pregnant. I'm guessing it was some type of young love situation, but truthfully, I had no idea. The biological traits and history could only be given for the mother's side. It had been a risky adoption, having no knowledge about what traits could possibly be running rampant through her genes, but we wanted a baby so bad. When I told Anthony about her outburst at the playground, he had listened with sympathy and offered me pity for having to deal with such an incident, but then suggested that we enroll Mackenzie in speech classes to assist with advancing her pronunciation of those tricky R sounds. Unlike Anthony, I always thought there was more to Mackenzie's behavior, that she wasn't displaying normal signs of appropriate behavior, that she had some tiny tick inside her, that when set off, would set a storm into motion.

CHAPTER EIGHT

GRACE GRASPED MACKENZIE'S HAND TIGHT, AS IF SHE WAS HOLDING onto the rail of a rollercoaster, gripping for dear life. Mackenzie's brown eyes seared through her, leaving her nearly toppled over from the eerie visions. They hit with a persistence that rattled her nerves. She saw a woman with short, choppy blonde hair reaching for the silver tree necklace that rested just below her collarbone. A red knit winter hat was pulled down close to her eyebrows. Her blue eyes were muddled with fear and confusion. Her already big eyes expanded and flickered back and forth, the final fright settling in.

"Grace? Are you okay?" Beth was standing beside her.

Grace continued to grasp Mackenzie's hand, which was now nearly crushed from the forgotten grip.

"Yeah, I'm sorry, I'm fine. I just . . . you look familiar, Mackenzie." Grace gathered her thoughts, trying to fill in the gaps of the odd exchange with words, hoping to detour them. "Have we met before?"

"Hmmm. . . . " Mackenzie tilted her head and surveyed Grace with contemplation. "No, I don't think so." She gave a sincere smile before tossing a section of hair over her shoulder.

Even in the absence of the visions, Grace knew she wouldn't have liked Mackenzie. There was something about the girl that seemed off, like she was too polished on the exterior. With all the girl was involved with, Grace was surprised they had never crossed paths during one of her visits to the school.

"Where else do you spend your time Mackenzie, besides school? Do you have a boyfriend?" Grace asked, taking the opportunity to see if the girl got nervous, or shriveled under pressure in the presence of a police officer.

"Ha! No, I certainly don't have time for one. Although, there is this new guy I met who's kind of cute." A girlish grin spread across her lips, making Grace second-guess her vision. Beth watched the exchange like she was at a sporting event, enthralled by the next pass of words.

"Kenzie, are you okay? You look a little pale." Beth walked toward her, extending a hand to feel her forehead.

"I'm fine, Mom. Now, let this nice officer ask me questions so she can wrap up her case." The girl was charming—too charming. Grace had expected a moody teenager, a spoiled brat. But Mackenzie was acting as polite and graceful as if she was well trained in etiquette, and apparently police procedure.

"So, who is this boy?" Grace asked, keeping her eyes on Beth to see her reaction and to prevent herself from being toppled over by visions of a woman that Mackenzie apparently had a hand in torturing.

"Oh, just some guy who's in a few of my AP classes." She angled her eyes toward her mother.

"You never told me about a boy, Kenzie," Beth said, trying to mask the surprise in her voice, well trained in teenage talk.

"It's no big deal, Mom, I've just been helping him with college applications and stuff."

"Where is he interested in going to college?" The question surfaced from Grace's lips. She was eager to catch the girl in a stumble.

"The usual favorites—Harvard, Yale, CalPoly."

"What's his name?"

"Evan. Evan McGuirk. Detective McKenna, while I'd love to chat with you about my love life or lack thereof, I really must get to work on my senior presentation," Mackenzie said, using a hand to smooth a long strand of hair along the side of her face. An eerie tranquility weaved itself through her words, and her face remained steady with only a slight tilt of the head that made her appear borderline disturbing. Her eyes followed Grace, as if they were hunting for prey. A child playing a game of chase.

Grace did her best to dodge the girl's gaze by looking around the room, at Beth, anywhere but in the eyes of the juvenile murderer. But the visions wrapped their grip around her, like a python sealing off the breath of its victim. Grace allowed herself to hold steady eye contact for what seemed like an eternity.

While she usually only saw visions of the victims themselves, Grace held on to see if there was a flash of a weapon used, or an identification of the location. There usually wasn't anything but a set of frantic eyes, or sometimes enough of a snapshot to capture an article of clothing. Like all her visions, they kept her up at night searching for proof so she could attach a killer to a victim.

The only crumb of evidence that presented itself in this vision was the backdrop of the victim's body. Grace picked up on the mound of icy snow like a pillow behind the woman's head. This was going to be a challenge, but like all the other times, Grace would lose sleep trying to crack a case where she held onto the biggest piece of evidence: the clarity and proof of what she saw when she looked into the murderer's eyes.

CHAPTER NINE

THE CONTROL ROOM GREETED GRACE WITH THE TYPICAL BEEPS AND hums of the radios and outdated machinery. The fan whirred in the background, a permanent noise at the station resulting from the lack of air circulation. It had become a staple of the station, the noise present in the still moments of the night and its noise comforting when the station was at its busiest.

"Hey, Joe," Grace said as she leaned against the piece of plywood that separated the control room from the hallway that led to the inner workings of the station.

"Hey girl, how's it going?" Lieutenant Joe Sullivan twirled around in his swivel chair, the loose wheels on the old furniture making his transition look sloppy as he rocked left to right like a boat being threatened by a few hefty waves.

"Good. How are you? Did you figure out what to do about your Christmas plans?"

"Eh, I got my daughter dragging me along to her boyfriend's family for dinner." Joe's fingers danced along the arms of the chair. "Hey, speaking of . . . I guess I'm supposed to bring wine. You know anything about wine, Gracie? All I know is that there are three options: red, pink and white, right?"

"I'll pick up a nice bottle for you, Joe. Don't worry."

"Thanks, kid. We didn't drink wine in my day. It was always Manhattans and martinis. Now they do all this fancy shit, matching meat with a certain kind of wine. I don't get it." He shook his head, clearly flustered.

Joe Sullivan was a good man. He'd been at the station for nearly forty years, and he was a dedicated supporter of the town, having been attached to several committees over the years. His heart had split in half the day he lost his wife two years ago; on his lowest days, everyone had thought for sure he would die of a broken heart. Joe had doted on his wife since they were in ninth grade at the local high school. They were the classic cheerleader, football player combo and his eyes never strayed from her since the day they met in freshman English class. He had one grown daughter who had ventured off to New York City for years, but returned when the news of her mother's death ripped through their family like a tornado.

"You just relax and I'll swing by the store on my way home tonight. I'll have a bottle of red and a bottle of white, that way you're prepared," Grace said, offering him a sincere smile. "In the meantime though, can I get you to run a check on a girl named Mackenzie Waterford?"

"What about Mackenzie Waterford?" Sergeant Barrington slipped into the conversation, filling his mouth with spoonfuls of Greek yogurt.

"Eh, just a missing person case I'm wrapping up," Grace said. "Why? Do you know her?"

"Of course I know her. My daughter has been competing against her since they learned how to read. The girl is a genius. Excels at everything she does. Don't tell my daughter I said that, though."

"Does your daughter hang around with Mackenzie?" Grace asked, trying not to sound too anxious to learn more about the girl.

"Eh, it's kind of a sore subject in our house. They're friendly, but Josie has come in second to Mackenzie for so long that she has a hard time completely warming up to her. Competition with kids these days, it's brutal." Sergeant Barrington shook his head and rested two hands on Lieutenant Sullivan's shoulders. "Hey big guy . . . what's up for Christmas?"

"I'll get those bottles to you." Grace winked and turned on a foot.

"Let me know how much I owe ya, kid," Sullivan said.

"Just get me that report stat, and we'll call it even. It will be my Christmas gift to you." Grace turned and made her way across the hall toward her office.

The fluorescent lighting spilled onto the linoleum floor, leaving a shiny pool of yellow framing her every step. She passed the break-room where a cluster of officers were huddled around a table of treats donated by one of the town residents as a Christmas thank you. She grabbed the mail that was sticking out of the metal box that hung outside her office. It always amazed her how many Christmas cards she received from victims she'd helped in the past.

She tore open the card on top of the pile as she made her way to her desk. Bits of glitter showered her black pants as she slid into her chair and pulled the festive card from its envelope. A sparkly red sled outlined in green glitter glided across the silvery background. *Merry Christmas* was scrawled across the top of the card in gold glitter. Two scratch tickets fell onto her lap as she opened the thick white home-made card. *May you and your family have a lovely holiday. Thank you for all of your help. Love, Elise and Morgan Donahue.*

Elise had been a victim of domestic violence. When Grace had responded to the call on that late Friday night, she had been paralyzed by the visions she saw when Elise's then-husband opened the door, claiming that all was okay and their daughter was just being a child and testing a call to 911. Morgan's voice had come across the phone in jumpy out of breath syllables. *My mom, my mom . . . just . . . got . . . hurt. . .by . . . my . . . dad.* Nine-year-old Morgan had been filled with hesitance when she called in, afraid to get her dad in trouble. In the end, she had saved her mother's life. This hadn't been Ray Donahue's first attack; in fact, the injury Elise sustained was minor compared to the women that made themselves present when Grace made eye contact with the abuser. A string of frightened female faces jerked Grace around when she was face to face with Ray Donahue, on the front step of his newly renovated colonial home on one of the nicest streets in town. Grace had worked with a local sketch artist to capture the faces of the women she'd seen in her visions. The sketches were scanned and added into the system that covered all of Massachusetts. With the convenience of social media, it wasn't hard to track three of the four women down, enough to convict Ray Donahue of assault and battery. There was still one out there who she had yet to find, and to this day, the set of deep-brown pleading eyes haunted her every time she closed her own eyes to go to sleep at night. She lived every day walking on eggshells, afraid to seal eye contact with the wrong person because she knew she didn't have it in her to walk away.

Grace picked up the next piece of mail from the pile. She unfolded a piece of paper that was folded in thirds and sealed with a round gold sticker. Barb's invitation to the police department Christmas party. While Barb was somewhat computer literate, she still insisted on sending printed invitations. The print danced across the page in flowing cursive black font:

Join your fellow officers at the annual Christmas party
Thursday, December 22nd at 6:00pm
Location: Breakroom
Light appetizers and beverages provided
Please bring a snack to share

A PICTURE of a wreath was stamped on the bottom and smudged in black ink. The lack of budget at the small-town station left Barb with black as the only ink option. The invitation looked more like a flyer for a car wash.

Grace remembered when the Christmas parties used to be catered with top-notch food and an open bar. Over the years, with budget cuts and an accumulation of unruly behavior at annual parties, the gatherings began to shrink and be more contained. It used to be that everyone felt bad for the poor officer who was stuck working the night of the party, but now everyone volunteered to work, if only to get out of having to go to the party that was held at the station with limited funds.

Grace used a foot to push off the floor, sending her into a wobbly glide toward the bulletin board that hung on the wall parallel with a map of the greater Boston area. She pulled a pushpin out of an old thank you note and pushed it through both the invite and the Christmas card. The board swung left to right, like a lazy pendulum. Her landline buzzed to life, startling her from her thoughts.

"Hey, Joe." The red light on the phone console had alerted her that the call was coming from the control room.

"I got nothing,'" Joe said. Grace could hear the background of *Leave it to Beaver*. Typically when the television was on, it had to be tuned into CNN, but every now and then a veteran officer would pull their rank and opt for less serious programming.

"That's what I figured." Grace rested the earpiece on her shoulder and unraveled the tangled phone cord with her free hand.

"Why are you after student-of-the-month, anyways?"

"Oh, just checking in on her before I officially close the case." Grace looked in the mirror that clung to the wall to the left of her desk, making a mental note to look into eye cream. Her mother had been pushing some all-natural stuff on her a few months ago. She used a pinky to stamp at the two puddles of darkness that lie underneath her bloodshot red eyes. Sleep was never one of Grace's easiest pursuits. "Wait, what do you mean 'student of the month'?"

"Just Google her on the computa'. She's everywhere. The kid's like some type of freakish scholar. She's pretty good at sports, too. I checked out her images on that Google search image button."

"Hey, thanks, Joe. I'll look into it." Before Joe could say goodbye, Grace was on a mission to find anything that would let her prove the girl's guilt.

Grace typed in "Mackenzie Waterford" and a collage of images flood the screen. All photos were of the girl in perfect lighting receiving some type of accolade, dating back to when she was as young as three years old. Several rectangular images stared back at her: Mackenzie with perfectly pointed toes and angled arms in a tutu as a toddler; the girl standing on a bleacher being presented with a soccer trophy; another photo showed Mackenzie being awarded a top score for some type of standardized test.

"Unbelievable. Does this girl fail at anything?"

Just when Grace had seen enough of the obnoxious photos, one of the images tugged at her. It was the eyes that pulled her in at first, the too-big eyes that took over the woman's face. In the photo, her hair was textured with chunks of brown, her natural color before she dyed her whole head blonde. Her face appeared much different than the vision Grace had seen of her, but she knew it was the same woman immediately by her giant blue eyes. A short, delicate smile offsets her substantial eyes, contorting her face into a peaceful expression, much different than the frightened, darting expression in the visions. A lanky arm extends from her small frame and drapes over Mackenzie's shoulders, pulling her into a tight side-hug for the camera. Anthony and Beth leaned into Mackenzie and the woman like bookends, smiling proudly. Mackenzie held a gold-plated plaque with one hand, and the woman gripped the other side of the dark wooden frame.

Grace zoomed in to read the font on the gold plate: *Student of the Year.* "Is this her teacher?" The words couldn't help but come to the surface, tainted in confusion. Grace had seen her fair share of shocking criminal work, but teacher and student crime was usually limited to the movies. "I guess Mackenzie Waterford isn't so perfect after all."

Grace opened another search tab and typed in "Bridgeton High School," clicking away until a list of faculty and staff appeared on the screen, side by side with bios and photos. She scrolled until she saw the distinguishable spiky short hair, precisely angled with the help of some type of cutting edge pomade. Grace imagined the woman getting her hair done at one of those trendy salons downtown, where flamboyant stylists two-step between dying and dicing hair, and spinning their clients around so they are face to face with a mirror that reflects a magazine perfect image of texturized, colored hair. *Jenny*

Silva, Art Teacher. "Art is not what you see, but what you make others see" was penned underneath the photo.

"Wow, fancy for a small town public high school," Grace said to herself, remembering the simplicity of the photos in her high school yearbook, long before schools had websites. "Thank God for the internet," she said. She was still of the age where she could appreciate Google searches and social media stalking because she had witnessed life before the surge of technology when the only way to track someone down was in the white pages of a phone book. "Is little Miss Perfect an artist, too?" Grace didn't remember seeing any colorful canvasses hanging in her room, and she didn't wear those chunky, quirky earrings like the ones that dangled from Jenny Silva's ears in the photo.

She pressed the speaker button on the phone, intent on keeping her focus on the screen without having to take the extra step in placing the earpiece up to her head. "Joe, can you run a report on a Jenny Silva?"

"Sure, but what's up with all the broads you're making me run reports on?" he asked, the sound of gum smacking between his words.

"I'll fill ya in later when I actually have a decent clue."

"Whatever you say, kid. I'll run this stat."

"Great, just ring me when you've got it. You might want to try Jennifer, too. And it's Silva. S-I-L-V-A."

"You got it."

Surprisingly, the technology at the small town police department was upgraded every few years, making it simple for a citizen's information to be pulled up in a matter of seconds. Joe would be able to type in the full name and green print would light up the black screen, granting access to all of Jenny Silva's personal information: address, license number and past violations, as well as previous addresses.

"Hey, kid." Joe came through the line, his voice gruff and accented with the weight of syllables standard for someone who has lived near Boston his entire life. Dropped R's and oddly pronounced cities passed down from generation to generation had left Joe without a choice but to sound like a hardcore Bostonian. "I've got a report up on the screen. No warrants, no history of crime. Just a few measly traffic violations back in 2013. Mostly failure to stop, it looks like. Gal's always in a rush."

"Is she from Bridgeton?"

"The name doesn't sound familiar, so I'm guessing no, but let's take a looksee at her other addresses." Joe clicked his tongue as he scrolled down to see the previous addresses. Being one of many Sullivans in the town, Joe comes from a long line of Bridgeton relatives. He left the confines of the town as little as possible, and had built himself a solid reputation of being one of the finer staples in the community of 17,000 people and 4,000 dogs. As he always said "I have everything I need in Bridgeton." He picked up his morning coffee at the Bridgeton Book Depot, the local store that prided themselves on having the best, if only, cup of coffee in town. He attended dinner at Rizzo's Italian Dining every single Friday night. If he wasn't there by 5:01, the staff started to worry. And when his wife was alive, they had designated seats in church. Everyone knew not to sit in the second pew from the back, the two seats closest to the aisle, because Joe and Marlene Sullivan would be there for four o'clock mass.

"Looks like she hails from California, by way of Somerville."

"Not surprising," Grace said, having her pegged as a girl who may have recently grown out of the hipster roots that were commonplace in Somerville. "When did she move to Bridgeton?"

"She's held an address here since—standby—two thousand . . . twelve."

"Good amount of time. Has she always been employed by the high school?"

"Good amount of time compared to who? She shouldn't even be considered a resident, if you ask me," Joe scoffed, his townie defenses jumping to life as they usually did when he was calculating the number of years required for a citizen of the town to be considered an actual resident and not just some gypsy floating through. Roughly ninety-percent of Bridgeton was made up of people who had lived there their whole lives and descended from parents and grandparents who had claimed the same. So, on the rare occasion when an outsider decided to dig up ground and plant some roots in the quaint town, a great deal of turbulence could be felt in the event that the outsider stirred up some trouble.

"Yes, Joe. I'm well aware of your thoughts on qualified residents in Bridgeton. What's her current address?"

"I've got thirteen Alebury Ave. That's over by the old pharmacy." Grace could hear the television in the background change from *Leave it to Beaver* to CNN. "You going over there? What kinda trouble is this girl in?"

"She's not in trouble yet, that I know of. I'm just looking into something for a friend, that's all." Grace made the words appear as magically as if she were a magician pulling a rabbit out of a hat. "You made me miss out on one of my favorite *Leave it to Beaver* episodes to do a favor for a friend? Kid, you're lucky I like you."

"Likewise, Joe. Thanks for all your help. I'll pay you back in cookies soon enough." Grace was already buttoning up her jacket and getting ready to head out the door.

"A girl after my own heart. Let me know if you need anything else." Joe hung up the phone and Grace swung open her office door so fast that she startled Sergeant Connolly, who was in deep conversation with a new patrol officer. The two paused and looked at her.

"Sorry," Grace said, adjusting the holster on her hip and forcing herself to slow down so she didn't look too suspicious.

"No worries." Sergeant Connolly locked eyes with her as he took a long sip of coffee. "You all set?"

Grace wasn't sure if he was mocking her or if he was onto her. His free hand rested low on his hip. His eyes scanned her body in a way that bordered on sexual longing and confused accusations.

"Yeah, I've got a meeting at the school." The words appeared out of nowhere, but reached the surface with a calm that made her feel that they just may believe her. The young patrol officer looked like a deer in headlights. This was probably his first real job out of school, and he most likely only saw good looking female detectives in the movies. Grace tried her best to downplay her looks, opting for a more natural appearance so the male dominated field wouldn't chew her up and spit her out like she was some sort of Detective Malibu Barbie.

"I'll be back this afternoon," she said as she slithered by them, maintaining eye contact with Mark as if they were in a duel.

As she stepped outside, the cold air hit her with force, its power leaving a tingling sensation in her nose. "Geez, when did it get so cold," she said under her breath as she walked to her car in quick steps. She shielded her face from the cold with the collar of her coat.

"Hey, Princess. Don't forget about tonight." Barb approached her, her voice cutting into Grace's tenacious march.

"Tonight? What's tonight?" Grace peeled her head up out of her coat like a turtle stretching its neck.

"Eric. Remember?" Barb used her gloved fingers to hold several paper bags filled with greasy food from Dewey's, the local fast food restaurant. She used a hip to shut her car door as she balanced a tray of drinks.

"Oh shit. This soon? You want me to go out with him tonight?"

"Gee, I didn't ask you to marry the guy but you could at least act a *little* excited about the date."

"No, that's not it. I just didn't realize you meant this soon." She shoved her hands into her coat pockets, and hoped that she could find an excuse to get out of the date somewhere in the depths of the lined coat. She had been completely enraptured in the Waterford case since meeting Mackenzie, and all she wanted to do when she got home tonight was share a pizza with Brody and research the hell out of the girl before she got away with another murder. "Don't worry, I'll be there with bells on."

"Okay, I'll have him pick you up at say . . . seven?" Barb shifted her weight to balance the food and drinks. "I'll give him your address." She started using tiny steps to make her way back into the building.

"Um, actually, I'll meet him there. Any idea where he wants to go?" Grace clenched her teeth, preparing herself for Barb's wrath. She had learned her lesson about getting picked up for dates a couple of years ago, when the guy got so drunk at the bar, she had to drive his car back to his house, then take a cab back to her place. She had promised herself she'd never be caught in that situation again. Some dating rituals were just meant to be forced out of today's society.

"Oh for the love of Pete! What is up with your generation wanting to be all independent and shit?"

"Sorry, Barb, but I'm not changing my mind about this one. I'm not risking my safety and putting myself in harm's way just so some guy can feel chivalrous for driving me around."

"Fine, I'll tell him to meet you at 21st Amendment. It's some yuppie bar in the city."

"Yep, I know where it is." Grace had been to the restaurant with her old high school friends a handful of times. The bar was a hotspot for colleagues from the financial district to meet up for happy hour and show off their corporate America slang and pressed office wear. There was one common theme at the 21st Amendment. It usually involved a group of giddy college girls sidled up to the bar next to a polished twenty-something guy from one of the city's bigger financial firms. The young girls who weren't quite of legal age would use their older sisters' IDs from back home. The guys would loosen their ties, after the end of a long day of punching numbers and attending useless meetings, and the younger girls would be wearing skinny jeans regardless of how skinny they were and always a baggy top that, if they moved in just the right way, would slink off their shoulder. The out-of-towner college girls almost always fell for a guy who claimed he went to Harvard. The pedigree was like crack to a girl from anywhere outside of New England.

"Thanks, Princess. You are a good cookie," Barb said, turning back quickly before she nearly slammed into the glass door of the station.

CHAPTER TEN

Most of the streets in Bridgeton were designated as one-ways, with the exception of a few main roads that traveled the length of the town. Alebury Avenue sat on the part of town that was designated as beachside, for obvious reasons. A row of narrow one-way streets were greeted by one main road that framed the edge of the beach. Grace had been told by a townie once that back in the seventies, Bridgeton Beach would get as packed as Miami Beach in the summer months. All Grace could picture was Farrah Fawcett look-alikes doused in baby oil, flaunting their string bikinis with Boston accents. She imagined men riding old beach cruisers in overly short swim trunks and golden hair. This time of year, all that decorated the sand were a few loose dogs trailing behind their owners and photographers who were eager to get the perfect winter beach shot complete with a line of sudsy waves reaching the shoreline just as the moon was illuminated by impeccable light.

Grace pulled into one of the many open spots along the beach wall. As she got out of the car, she wondered where people parked back in the Bridgeton Beach heyday. Her car was parked three streets away from Alebury, just enough to make it look like she was going for a stroll in the middle of the day. A woman pushing a double stroller gave her a subtle smile as she pushed two sleeping babies shielded by clear plastic covers.

Bridgeton was the type of town where you could drop a name in a coffee shop and a million opinions and voices would explode about the person, like a real-life Google search. It would be as easy as asking the woman if she knew where Jenny Silva lived, but Grace couldn't let anyone know about her mission just yet because there was always that slight chance that her vision was wrong and that Jenny Silva was actually someone else. She had yet to have a misleading vision, but Grace couldn't be too safe when it came to her position as a detective. When Grace was a little girl, she would spend countless hours in front of the television, her nose nearly touching the screen so she could absorb every clue that Charlie's Angels found. After each episode, Grace would log the clues in her solid blue Trapper Keeper. Even at the young age of nine, she wanted her classmates to take her seriously, opting for a solid color instead of the fluorescent unicorns and puppies that her female classmates had.

Alebury Avenue happened to be on one of the only dead end roads in Bridgeton, and Jenny Silva's house was inconveniently tucked in right at the end of the street, making it impossible for Grace to look nonchalant as she attempted to spy on the house. It was the middle of the day and, while people would soon be taking their Christmas breaks, the street was dead. Only a couple of the driveways had cars, though that didn't necessarily mean people weren't home. In a town like Bridgeton, there were several one-car families, as public transportation was a convenient option for those who commuted into Boston. Still, something about the street seemed still and unmoving in a way that instantly put Grace on edge.

The grass had taken on its winter coat after seeing its first snow over the past weekend, absent of the vibrant green shade that gave the neighborhoods that extra contrast in the nicer months. Shovels leaned against the sides of several houses, awaiting the first major snowstorm of the season, and buckets of salt sat at the bottom of the front and side steps. Few houses in Bridgeton had a fresh coat of paint, revealing chips and decay that showed the age of the old Colonials and Capes. The houses that were closer to the beach were naturally smaller and closer together, having traded yard space in for the coast that was steps away from their front doors.

Grace couldn't miss Jenny Silva's house if she tried. It was purple and so small that it looked like it could be the in-law home of the cape that sat beside it. There was a celestial sun hanging from the front door and a row of pots filled with frozen soil and sunflowers. Three wobbly looking steps led to a small side porch. Grace guessed that this was used as the main entrance, as there was a mailbox hanging loosely alongside the storm door. An orange bag filled with circulars sat on the top step next to a couple pieces of mail that had fallen out of the overstuffed mailbox.

"Looks like this is Jenny Silva's house," Grace muttered to herself as she picked up the loose mail from credit card companies and a catalog from a Boston art school. She tapped on the door lightly, a stark contrast with the normal beating that officers gave to make their presence known. She leaned her ear against the door and used her index finger to press the round doorbell. Based on her experience, the majority of doorbells in this town failed to work, mostly because of the age of the homes but sometimes people simply didn't want to deal with mailmen ringing their doorbells in the middle of the day to alert them to a delivered package. Grace remembered overhearing a conversation between two moms at the checkout line of Target one day. *"I mean seriously, I had to disconnect our doorbell because the stupid mailman was delivering packages during naptime. Like, hello! My kid is sleeping. I need all the me-time I can get."*

When Grace was sure that neither Jenny Silva nor anyone else would be answering the door, she leaned over the porch railing that overlooked the tiny backyard. In what little piece of land that Jenny Silva had, she had made sure to fill it with plants and pots and garden creatures. A few garden gnomes stared up at Grace in an all-knowing way. "Do you guys have something to tell me? Have you seen any weird activity around here lately?" Grace asked the gnomes with a quiet chuckle. This wasn't a laughing matter, but sometimes she had to look at her life with a sense of humor. Her visions had become such a natural part of her life that she seldom found the amusement in how God chose her to be the recipient of such a powerful gift.

A Nerf football lay flush against the exhausted wooden fence that had frayed triangle edges pointed up from the earth, but leaning slightly to one side like an old man walking with a limp. From what Grace had seen of the woman so far, she didn't picture her with children and was certain that the football had been thrown too far from the neighboring yard. The house next door was bigger and boasted a larger yard that was filled with signs of childhood. Two sleds lay on the bulkhead. The outline of a trampoline was resting underneath the protection of a tarp, off limits for the winter months. Grace rapped on the door again, louder this time. "Hello? Is anyone home?" The words sounded so odd coming from her mouth, like an old detective movie.

"You lookin' for Jenny?" The voice pierced the air, punching her in the gut. She whipped around so fast, she almost lost her balance on the uneven wooden slats of the porch.

"Yes, I am."

"Hey, you're that gal detective. The one that works at the high school sometimes," the older man said as he looked up from pouring salt on the walkway that led up to the house next door. His body was leaning over as he looked up, angled in the shape of a C. Grace shouldn't have been surprised that the man knew her. She was in the local paper nearly every week for town events. She assumed most people didn't read the paper, but based on the age of the guy, he was most likely of the generation that still tracked their news with a subscription to a hard copy. "I'm Walt Brennan. I spend most of my days here watching my two grandsons while their dad goes to work. I live the next street over, on Riptide Way."

"Oh, nice to meet you, Walt." Grace was taken aback by the amount of information the man had shared, but that was typical of the retirees in the town. They loved to talk and most of them spent their days catering to their grandchildren to offset the high cost of daycare. "Do you know Jenny Silva?"

"Yeah, nice girl. Loves her plants. I've got a bit of a green thumb myself. She asked me for advice one day about sunflowers. I told her it wasn't the best place to plant them, since she doesn't get direct sunlight there, but as you can see, the girl was determined. Haven't seen her for a couple of days, though. I was under the assumption that she was on an early Christmas break or something, since she's a teacher and all. Heck, I need a Christmas break after spending all day with these boys. I tell ya, I'm not as young as I used to be. I always tell my son I woulda never been able to have kids at the late age he had them. You don't have the energy you have in your thirties as you do in your twenties. Me and my wife got married when she was eighteen and I was twenty. Made a baby on our honeymoon . . . am I babbling? Sorry, I get a bit caught up when I'm presented with the opportunity to talk with a beautiful young woman." Walt said with a smirk. "Don't tell my wife, though. She's inside napping with the boys."

"I won't say a word."

"Why are ya looking for Jenny, anyways? Are you off duty? Is she a friend? I can't imagine she's in any kinda trouble. My wife always complained about those tattoos she has winding up her arm, but I don't think she's the criminal type."

"Yeah, I just got off shift and thought I'd stop by. We became friends at one of the school functions a few months back."

"Ahhh, well. I'm gonna head inside before the storm comes. You should do the same. I hear we're supposed to have a rough one." Walt set down the bucket of salt and rubbed his hands together. "Don't tell my wife you saw me without gloves . . . she gets on me about my thin skin tearing in my old age." A full smile spread across his face, revealing a warmth that was matched by his deep brown eyes. Grace could tell from across the yard that Walt had been a looker in his day. Most likely Italian, with thick lashes that may have thinned over the years, but still framed his eyes in a way that softened his face. He still had a full head of hair. There were a few strands of the dark brown of his youth peeking out from behind shades of silver and white. He wore a navy blue peacoat that reached his mid-thighs, its brown buttons fastened unevenly along his chest.

"Your secret is safe with me." Grace shot him a smile. Walt

Brennan was chatty, but there was something safe and warm about the old man.

When she was sure that Walt was safely tucked inside the house, Grace reached for the loose brass doorknob that stuck out from the pale yellow door. She barely had to touch the knob before the door flung open wide, welcoming her into Jenny Silva's world. She gave one last look over her shoulder to make sure no one was witness to her welcoming herself into the stranger's house.

"Jenny? Jenny, are you home?" Grace said the words as a precaution. She knew deep down that she wouldn't get a response, but if someone—anyone—was there, she had to make it look like she was there out of concern and not breaking and entering. She was in dangerous territory, attaching herself to a case that technically didn't exist anywhere but in the captivity of her mind.

A round pine table sat beside a window near the doorway, flanked by four chairs all painted in different bright colors. The backs of the chairs were tattooed with black henna stenciling. Grace walked into the kitchen slowly, keeping one hand on her holster. Only a small chunk of the table could be seen from underneath the clutter of papers and books. A sketchpad lay open next to a coffee cup with the quote *"art is never finished, only abandoned"* in bright red print. A dried up tea bag sat in a heap next to the cup.

Grace knew that she wasn't following proper police protocol, that she should never mess with a potential crime scene, but how was she to know if these visions were accurate if she couldn't make contact with the evidence. She pulled a pair of gloves out of the pouch tucked next to her holster and tugged them on as a precaution. A wet imprint was left behind from the tea bag on the table. Based on the knowledge that Grace had gained from years of watching her mother experiment with herbal teas, she knew that it took about twenty-four hours for a bag to completely dry out, including the object that it was set on. The thought that someone was here within the past twenty-four hours sent a chill down her spine. She plucked the tea bag with gloved fingers and dangled it in front of her like she was taunting a cat with a mouse. A tiny dollop of liquid remained on the table beneath the bag.

"Definitely a somewhat recent cup of tea," she said under her breath as she placed the bag back down in the small puddle.

A row of canisters holding a variety of spices and baking supplies stood in a line along the laminate countertop, uneven heights peaking and dipping like a miniature city skyline. Grace picked up one of the canisters and flipped it open. Some of the quinoa that was stuck to the lid fell out in little sprinkles.

She eased her way into the house, making her way down the narrow hallway that housed a long line of hooks for purses and coats. Across from the hooks was a thin wood-paneled closet door, its latch undone and the door cracked open slightly. A messily folded pile of clean sheets filled one of the shelves and a laundry hamper took up the limited space at the bottom of the closet. A few articles of clothing were dangling out the side of the overstuffed container.

"MEOW."

The noise startled Grace, causing her to slam the door shut, turning fast so her back was pressed against the thin wooden door-frame. A small gray cat swaggered toward Grace from one of the adjoining rooms.

"MEOW," the cat roared as it rubbed against her legs, leaving a trail of fur behind on her black pants. Its voice had strength for something so petite, but it was friendly enough as it continued to meow and figure-eight its body between Grace's ankles. She looked down the end of the hallway to see two empty bowls resting on a plastic mat.

"You hungry, kitty?" Grace asked as she crouched down and scratched the cat's chin. "Let me see if there's any food lying around for you." Grace found herself back in the kitchen, inspecting the cabinets for food. It seemed like everything she came across was organic or wrapped in recycled packaging of some sort. Her eyes surveyed the contents of the refrigerator as a last resort. Half-eaten containers of berries, Greek yogurt and soy milk was all that sat on the bare shelves. She looked on the side shelf and spotted some Tupperware containers that were filled with a chopped up concoction. *Van Gogh* was scrawled in black marker on the red lid of one of the containers. She grabbed one that was half empty.

"Well, if you're not Van Gogh, I feel really bad for the poor soul who is," Grace said as she opened the lid and sniffed the mushy substance. The cat meowed again and climbed his front paws up Grace's shin. She walked the container over and dropped the mass into one of the bowls, then topped the other off with water. The cat immediately went to town eating the food like it was starving. "How long has it been since you've been fed, buddy?"

Grace peered into the two rooms that branched off the end of the hallway. One was clearly Jenny's bedroom. A queen-sized bed sat in the middle with crumpled purple sheets and a deep-purple comforter. A few sweaters were dangling off a dresser on the opposite wall. As Grace walked across the room, the boards creaked beneath the round area rug that took up most of the hardwood floor. She ran a hand over one of the sweaters and she could feel through the glove that it was still damp. The sweater was bright red and loose around the neck, making it look like it would hang loosely off the shoulder of a small frame. A loud crash erupted outside the door to the house and Grace froze, unable to move her body. Her heartbeat accelerated so much that she felt the pounding in her ears. Her hands clenched at her sides as she thought of reasons to give for being there. What if Jenny had a boyfriend, a friend, or even a parent that stopped by looking for her and they found her inside Jenny's house?

"Shit," she said under her breath. She tiptoed to the door of the bedroom, but the floorboards gave her away, creaking beneath each step. Like the trained detective that she was, she moved her body along the walls, shielding herself from potential shots fired. Making her way to the kitchen she paused again, waiting long enough to ensure there wasn't another sound. Peeling back one of the sheer white curtains from the small window of the side door, she looked onto the porch to see a pile of mail and a knocked over pot. "Thank God," she said to herself. "Nice aim mailman."

The only other room in the house that had gone unsearched appeared to be the designated art room. Canvas oil paintings and sketched drawings covered the walls like wrapping paper. An easel sat at the center of the room, its legs stabbing into the blue carpeting on the floor. Grace found it odd that Jenny would choose the only room in the house with carpeting as the room that paint gets spilled in, and started to deem the girl as either very messy or not too talented when it came to interior decorating. The only décor besides plants and magnets with quotes, was the artwork that she had brought to life. There were several sketches of faces and paintings of plants and flowers. There was one lonely painting of Van Gogh, and Grace could confirm her talent, as the green eyes that sat like two marbles on the cat's face, were spot on. She managed to bring the eeriness to life.

The easel was flipped to a drawing that was halfway completed. It was one side of a man's face. The features didn't look familiar to Grace at first, until she recognized the shape of the one completed eye. It hit her like a ton of bricks and suddenly her whole body felt heavy, like she was sinking to the bottom of an ocean.

CHAPTER ELEVEN

BETH

I KNEW SOMETHING WAS GOING ON. NOT IN THE WAY THAT ONE WOULD imagine—I didn't find a lipstick stain on his collar, nor did I find a number folded up in one of his pockets. It was something in the way he became, as if he no longer noticed me when I entered the room. I had become a fixture, like that marble-topped table we bought together so many years ago. I tried sprucing up my appearance; I even got a few highlights thrown in with the help of one of Mackenzie's friends who wanted to go to cosmetology school.

I found out it was her when I drove by the school on my way home from the office one night. I happened to be going that route, thinking maybe I would swing by and catch Mackenzie during soccer practice. I hadn't suspected anything. In fact, just that morning I thought things were looking up; Anthony had taken the time to give me a peck on the cheek before leaving for work.

When I saw his car in the parking lot, I figured it was a safe bet that Mackenzie was practicing and he was there supervising. Maybe he'd let Mackenzie drive them home, to practice her driving skills. Nothing struck me as odd, until I stepped out of the car and realized the soccer field was empty, except for one lone girl practicing. A girl whose frame and form were clumsy and unfocused, so naturally I knew it wasn't my daughter.

I knew that the art classrooms had a back entrance that spilled into the staff parking lot because I had picked up Mackenzie there on several occasions. Surprisingly, Mackenzie hadn't been much of an artist. It seemed to be the one thing she didn't excel in, so she had devoted extra hours after school to learn painting techniques and color palettes. I never understood it. Most people accept it when they aren't good at one thing. Mackenzie was different. She couldn't comprehend the fact that we weren't designed to be perfect. We are human. When asked about her art class, Mackenzie would always rave about her teacher, Miss Silva. I knew they had grown close and I welcomed it because, as far as I knew, Jenny Silva was a good influence on Kenzie. Her classroom was always messy and she had that classic artist persona about her —a little quirky, a little mysterious and far from perfect.

There was one semester that Kenzie took the class and the focus was "Finding art in imperfection." I remember peeking at the syllabus once when Kenzie left her schoolbooks sprawled out on the table. I thought about how fitting that would be for Mackenzie to learn, like the lesson was designed for her. When I saw Jenny Silva pressed against the building by my husband, I can't say I was all that surprised. I mean, she was young, pretty and different than me. My intuition was right. My husband was having an affair.

But, what I would learn later was so much worse.

CHAPTER TWELVE

"Yes, Mom?"

Grace picked up the phone fast. The thoughts in her mind darted back and forth, bashing up against various explanations and possibilities. She was at the stoplight at the only intersection that allowed access into and out of Bridgeton. Filled with regrets from committing to the date with Barb's nephew Eric, Grace had forced herself to leave work and head home to get changed for a dreaded night out.

"Honey, I'm on my way to your house. I need to get that book I lent you a few weeks ago. You know, the one about the all-natural cleansing and how it's enhanced by daily meditations—"

"Yeah, mom, but now's not a good time. I've gotta get ready . . . I'm not even home yet."

"Don't worry, I won't interrupt your dinner date with Brody. And it's too late, I'm already letting myself in." Ellen McKenna's voice came through sing-songy and high pitched. Grace looked over at the sketch she had stolen from Jenny's house. She figured she was safe taking it because if Jenny Silva happened to be alive, it's doubtful that she would want the picture of Anthony.

"Okay, fine. I'll be home in about ten minutes," Grace said, trying to rid her voice of any impatience she felt. If she didn't get her mother out fast, she was going to have to explain why she was getting ready to go out. And that could start a whole new rant about how important it was for Grace to date and expand her social life.

By the time Grace made it home, it was four-thirty and darkness had already blanketed the streets. As expected, Ellen was busy at work in the walkway leading up to Grace's small front porch. The woman always took it upon herself to pretty up Grace's place, which usually involved hanging dream catchers throughout her house and spritzing lavender oils on her pillows and sheets when she wasn't looking.

"Hey, Bug." Ellen looked up from stabbing a decorative metal Santa into the earth. She had called Grace "Bug" for as long as she could remember, the name shortened down from Gracie Bug.

"Hey, Mom. I thought you came for your book?" Grace kicked her Jeep door shut while she balanced her lunch sack and workbag in one hand and her coffee mug in the other.

"Stay right there! Don't move!" Ellen placed a determined flat hand out in front of herself.

"Mom, I don't have time for this. I'm in a rush." The impatience rose in Grace's voice. She was not in the mood for her mother's silly antics.

"Oh no. There's always time for—" Ellen bent down and struggled to plug in the thick orange extension cord that was draped across the front porch, "—Christmas lights! Voila!" She waved her arms in front of Grace as a row of colorful lights outlined the small house.

"What is this?" Grace said, unable to help being uplifted by her mother's positive energy and the hundreds of twinkling lights before her.

"I thought it was time you start showing a little Christmas spirit. You know, Bug, if your house is lit up, maybe some of your neighbors won't think you're a single workaholic who doesn't have time to be invited to holiday parties. I'm just sayin." Ellen raised another hand, putting up her defenses.

"Mom, even if I had time to socialize with my neighbors, you know how I feel about Christmas."

Ever since that Christmas by the skating rink when she was paralyzed by her first vision, Grace had a bad association with the holiday. She had even given up wanting to be a professional ice dancer, because every time she thought about the ice, she inevitably thought about the red-haired woman being swallowed by the water.

"I know, honey, and I'm not saying that your gift is an easy thing to deal with, but I don't think you need to take it out on the most wonderful time of the year." Ellen opened her arms and did a little jig mimicking the Christmas song.

"I appreciate your effort." Grace surveyed the lights that hung slightly uneven along the entryway of the house and branching out along the outline of the roof. "How did you even get those up by yourself?" Grace started to loosen up, forgetting about Mackenzie Waterford for a few seconds.

"Never underestimate the power of a woman with a staple gun and a ladder." Ellen smiled as she picked up the tool and held it up.

"Where did you even get that?" Grace asked. Her mother barely knew how to work a pair of scissors, let alone a staple gun. Grace ducked away from her as she held it up high.

"Steven. Your neighbor." Ellen pointed the staple gun at the small red house next door.

"You're talking to my neighbors?" Grace said, realizing that she had never even been next door to thank them for leaving her a basket full of muffins when she moved in nearly two years ago.

"Well, one of us has too. Besides, his wife just passed. I thought he'd want to help a young lady like me to get his mind off things."

"His wife died? When?" Grace felt like a horrible person. She had been so consumed with her own life, she didn't even stop to see what was going on in the world.

"Like two months ago. Get with it, kid." Ellen set the tool down and grabbed the lunch sack and coffee mug from Grace's hand. "Let's go inside, my hands are freezing."

If Grace didn't slow down soon, she was going to miss out a lot more than the passing of her neighbor's wife. She promised herself that as soon as she figured out this Mackenzie Waterford thing, she'd settle down. Maybe even take a yoga class or something.

CHAPTER THIRTEEN

As expected, The 21st Amendment was bustling with the typical crowd. Grace took a deep breath as she pulled open the heavy door, nearly smacking herself in the face. It took seeing a few stars from the exertion to make her realize that she had hardly eaten anything all day because she had been so consumed with Mackenzie Waterford and Jenny Silva. She was starving.

The crowd was thick, but Eric wasn't hard to find. He sat perched at one of the high-tops near the bar. His legs were thick and splayed open in typical man fashion. One hand rested on his cell phone, the other was wrapped around a Diet Coke. Barb must've shown him pictures of her, because he nearly fell off the barstool, he stood so fast when Grace sandwiched her way between a chair at the bar and another high-top, and appeared before him.

"Eric?" she asked in that way that was always awkward on a first date. The usual way around it was to talk about the person who set up the blind date. That had been Grace's plan; keep the focus on Barb. She was an easy enough subject to keep a conversation on. The woman was a spitfire.

"Grace McKenna?" Eric leaned in like he was going to give a hug, but instead thought better of it and extended a hand. Grace noticed his hair first, the tiny glints of red just like Barb's, shimmering against the low lighting of the bar.

"Nice to meet you." Grace settled her eyes onto his for the first time and when she did she realized she had made a big mistake. Her mind was penetrated by a half dozen flashes of a girl who looked no older than seventeen. Two pink-rimmed hazel eyes stared at her on a backdrop of a round pink face. Tears carved out the girl's puffy cheeks as they dropped off her slightly jutted chin. Grace was frozen for a moment, the background of the bar noise pulsating in her ears.

"Hey . . . are you okay?" The placement of Eric's hands on her shoulders was enough to pull her out of the trance. Her natural instinct was to shake off his contaminated hands, but she stopped herself.

"Yeah. Sorry. Just a bit tired. Long day at the office, ya know." Grace slid onto the barstool opposite him and almost instantly started fiddling with the appetizer menu so she wouldn't have to look into his eyes. In most cases, when she saw a vision, it was a passing stranger on the street and she could walk away and feel the wrath of their wrongdoing cemented on her memory forever. But with Eric, she was trapped. She had to sit through a date and act like he was a normal guy. Grace started counting down the minutes in her head, calculating how long she would have to sit through their date. More importantly, she had to figure out how she was going to tell Barb about her nephew.

"I hear days at the station can be draining." Eric used a finger to sop up the liquid that was sweating off his icy glass. "At least, that's what Aunt Barb says."

"Yeah, Barb is a hard worker. Knows the place inside and out. Hell, I probably wouldn't be able to do my job if it wasn't for her," Grace said, as her heart grew heavy. She knew that Barb thought of Eric like a son and they had spent a lot of time together. The woman would be devastated when she found out that her beloved nephew was definitely a pedophile, possibly even a murderer.

Unfortunately, most of Grace's visions presented themselves when it was too late, when a victim had already had their last breath. But there was always that chance that maybe Grace could've met Eric at the right time; maybe the hazel-eyed girl was still alive. Based on the photos she had seen Barb flaunting, this girl wasn't one of his daughters, a tad older. That left a massive question burning inside Grace. *Who is the young girl with the beseeching hazel eyes?*

"Can I get you anything to drink?" A pretty waitress appeared at their table, placing two menus in front of them. She was wearing a form-fitting black tank top, matching the rest of the servers in the bar. Grace wondered how these girls were wearing skimpy little tops in the midst of December when a storm was brewing, but quickly realized that she was hot in the overcrowded watering hole. She slid her jacket off and let it fall limply on the chair behind her.

"I'll have a soda water with lime," Grace said as she looked over at Eric's non-alcoholic beverage, remembering what Barb had told her about his dedicated recovery. She couldn't help but wonder if the hazel-eyed girl was a victim during one of Eric's binges, or if he had been sober. Either way, something was wrong with the man.

"Have you had a chance to look at the appetizer menu?" The waitress looked directly at Grace as she absent-mindedly clutched the menu in her hand.

"Yeah, we'll take the . . . do you like stuffed mushrooms?" Eric asked. Grace could tell he was trying hard to be courteous. He was nervous. Maybe that's what happens when you're a criminal and you go on a date with a detective. Not the sharpest tool in the shed, Grace thought to herself.

"Actually, no, I don't." Grace took a chance at shutting down his game of chivalry. "How about the quesadillas?" She looked at the server, not even asking Eric his opinion. The girl's heavily lined eyes looked back at her, a tad shocked by Grace's shortness.

"You got it. Do you still want the stuffed mushrooms?" She looked over at Eric, hesitant.

"Um, no, that's okay. Quesadillas it is. Whatever the lady wants." An annoying smile appeared on Eric's lips. *Enough with the cheesy lines,* Grace thought to herself. She couldn't help but wonder if she would be falling for this, had she not seen the vision. She raised her right eyebrow at him, the move practiced and rehearsed for moments like this.

"And will you guys be having dinner as well?" The girl asked, tossing her long, shiny brown mane over one shoulder as she hinted to the crowded restaurant. A small tattoo on the inside of her wrist revealed itself with the movement. *Strength* was inscribed in small black print.

"No, just an app is fine." Grace stepped in, knowing full well that if they weren't boosting their check with two over-priced meals, then the server would rush them out to accommodate another couple who would be more likely to leave a bigger tip. She could feel Eric's eyes burning a hole through her, but she refused to look.

"Is everything okay? You seem a bit on edge. Bad day at work?" He wrapped a hand around his sweating glass. "I can only imagine what it's like being a female police officer. Gosh, you must get hit on all the time, huh?"

"Will you excuse me for a minute? I need to use the restroom."

Grace slid off the chair and made her way through the crowd that parted for her, as if they sensed her mission to get somewhere, anywhere but across from Eric. Luckily the bathroom was small, uncomfortable enough for a crowd of ladies to gather in and get in her way. Plenty of privacy to smooth out the thoughts that were bumping around in her head. She placed her hands on the side of the small white sink and looked in the oval mirror that hung above it. A few water spots on the mirror made her face look contorted, almost like she was in a watery dream-like state.

"Why? Why me, God?" she asked the reflection that looked back at her. She stared into her own eyes as if she were trying to reach for answers. The so-called gift that she was born with was once again going to keep her up all night. The part that scared her the most was that when she looked at her future, all she could see was a lifetime of witnessing other people's pain. It was like that feeling she got whenever she saw people fighting in a physical brawl. She felt it deep in her gut, the sadness that gripped her when she saw others hurting. Sure, it was part of her job as a police officer; she saw domestic disturbances several times a week, but with those clean-cut cases she had the power to stop them. With the visions she was in a constant state of inquisition and melancholy.

She took a deep breath and ran a finger across the small scar that ran through her right eyebrow. Whenever she was feeling weak or at a loss, she would rub the scar and think back to that day when she felt the grip of anguish that could be left on one's heart when witnessing violence. She had been plucking dandelions in the small shared yard of the apartment complex that they were living in at the time. Ellen had one eye on six-year-old Grace and one eye on the community garden she was assisting with in the common area. Grace heard some boys arguing on the basketball court nearby. She looked in their direction as she blew the fuzzy head off a white dandelion. "Titty baby! Titty baby!" The two boys chanted as they surrounded the third, smallest boy. They gathered around him closer and closer, until both of the teasing boys were on top of the defenseless boy, pummeling him repeatedly. Grace could still hear the boy's screams when she thought about the incident today. Before the boys even had a chance to look up from the scuffle, she was on the two bullies, clawing at their faces with sharp, unfiled nails and pulling at their hair with such strength she had a clump of varying shades of brown in her grip. She had formed her hands into fists, her spiky little knuckles protruding as an extra weapon and punched at the boys with the force of a ruthless fighter. The fight started to come to a close as one of the boys tried shielding his face from Grace with a beefy forearm, the metal edge of his watch creating a slice through the outer edge of her right eyebrow. A stream of blood trickled down the side of her face and landed on the beefy boy below her, leaving little red droplets on his Pac-Man T-shirt, the yellow cartoon spotted with red dots.

"I was protecting him, Mama." She pointed at the little boy. "They were being mean to him."

"Honey, I know that you felt really bad for the little boy . . . but you can't save everyone.

Grace thought of her mother's words from so many years ago, as she appraised the scar and tried to figure out how she was going to get out of this date and tell Barb about her awful nephew. "Damn it God . . . why me? Couldn't you have passed this on to someone else?" Grace wasn't church-going and God-fearing, but she did believe in something; there had to be a reason why she was the recipient of such perception. "Put your big girl pants on and be strong," she said as she gave herself one last look in the mirror, smoothing out the knit sweater that ran the length of her backside and halfway down her thighs. The less she offered to show Eric, the easier it would be to keep him from being interested in her. It's just the way men worked. Eric didn't seem like the type of guy who would put in the effort to chase her and dote on her until she gave in.

As she pushed the narrow wooden door open, it nearly swung into a girl with long blonde hair and too much makeup. The girl gave her a dirty look and bumped her arm as she walked by. Grace had to force herself not to hiss profanities over her shoulder. The crowd had thickened in the five minutes since she had gone into the bathroom. She could hear talk of the upcoming storm drifting off of different conversations as she made her way back to the table. It was as if the anticipation of a snowstorm sent a ripple of energy through the room, creating a heightened buzz. Everyone was prepared to be landlocked for a few days, some even free of work and school commitments like they were packing up for a long vacation.

By the time Grace made her way back to the high-top, Eric had already moved on. He was looking up at their waitress with eyes so ravenous Grace could've sat down at the table, had a meal, and he wouldn't have noticed her presence. Grace could see the waitress giggling as he most likely passed along some cheesy line while he caressed her hand. *You've gotta be fuckin' kidding me,* she thought. She could kill Barb right now. Not only did the woman set her up with a criminal, but he was an impatient cocky hornball on top of it.

"Well, I guess I'm interrupting something, so I'm gonna head out." Grace tore off a slice of the fresh quesadilla and popped it into her mouth, sliding her arms into her navy blue peacoat.

"No, it's not what you think. I swear." Eric looked up, startled as the girl melted away embarrassed, blending in with the crowd.

"Listen, I didn't want to go on this 'date' to begin with, but I thought I'd do your aunt a favor. Barb's a good woman, you know. She's just looking out for you. And this is how you thank her?" Grace pulled off another slice of the cheesy appetizer, ravenous from the long day and having forgotten to eat anything. She didn't care about manners. She'd reserve those for someone else.

She pushed her way through the crowd and slammed out the front door. The cold hit her like a blast, pushing the breath out of her. She walked to her car and looked up at the stars. "Why God . . . why me?" she said, as the first snowflake fluttered down from the sky, landing on her eyelash.

"Wait up! Grace, come on—wait up!" Eric's voice came from behind her. She could tell he was running by the breathy gasps between his words. She started walking faster, placing one hand on her holster. She hoped to God she didn't have to claim self-defense on a blind date, but based on what she'd already seen of Eric, she couldn't be sure. She carried her department-issued Sig Sauer 40 with her at all times. When people knew you were a cop and you were out in public places in civilian wear, you were either bashed and treated with little respect, or you were pulled into unsafe situations. Grace had always preferred to carry her gun, who she had named "Siggy," to remove the threat of violence. Siggy always had her back, so she deserved a name.

"Listen, Eric. I know who you are and I know what you did." Grace used her shoulder to drive him into the brick wall in one fluid motion. He was by no means feeble, but he didn't have the build of a world-class athlete, either. She had seen the slight protrusion of a beer belly, most likely left over from his years as an alcoholic.

"What are you talking about? Are you crazy?" Red blotches made their way up his neck and covered his face like a chameleon taking on its defensive coloring. His eyes darted everywhere except on Grace, and she was grateful for that. Lack of eye contact was a sure sign that the person was guilty or lying. She had learned that the first day at the academy. And she certainly didn't want to see his doings with one shared glance.

"Don't make me have to tell Barb what you've done. I'm not fucking around!" Grace couldn't help herself. She'd had enough. She was sick of seeing through the eyes of murderers, abusers and rapists. She was sick of hiding, and it was time she took matters into her own hands. She used a thumb and forefinger to grip his neck, stubbles of red hair stabbed at her hand as she squeezed just hard enough to make him beg, but not hard enough to leave a mark. Another skill learned at the academy. "Now say it . . . say what you did," Grace hissed, the words sounded so raspy and almost inhuman that she surprised herself. She squeezed harder.

"Is this about Allie?" He looked at her through two reddened lenses. She looked away. She didn't need to stamp the vision on her memory again when he could tell her the truth.

"Yes. Now talk, or I'll use my gun. It would be pretty easy to claim self-defense on a child abuser."

"It was just once, I swear. I had been drinking. I'd never do that if I was sober." His voice came out in shaky syllables, his arms still pressed flat against the brick wall.

"WHAT DID YOU DO?" Grace was fired up now, she couldn't stop. All the years of maintaining her composure had taken a toll on her. It was like a dam opening at the edge of a lake, a swell of water came rushing out much like her anger was doing right now.

"Can I sit?" He looked at her with pleading eyes and gestured toward the curb that married the street and the sidewalk.

"Fine." She kept a grip on his right arm and pressed his head down like she was loading him into the back of a cruiser. She figured he might as well get used to it now.

"But . . . how? How did you know?" He looked at the ground, spitting on the street between his legs. "Is that why you agreed to go on a date with me? To interrogate me?"

"That's not important. What's important is what you did and why you did it, and keeping you from ever doing it again."

"I know what I did was wrong, but it wasn't like that. I would never intentionally hurt someone. I don't—I don't know what happened that night." He dropped his head in his hands, hiding his face as the shame sunk in. "I mean, I have two daughters of my own. I'm a good dad. Really, I am."

"I'm not going to ask you again. What did you do?"

"Carrie and I had just gotten home from our monthly date. We were trying hard to work things out between us. We thought that setting up a monthly date would help us with achieving that couple time that our counselor had been urging us to do. We got married young, never had a chance to be kids, I guess. After ten years of marriage, things fizzled. Started going downhill."

"You've got five minutes to tell me what happened. Speed it up." Grace looked down at her watch.

"Okay, okay. The girls had gone to bed, it was late by the time we got home. Carrie had gotten a little tipsy so I told her to just go upstairs to bed and I'd walk the sitter home." He let out deep breath, shrill and choppy. "She came on to me first, I swear." He held up his hands and looked straight ahead. Grace found that hard to believe, but sometimes teenage girls formed crushes on older men, even when they weren't the easiest on the eyes. Maybe the girl didn't have a caring father and she was looking for love or seduction in a father-like figure.

"Never an excuse. What happened?"

"I got carried away. I pinned her against the brick wall in the nearest alley. We live on a busy street with lots of little alleys." He shook his head and sealed his lips together and for a moment Grace thought he was going to get up and run, but instead the words flooded out of him. "I didn't realize I was being so rough, I thought she wanted it. I really did. I was flattered that this beautiful young girl would even look at me, let alone go in for a kiss. I couldn't help myself. It's like someone or something was taking over my body. I'm not like that. I'm really not. And then I noticed that she had been crying. I had been hurting her. Somewhere in the distance I could hear her yelling 'STOP, STOP,' but whatever it was inside me blocked it out."

"So then what happened?" Grace suddenly felt nauseous.

"I threatened her. I told her that if she ever told another soul that I would turn it all around on her."

"You raped a minor! For God's sake, how did you expect you could possibly turn it around on her?" Grace cracked her knuckles, her face heating up with rage, warming her body in the cold air.

"She was naïve. I told her I'd tell her father. I knew her father and I knew that she was petrified of him. He is one of those insanely strict parents. I knew she wouldn't tell."

"What do you have to say for yourself?" Grace asked, feeling no pity for him as he started sobbing between deep heavy breaths.

"I'm a horrible person. I should go to hell. Just arrest me."

"Yeah, you're right about that. But, arrest you? What kind of case do you think I'll have arresting you for a rape you committed, I don't know . . . how long ago?"

"It was two years ago. She's nineteen now. Just finished her first semester of college."

"Exactly. Unless she can pull up cameras that witnessed the incident happening, then she isn't going to have evidence that will hold up in court." Grace looked at her watch. "Do you realize that you have messed with an innocent girl's life? Do you realize that she will be haunted forever because of your selfishness that probably lasted all of three minutes?"

"You think I don't hate myself for this every day?" He wiped his nose with the back of his jacket, a cluster of snowflakes landed on his eyelashes and melted almost instantly from the heat of his tears. "I lost everything. My wife. I only get to see my girls every other weekend."

"Wait a minute. I thought nobody knew about this?"

"Nobody does . . . that I know of. Our marriage was already falling apart and after that things got even worse. I couldn't live with myself. I didn't think I deserved my wife. She deserved better than to be with someone like me. And I had trouble facing my girls. God knows what I would do to someone who did that to one of them. The guilt has wrapped itself around me, sucking the life out of any good that I had before. I haven't touched a drop of alcohol since then and I never will. Something came over me. I'd like to say that it was the booze. I'm not that person, I swear I'm not. And I'm going to be paying for this for the rest of my life. You're a cop. Don't you have to arrest me now? You know what I did, you must've found out somehow, so you have evidence." He looked at Grace, his hooded eyes pleading like a toddler asking for candy.

"It doesn't work that way."

"But, how did you know?"

GRACE CLUTCHED the steering wheel as she made her way through the tunnels that connected Boston to its outskirts. In most cases she would feel claustrophobic in the enclosed space, the narrow roads making her feel uneasy every time she rode alongside another vehicle. But during snowstorms, the tunnels were a place of shelter from the slippery blanket of white covering the outside roads that would inevitably cause a pileup of cars whose drivers panicked and slid into one another.

A pool of sweat had accumulated on the ridges of the steering wheel, a symptom of the visions. Her body temperature rose in conjunction with the visions, a contrast to the crisp cold air that accompanied the snowflakes to the ground outside. She was torn between what she saw and what she should do. She struggled with the decision to tell Barb. Her nephew was a rapist—a remorseful one, sure, but there was still the possibility that he could do it again. Grace couldn't rule anything out. If she let him go, forcing herself to forget his story, there was the risk that he could relapse and ruin another girl's life forever. Did she want to take that chance to prove her own sanity?

The sight of twinkling Christmas lights interrupted her thoughts as she pulled into the dirt drive that led to the cozy house that she called home. For a moment she felt a wave of Christmas spirit sweep through her, warming her heart and bringing memories of her and her mother celebrating the holiday together, just the two of them. She could almost feel the hot chocolate warm her body, an annual treat that she and her mother shared on Christmas Eve every year. They would dance to the sound of Perry Como's voice belting out

Christmas songs as they decorated the freshly cut tree. Her mother barely made enough to support them, but she was dead set on buying the biggest, freshest looking Christmas tree every year. Over the years, they had accumulated enough ornaments to keep up with the growing pine that would take up half of their living room and serve as their own personal air freshener from the day after Thanksgiving until January first.

The lights that hung from her house were messy and uneven, but they still lit up the Christmas spirit within her heart. A smile danced on her lips as she heard the sound of bells crashing against her wooden door. Ellen had taken the liberty of hanging a bell decoration on the doorknob, the long leather belt lined with silver bells rocked side to side as she stepped into the warmth of her home. Brody raised his brows from his flat out position on the floor. It took him a moment before he recognized her standing there, then with all the effort the one hundred and fifty pound dog could muster, he got to his feet, sliding all over the linoleum floor. He hopped left to right, banging the unfinished table that sat flush against the wall.

"Hey, Brody bear. How's my boy?" She crouched down as he sat and waited patiently for his greeting, his body bracing hers as she leaned into his furry black frame. She scratched in all the places he expected as part of his daily greeting and finally moved out of the way so she could pass by. Grace used a remote to turn on the flat-screen that was hanging above the small fireplace while simultaneously sliding into the chair next to the table where her laptop was permanently charging. The silence was penetrated by the local newscaster's steady voice rattling off the daily news. Grace had the bad habit of turning the television on the second she entered her home out of loneliness and an attempt at keeping up on accounts that may soon involve her. It was always important to be well informed with what was going on in the area. Brody let out a deep breath as he slid down on the floor by her feet, resting his massive head between two shaggy paws. "You want some takeout, bud?" Grace clicked on her favorites bar and pulled up the Rizzo's Menu. "What do ya think, pizza or sub tonight?" Brody lifted his head and peered up at her, an acknowledgement to her question.

"I think a steak and cheese sounds good too, buddy." Grace punched in her memorized credit card info and instantly pulled open another window, launching into the world of Google. The sound of her fingers dancing busily across the keyboard meshed with the sound of the newscaster's monotone delivery, until a few escalated words pulled her from her Google search. *Boston Police department confirms the abusive activity of a local babysitter. The nineteen- year-old suspect was caught on camera holding a two-year-old hostage in her own home.* The background of the footage showed a brownstone planted prominently on Beacon Hill, as officers guided the young girl out of the building and into the cruiser. She didn't look much different than Mackenzie, hiding behind a long, dirty blonde mane and clothed in a neat, reserved cardigan over a pair of slimming jeans.

"What the hell is wrong with today's youth?" Grace said the words out loud, massaging Brody with her left foot.

CHAPTER FOURTEEN

THE SNOW FROM THE NIGHT BEFORE COVERED THE STREETS IN A SOFT white blanket. Grace carved out fresh tracks in the light layer that had veiled the ground since the last plow went through. It had dimmed down to a light sprinkle, the snowflakes trickled down in a soft gentle dance. Grace loved the feeling of tranquility after a heavy snow, when the world was still and people were tucked into the comfort of their homes. While the rest of Bridgeton seemed to be still, its residents safely snuggled under the warmth of comforters, the ocean crashed to life. Grace sat at the longest red light in town and watched the waves reach for the seawall, the salty water spraying on her windshield blending with the tiny flakes that had fallen and clung to the glass.

As usual, Barb's car was parked in the spot that she designated for herself, so close to the front steps of the station that she could practically step onto the brick staircase from the bright red Mustang, tattooed with a license plate that said "RED." For the first time since Grace had known the woman, she was nervous to see her. She could feel the butterflies dancing in her belly as she tossed her bag across her body and made her way past Barb's car. She took a quick look into the Mustang and noticed a small photo tucked into the glass shielding the speedometer and gas light. The photo looked like it had been cut, one of the edges slightly frayed and uneven. Two giggling girls looked up at Eric in awe, as he had one eye on them and one on the camera. It was amazing to Grace how people could lead double lives, having the good side of themselves on display for the world to see, and the other side tucked away and hidden.

"Shit, this is gonna be tough," Grace said under her breath as she pulled the heavy front door open and walked into the station. As expected, Barb was on her like a dog after a bone. Grace had never seen the woman move so fast, as Barb nearly jumped up from her chair and followed her down the hall and into Grace's office.

"So, how was it? Isn't he a gem? Gosh, I remember how charming he was as a little boy. I can imagine how he is on a first date." Barb leaned against the wall, crossing one ankle over the other as Grace busied herself with unloading her bag and flipping through random files.

"It was good. He's a very nice guy." She didn't look up to receive the eye contact that Barb was nearly hurling at her.

"Oh, you little vixen! I knew you two would hit it off! I didn't think it would be on the first night, but I gotta say . . . I'm proud of ya, Princess. It's about time you got out there. You're only young once. So, when's the next date?" Barb was jumping to conclusions like a frog hopping from one lily pad to the next, not stopping to breathe.

"It's not like that, Barb. We just had an appetizer and called it a night." Grace grew brave and looked up to seal eyes with the woman. "I was tired. It was a long day." She was a terrible liar and Barb knew her well enough to sense it.

"You didn't like him, did you? Not your type? Ugh, don't tell me you're one of those girls who doesn't like nice guys . . ." Barb slid into the chair that was on the other side of Grace's desk.

"No, that's not it. Like I said, I was really tired." Grace seemed to shrink under Barb's watchful eye.

"For God's sake, Grace, you aren't even forty. You can't use the tired excuse yet, not to mention you don't have kids to blame that on." Barb's face was starting to break out into little splotches of red. She only called Grace by her name when she was upset, and the shade of red that was now covering her face was a sure sign that she was not happy. Barb had a way of protecting her own, she would defend her friends and family with all she had inside her. She was like a red-haired pit bull. If she only knew what she was up against this time. "Gosh, I at least gave dating a go until I was in my fifties, and here you are giving up because you're scared of God knows what. What—are you afraid you might find happiness?" Barb's voice was escalating and Grace could feel anger start to boil within her. Eric seemed to have his aunt, his innocent children and possibly his ex-wife fooled into thinking he was a decent guy. Grace had seen her mother in the quiet moments when she would drift off, surely replaying the night that she had been raped and robbed of her right to her own body. She took a deep breath, but all she could see were the tears in her mother's eyes as she tried to break away from the grip of a stranger.

Grace was tired. Between the recurring images from Eric and the struggle with piecing together Jenny and Mackenzie's relationship, she had barely slept, and her blood was beginning to boil as anger and lethargy coursed through her.

"Enough, Barb! Your nephew is a rapist!" The words accelerated out of her mouth, but landed flat in a bed of silence. She looked at Barb, aware of the damage she had done, scolding herself for not just covering for the guy this one time. "He's a rapist, he raped the girls' babysitter." The syllables came out of Grace's mouth in a low whisper. She saw the way Barb's face contorted from realization to anger as the words hit her, at first slow and gentle and then nearly knocking her over in absurdity.

"Are you out of your goddamn mind, McKenna? Have you been watching too many of those stupid crime shows? Where in God's name would you get an idea like that?" Barb asked, her face transformed into a look of disgust as she scanned Grace from head to toe, surely questioning what happened to the woman she had considered a friend. She held up a hand, "Please don't tell me you're accusing him of raping you?"

Grace knew she was stuck. She had opened up a can of worms and there was no going back. She couldn't tell Barb that the vision crept inside her mind when she looked into the man's eyes, she couldn't take it back and say she was kidding, all she could do was apologize.

"I'm sorry, I know this is hard for you to grasp, Barb. I'm sorry." And with Grace's words, Barb turned and slammed the door so hard, the bulletin board swayed side to side on the wall.

Grace dropped her head into her hands, closed her eyes and took several deep breaths. "Why me, God? Why me?" As if on cue, there was a knock on her office door. "Come in," Grace said after taking one last deep breath while wiping away the tears that had started to form in the corners of her eyes.

"Hey, Grace. How are you doing?" Chief Welch said as he leaned in the doorway gripping a Dunkin Donuts cup in one hand.

"I'm good. How are you?" Grace looked up and peeled her shoulders back, forcing herself to appear strong and stable.

"So, I just wanted to touch base about the Waterford file. False alarm, huh?" He rubbed what little stubble he had on his chin. "Guess that's a good thing. Hate to see kids go missing. Seen too many in my day." He inched his way into her office taking in what little décor she had. "You do a good job around here, Grace." He used an index finger to lift the top of the Christmas card.

"Thanks." She stood from her desk, crossing her arms around her chest. She couldn't help but be flattered by the compliment.

"You should be proud of your accomplishments here." He took another swig of his coffee. "I'm sure you've seen the posting for Sergeant Lieutenant Detective."

"Yes, I have." Grace had seen the posting but hadn't thought too much about it. She assumed that one of the officers with more time in service would be tough to go up against.

"I think you'd be stupid to not put in for it. That's all I'm saying." Chief Welch took two backward steps and quietly opened the door. "Just think about it, okay?" he said before allowing a big smile to spread across his face.

For a morning that started out crummy, the day was looking up for Grace. She imagined herself getting promoted and pinned by the chief as her mother watched on with a tear in her eye. She had spent her life trying to make her mother proud, to prove to her that she did the right thing by keeping her after the most violent act of her life. Grace knew that while she had the same eyes as her mother, she surely had several of the traits of her father, including the shape of her angular face and the fullness of her lips. Her mother had a heart-shape face with a set of lips that were so thin they looked like a skinny line had been drawn across the lower half of her face. She was sure Ellen couldn't help but see the differences in their appearances, knowing full well that anything that didn't mimic her own features was likely a result of her rapist's DNA.

She Googled Mackenzie Waterford again, this time searching for links instead of photos. After several rows of search results, she clicked on the girl's Facebook page. "Of course. Facebook. The bible for all teenagers," Grace said under her breath. She had recently heard somewhere that the younger generation thought Facebook was outdated and uncool and Twitter was the new thing, but that didn't appear to be the case with Mackenzie. She scrolled down the timeline. A few messages from friends greeted her.

TAYLOR: *Hey girl, missed you in AP chem yesterday. Where were u?*
December 20, at 8:30pm

MATTY O'SHEA: *Great speech! You rock!*
December 20, 2015 at 11:13pm

THE REST of the posts were an assortment of professional female soccer players, news clippings on college entrance exams and a few cute cat photos. Based on Mackenzie's lack of replies, it appeared that the girl didn't spend all that much time on social media. Either that or she was covering her tracks. Just as Grace started to scroll through her list of 213 friends, she remembered Mark saying that he had a sister about Mackenzie's age. Grace took a moment to let her fingers dance on the desk, before picking up the phone and dialing Mark's extension. When the call went to his voicemail, she dialed the control room.

"Hey, Joe."

"Hey, kid. What can I do you for?" The warmth of his voice comforted Grace the instant it came through the line.

"Hey, do you know if Sergeant Connolly is in today? I've got a quick question for him." She felt the need to defend herself for asking about him because she'd been so used to Barb making assumptions about her love life.

"Nope. Today's an off day for him. He'll be back in tomorrow." Joe fired the answer at her before even having to think about it. "If you really need him, you can probably find him at the gym. The guy works out like he's training for the next Sylvester Stallone movie or something."

"Ahhh okay. Thanks, Joe."

"You got it, kid."

Grace slid her desk drawer open, the squeaking of the metal piercing her ears. Folded up into a tiny square was the hot pink Post-it note with Mark's cell number on it.

Hesitantly, she dialed the number and after four rings, Mark's voice picked up, breathy and in short bursts. There wasn't much that Joe Sullivan wasn't right about. "Sergeant Connolly," he said.

"Do you always answer the phone like that when you're off duty?" Grace asked, feeling an elevation of confidence.

"I like to think I'm never off duty." He came back with a light chuckle. "What's up, Grace?"

"How did you know it was me?"

"Well, it's the year 2015 and we have caller ID, and you happen to be one of two females who work at the Bridgeton Police Department. And let's face it, no one quite has Barb's deep Boston accent." His voice was fluid now, having had a moment to drop his weights or lower the level of the treadmill. Grace pictured him pacing back and forth in front of a mirror in a home gym, the back of his shirt drenched in sweat.

"Well, I remember you mentioning that your sister attends Bridgeton High. I was hoping maybe I could chat with her for a bit about the Waterford case."

"Wow, so is that Waterford girl still missing?" He asked, his interest genuinely aroused. "I thought for sure that would be a false alarm."

"Well, technically it was, Mackenzie is home and safe. Turned out to be just a miscommunication between her and her parents." Grace paused for a moment, having not even given any thought to how she was going to explain her interest in the closed case to Mark. "There's just something I want to clear up. Something is a bit off."

"I gotcha. You gotta go with your gut." Mark's words were coated in comfort and Grace had started to think this was going to be too easy. "So, what do you say we meet for coffee. I'll pick Rain up around two-thirty after she gets outta some Christmas break class she is taking. We can meet at that little coffee shop just outside of town. I'm assuming you want a private location, away from the crowd of kids who typically hit up the café in the town's center."

"You read my mind." Grace had imagined this conversation to be a lot more difficult than it was proving to be. Mark was always so quiet, even mysterious around the station. Over the phone she felt the ease of speaking with an old friend. "Wait, did you say *Rain?*"

"Ha! Yeah, I did. My mom kind of switched her gears a bit when she had my little sister.

"Different dads?" Grace couldn't help but ask the question. She had already been intrigued by Mark, now she was putting together the details of his family.

"Yep," he said brusquely. "So, I'll see you there around two-thirty. Sound good?"

"Sounds great. Thank you so much, Mark. I really appreciate this," she said, grateful for the subject change.

"No problem. Rain is used to being questioned by her big brother, so this should be no big deal," he said with a chuckle.

CHAPTER FIFTEEN

A CLUSTER OF BELLS CRASHED ON THE DOOR OF WAVE CAFÉ AS GRACE pushed her way into the warmth of the coffee shop. She could hear a girl giggling before she looked up from stomping the snow off her boots. In the corner of the café, Mark was immersed in the story that Rain was telling him, her arms animated and her face contorting as she mimicked someone. They looked more like a father and daughter than brother and sister. Grace slid her hat off, shaking off the clump of snow that had dropped on her head when she opened the door. Mark waved in her direction, motioning to the third seat that he had already considerately pulled up to the table for two.

"Hey," Grace said as she slid out of her long puffy black coat, hoping not to shake off any more snow on the floor. She already felt bad about the trail of melting flakes that had followed her from the door to the table.

"Hey, Grace. This is Rain, my baby sister."

"Oh my God, will you please stop calling me your *baby* sister? I'm practically an adult!" Rain said, her eyes rolling with each word. "It's nice to meet you, Grace." Rain stood up and shook Grace's hand. Clearly, Mark had taught the girl well.

"You'll always be my baby sister," he said, making a pouty face. Grace felt like she was meeting a different Mark than the one she knew at the station. He was always so serious, so quiet and now here he was, clearly smitten with his sister.

"It's so nice to meet you, Rain. Thank you so much for taking the time to chat. I'm sure you're swamped with schoolwork," Grace said, sliding her wooden chair to the empty table.

"Rain here is one of those geniuses who barely has to put in any effort and she excels. Aren't you, Rain?" Mark said, doting on the girl. "She literally has a photographic memory."

"Not quite." Rain shrugged off the compliment.

"Do you guys want a coffee, tea?" Grace asked.

"I'll get it. You two get acquainted." Mark stood, stabbing his hands in his pocket. "I already know what you want, little missy. Iced peanut butter mocha with an extra shot of espresso. Grace?"

"Oh, I'll just have a medium coffee, skim milk and sugar."

"You got it," Mark said as he sauntered up to the counter. Grace watched as a gaggle of college girls at a corner table stopped mid-conversation and stared at Mark as he walked past. She could practically see the drool trickling past their glossy lips.

"So, did Mark tell you why I wanted to meet with you?" Grace turned toward Rain, taking in the girl's shiny black hair and big brown eyes. The common features that Mark and Rain had stopped at the dark hair. They were both highly attractive, but she didn't doubt that they had different fathers.

"No, he didn't. But, I know I'm not in any kind of trouble. I made him promise me that," Rain said, a bright white smile penetrating her olive skin.

"No, you certainly aren't in any kind of trouble. I really just wanted to ask you a few questions about Mackenzie Waterford. Do you know her?"

"Ha! Everyone knows Mackenzie Waterford. She's pretty notorious at Bridgeton High."

"I kinda got that impression. Do you have any classes with her?"

"Yeah, I'm in a lot of AP classes and, as I'm sure you've heard, so is Mackenzie. So, we tend to overlap a few classes here and there."

"Really, so you know her pretty well?"

"As well as I can. She has a ton of friends but kinda keeps to herself at the same time. If that makes any sense." Rain paused for a moment, using one hand to gather her thick mane and twist it between her fingers, before letting it drop on one shoulder.

"Yeah, I guess some people are like that," Grace said, as she looked up to see Mark hovering over her, holding out a steaming cup of coffee.

"Here you go," he said, sliding into the third seat. "And here is your ridiculously high-calorie, overly expensive drink," he said, rolling his eyes as he sent the fancy iced drink across the smooth surface of the table to Rain. Rain didn't miss a beat and rolled hers right back.

"Are there any friends or relationships that you remember Mackenzie having that seemed a bit off? Maybe something you noticed that was odd. Something you could pick up on from a distance, or heard a rumor about."

"Ouch." Rain used two fingers to squeeze the top of her nose. "Brain freeze, brain freeze." Her face contorted into a look of pain.

"That, my baby sister, is why you don't drink these frozen drinks—especially in the middle of winter." Mark leaned back in the chair, self-assured and satisfied.

"Oh, shut it. I just drank it too fast," Rain said, gaining her composure. "Now that I think about it, she has this weird relationship with our art teacher. It's like the two of them are BFF's, even though there is obviously a huge age gap. I mean, I wouldn't want to hang out with any of *my* teachers."

Grace was so satisfied with this admission that she nearly broke out into a huge grin, but stopped herself. "Really? How so? I mean, how are they close? Do they spend time outside of school together?"

"I can't say for sure, but it's weird. Like, we'd be in class learning about something stupid like what thickness of brush we should use to create certain lines, and Miss Silva would ALWAYS call on Mackenzie to be an example. And the two of them, I don't know . . . they would like have this secret language, giggling and acting all weird. In front of the whole class. The rest of the class got pretty annoyed by it, but we kind of always expected Mackenzie to be the pet. That's the way it always is with her. She has to be perfect at everything."

"So I've heard." Grace peeled her eyes off of Rain and transferred them to Mark, who was staring openly at her. For a moment, Grace was mesmerized by the way his hazel eyes glistened against the backdrop of an incredibly bright white. He gave her a small sideways smile, revealing a cleft in his chin.

"I do remember when we went on a field trip to the MFA, the two of them arrived and left together. I'm not sure if anyone else noticed it, but I did for sure. It was kind of obnoxious, ya know? Miss Silva drives this old school blue VW Bug, and it's got all these hippy stickers on the back, so I remember reading all the peace-loving bumper stickers from where I was standing, and then I noticed that Mackenzie got out of the passenger side and I was like *weird. . .*" Rain sat back in the chair, and pulled one leg up, making herself comfortable. "I mean, I remember thinking it was exceptionally weird because Mackenzie is soooo not the hippy type. She's all reserved and buttoned up, if you know what I mean. Kinda like her parents. And then there's Miss Silva, who has literally showed up to class with two different shoes on and just chalked it up to being *artistic expression*. It's kinda what I like about Miss Silva, though. She's so loopy, just a classic artist ya know?"

All Grace could picture was the image of Jenny Silva's tormented eyes, the struggle that the woman was enduring, whether it was physically or emotionally.

"Knowing Miss Silva, she's probably at some hippy retreat during Christmas break or something." Rain absentmindedly fingered the colorful stringy bracelets on her wrist.

"Could you do me a favor, Rain?" Grace's heartbeat escalated with the girl's innocent admission.

"Of course."

"If anything else comes up, in art class . . . in anything involving Mackenzie, could you do me a favor and call me right away? Anything that seems a bit off to you." Grace pulled a business card out of her pocket and slid it across the table. "But, I just ask that you keep this between me and you—" Grace caught herself, "—and your brother, of course." She looked over at Mark and caught his stare again; this time it was accompanied by a wink.

"Sure thing." Rain took the card and slid it into the front pocket of her backpack. "You people still use business cards? Sooo old school," Rain joked as she uncrossed her legs and started to stand.

"Shut it," Mark teased. "Is she free to go now?" He turned toward Grace who was giggling at the interesting dynamic between the two of them.

"Yes, you're free. Thank you so much. You have no idea how much I appreciate this."

"Yeah, and get back to whatever sport or extracurricular activity that you have this afternoon, you overachiever," Mark said as he stood and pulled the girl in for a hug, while looking over at Grace. "What kind of kid participates in school activities on break?"

Grace started to stand and heft her bag on her shoulder as Mark watched Rain walk out the door of the café.

"Hey do you mind sticking around for a little?" he asked.

"Yeah, of course. What's up?" Grace slipped back into the seat, touched by a tickle of butterflies in her stomach. It was one thing to be sitting at a table with Mark and his sister, it was another to be alone with him. Seeing the endearing relationship that Mark had with Rain had only escalated the adoration that she felt for the guy. Grace felt herself slowly falling into the depths of a crush, one that she was trying her hardest to swim away from.

"My sister is cool, just so you know." Mark took one last sip of his coffee before stuffing his napkin in the cup.

"What do you mean?" The confusion on Grace's face was enough to make Mark laugh a little.

"I mean, she won't tell anyone about the conversation that you two had today or any of the conversations you plan on having in the future. I've trained her right." Mark threw another wink at her.

"Oh, okay. Sorry . . . I wasn't sure what you meant." Grace felt a touch of embarrassment make its way to her skin; the heat was sure to leave a gentle burn resulting in splotches of red.

"So, what's this all about, anyways?" Mark asked directly.

"It's just . . . well . . ." Grace stumbled on her words, having not rehearsed how she would answer his inevitable questions.

"Is it that gut feeling? You can tell me. Trust me, I have them all the time. Especially when it comes to cases," he said, maintaining eye contact with her. "I know I'm not a fancy detective, but I've still gotten my ears wet on a few cases."

"Yeah, yeah, it's just intuition I guess. Something just doesn't seem right." The words started to relax her as they came out, and she became more comfortable in his presence. "I guess I just feel unsettled about this Mackenzie girl. There is something so off about her." Grace tried her best to keep herself from describing the visions that tugged at her throughout the day, like a dull headache that wouldn't go away.

"I know how you feel. Sometimes when I release a criminal for something as simple as a speeding ticket, I'll get this sick feeling that they're some kind of crazed murderer and I'm just throwing them back in the world to do God knows what. I mean, imagine all the pedophiles out there. I'm sure we don't know about half of them. It's kept a secret for their lifetimes because the kids are too scared to say anything." Mark paused, smoothing his hands on the surface of the table. Grace could see the line of veins protruding from his skin, evidence of his time at the gym. "Sorry, I get so worked up about this stuff. Now I'm babbling."

"No, no I totally get it. I mean, that's why we're in this field right?" Grace said, feeling a layer of the initial awkwardness removed from between them.

"Yeah. Hey, do you want something to eat? They have amazing sandwiches here."

Grace realized for the first time that she hadn't eaten anything since her romantic meal with Brody last night. She could feel an empty hole in her stomach, begging to be filled. "Um, sure."

"Let's go check out the board. They usually have specials." Mark stood and followed her lead to the counter. A massive chalkboard took up the entire back wall, filled with daily specials and favorites, written in artistic colorful chalk.

"The usual, Mark?" The girl behind the counter looked up from wiping the surface with a rag.

"Yes, please. Can you make sure there's no bacon on it?"

"As I always do," the girl said as she went to work loading a wheat pocket with various vegetables.

"Wait, you don't like bacon?"

"Vegetarian since 2007. You caught me." Mark held up his hands before stuffing them deep into his pockets.

"Wow, I'm kinda shocked. I'll take the same thing. No pickles, please."

"I know I don't look like the typical vegetarian. Are you one, too?"

"God no! But I'd feel horrible eating the delicious livestock that they have available here, right in front of you." Grace looked up at the sign boasting of chicken, bacon and egg sandwiches.

"It's okay, trust me. The rest of my family has no problem stuffing their faces with meat right in front of me and Rain." Mark folded his hands across his chest and took on the habitual stance of a police officer. "Yes, my baby sister is the one who got me hooked on saving the world one furry creature at a time. Although, I can't say that she has listened to a damn thing that I've said about lowering her sugar intake."

"She's really got you wrapped around her finger, huh?" Grace asked, her smile bordering on a teasing grin.

"Hey, if you saw the videos she showed me, you'd be wrapped, too. The torture those poor animals endure. And it's not like we need to eat meat in order to thrive. Sorry I'm going on a tangent."

"It's okay, I get it. I'm an animal lover myself. I just haven't quite made the commitment to give up my Friday night steak and cheese just yet." Grace accepted the tightly wrapped sandwich that the girl behind the counter presented to her and she followed Mark as he led them back to the table, clutching his own sandwich like a football. "It's sweet though," Grace said as she peeled the white tape off the parchment paper and began surveying the ingredients of her sandwich.

"The fact that I refuse to eat meat to prove a point?" Mark took one massive bite as half of the sandwich disappeared into his mouth.

"No, the fact that you have such a great relationship with your *baby* sister." Grace delicately nibbled the edge of her sandwich, trying hard not to drop any loose ingredients on her lap or the table.

"She's a good kid. Much better than I was when I was her age," Mark said, wiping a droplet of spicy mustard off the corner of his mouth. Grace thought back to herself when she was that age and the quiet life she and her mother lived. She had become so used to the holidays and special occasions being celebrated with just the two of them in the comfort of their modest home and back and forth mother-daughter banter that she couldn't imagine what it would be like to have a sibling.

"Do you have any other siblings?" Grace took a leap and dug a little deeper into the secret life of Mark Connolly.

"Yeah, two younger brothers. They share the same dad as Rain and they're good kids too, but I guess it's the protective man in me that feels the need to always look out for Rain. I'm sure she's highly capable of taking care of herself, but I can't help but look after her." Mark swiped some of the fallen pickles off the wrap and dropped them in his mouth. "What about you?"

Something about the way he ate made Grace's stomach catapult into a series of somersaults. It was as if everything he did in life was done with an insatiable hunger. His passion for exercise, his enthusiasm for his job as a police officer and even the way he nearly inhaled the sandwich that was put together with his chosen and well-thought-out ingredients. Grace couldn't help but imagine what he would be like in bed.

"Nope. Just me and my mom," Grace said and for whatever reason she was compelled to continue. "My dad's never been around." She paused bracing herself for what she was about to say. The words had never felt comfortable leaving her lips. "He . . . actually raped my mom. When she was in college." Grace's eyes darted from Mark to the table and back, unsure of whether he was going to think she was some type of freak for sharing such a personal piece of her life, or whether he was going to give her unwanted sympathy.

"Are you serious?" He clenched his fists, forming two red potatoes.

"Hey, I wouldn't be alive without such an act of hate, right? Just think about it like that."

"I know, I know. I just have an extreme hate for rapists. It's such a sick thing to do." He eased his fists open into two palms face down on the table. His eyes curved on the edges, softening his anger and supplementing it with a genuine candor.

"Well, what's done is done and the past is the past, as they say," Grace said, trying to close the conversation. "On another note, I've taken up far more of your time than I planned on. Didn't you say you only had a few minutes to meet?"

"Oh shit," he said as his eye caught the enormous watch on his wrist. "I'm late. I've got a training appointment."

"Training for what?" Grace wondered if there was some station training she'd forgotten about.

"I've got a client at the gym . . . at my home gym," he said, zipping up his jacket and pulling on a thick pair of winter gloves. He looked like he was ready to shovel his way out of a snowstorm.

"You train on the side?" Grace said, following his lead to the door.

"Yeah, it's kinda my passion." The shy crooked smile that Grace seemed to be falling for spread across his face as he pulled a blue winter hat on his head, the color accentuating the yellow flecks in his hazel eyes.

"I could use a little training myself," she said, feeling her thighs rub together in her black cotton pants.

"You have my number." Mark walked her to her car, and rested a hand on the hood as she unlocked the door. There was an awkward pause before Grace opened the door and started to slide into the driver's side. "So, I guess I'll see you at the station tomorrow. I start up my four day tour again."

"I'll be there," Grace said.

Mark used a hand to gently shut her door and she watched him walk down the road in her rearview mirror until he became a small black silhouette.

Grace allowed thoughts of Mark to infiltrate her mind before she summoned all the discipline she had to focus on what she needed to do to prove that Mackenzie Waterford was guilty. Guilty of what, she wasn't sure, but she was determined to find out.

CHAPTER SIXTEEN

BRIDGETON HIGH SCHOOL APPEARED TO BE AS OLD AS THE TOWN ITSELF, the structure of the building lopsided as if it were literally dropping into the cemetery that sat across the street, sealed off by a black wrought iron fence.

Bridgeton School District always took long Christmas breaks, but they used the school for activities during the time classroom learning was on hiatus. The idea had actually been something that Grace herself had spearheaded during one of the meetings designed to keep kids busy and away from drugs. While some of the teachers weren't too enthused about the extra hours they'd have to volunteer their time staffing arts and crafts and cooking classes, the program was a hit with the parents.

It was nearing four o'clock, so Grace wasn't sure she would have any luck in getting a principal or staff member who wasn't rushing out the door eager to get on with their lives away from a bunch of kids. Surprisingly, about ten cars still sat in the small staff parking lot. A couple of little girls came flying out of the building in a tornado, their cheeks pink like roses and each with their arms wrapped around what appeared to be some type of paper-mache animal.

She pulled into the staff lot next to Miss Smith's white minivan and placed the parking tag on her rearview mirror, the red print affirming her stature as town police facing outwards. On a weekly basis, Grace spent several hours at the school working with the teachers of the incoming freshmen, assisting with anti-bullying policies and giving informative sessions on drug and alcohol abuse and crime. She even had to spend five hours a year training the faculty and staff on the proper protocol for dealing with a school shooting. It was necessary training, but heartbreaking at the same time. When did the world become so tainted with crime in innocent environments like schools, malls and movie theaters? The big crime news when Grace was growing up was mostly associated with gangs and small, targeted groups involved in drugs. Her boots crunched on the salt pathway that led to the main entrance of the building.

"What brings you here during Christmas break, Detective McKenna? Don't they ever let you off the clock?" Mr. O'Neil's gentle voice came out in perfect pronunciation as he stopped next to her on his way out of the building and toward the parking lot. Mr. O'Neil had been an economics teacher for as long as Grace had been alive, and he was compulsively on time to trainings and meetings, always the first one in attendance sitting in the front row waiting patiently. He was a nice man, dedicated to his career in a way that one without a wife or child normally is. Every time Grace ran into Mr. O'Neil, she couldn't help but wonder if one day she would be like him, married to her career and absent of a family. She imagined he had been one of the first ones to volunteer to staff the Christmas break activities. He clutched a Tupperware container in one hand. Grace could see the red and green sprinkles through the container labeled *Christmas Cookie Class* in perfect handwriting.

"Oh, I'm here on some routine business. Just having my monthly check-in with Principal Woeburn." She could see the panic in Mr. O'Neil's eyes simmer down, content that he hadn't been late for a meeting, let alone miss one altogether.

"Well, he's still going strong in there. He's another one who doesn't like to take a break," Mr. O'Neil said as he waved her off. "Have a wonderful Christmas, if I don't see you again. I'm off to visit some family in Connecticut." It made Grace happy that he had a place to go for the holidays. It was good to know he had something outside of the school and students. Maybe there was hope for her having a social life someday. "Hey, wait a minute. I'm so rude not to offer." He turned around and stepped toward her, as he peeled the lid off the container. "How would you like one of my famous Christmas cookies?"

"Thanks, Mr. O'Neil. Sure, I'll try one," Grace said as the smell of sugar hit her nose and woke her up.

"I'll let you in on a little secret, though," Mr. O'Neil said. "I don't have a secret recipe. Got these from some fancy cooking website." He winked at her and sealed the cover. "Don't tell the kids."

"Your secret is safe with me, Mr. O'Neil. They certainly taste delicious. Have a Merry Christmas." She winked back to him just as she waved to another familiar faculty member. Mrs. Holland waved to her as she was in mid-conversation with another young teacher that Grace hadn't recognized.

Grace wondered if Mrs. Holland had been friends with Jenny Silva. Or maybe the art teacher kept to herself, distant from the others. Grace had assumed the latter, considering that she herself didn't know Jenny Silva, given the amount of time and years she has spent tasked as the Bridgeton School Liaison. She liked to think she knew all the faculty and staff in the school district, but there was still about a quarter of the staff that she hadn't met. Some names she had heard in passing, but she struggled with putting a face to the name. Jenny Silva remained a mystery to her, in more ways than one.

As promised, Ray Woeburn was sitting at his desk diligently working.

"Knock, knock," Grace said the words as she tapped on the doorframe, the door cracked open just enough to prove his theory of having an "open-door policy," but not enough to make a teenager with a problem feel all that welcome.

"I'll be there in a sec, Marcy. Just wrapping up this new end of year system," Ray said not looking up from his computer.

"Actually, it's not Marcy. It's Detective McKenna."

"Oh geez. I'm so sorry, Grace." Ray swiveled around and catapulted off his chair. He marched toward her, extending an arm as he rested a hand on her shoulder and ushered her in the room. "Take a seat. Please." He waved his hand toward an old living room chair that sat in the corner of his office for those times that he wanted students to feel a certain level of comfort when they confessed their problems. Ray Woeburn didn't have the best interpersonal skills, but he was a good, solid principal, always looking out for the best interest of the students. And anytime Grace needed something, he dropped everything to assist her. "We didn't schedule a meeting during Christmas break, did we?"

"Actually, I was tallying up my traffic violations for the year and I noticed that one of your teachers, Jenny Silva, has an awful lot of violations. Now, I don't typically do a visit like this, but I wasn't sure if this was part of a bigger issue." Grace didn't know where this was coming from, but it seemed to be working. Jenny Silva only had a few traffic violations as far as she knew, but she rationalized with herself that she was working toward a much bigger problem here and if she had to tell a white lie, then she was okay with that.

"Hmmm." The principal twisted in his chair, crossing one leg over the other. "Well, I can't say I'm surprised." He held two hands out, palms facing Grace. "Don't get me wrong, Jenny is an A-plus teacher in my book. She's one of those teachers who are passionate about her subject . . . I guess almost to a fault, in some cases. She gets so caught up in art and coaching the students on the importance of imagery and all that. Sometimes I think she forgets where she is. Like, maybe she actually believes she is living inside one of her images or something." He tried holding back a chuckle. "To put it bluntly, Miss Silva can be a bit of a space cadet at times. And I mean that in the most sincere way, if that makes sense." He clasped his hands over his elevated knee and paused. "Is she in some type of trouble?"

"No, no, just double checking. Do you happen to know if Miss Silva has volunteered for any of the Christmas break activities?"

"Well, let me check. I have the sign-up sheet right here." He rolled closer to his desk and flipped open a binder titled *Christmas Break Activity Schedule Sign-up.* He used an index finger to guide him down the list. "Looks like she had originally signed up to teach an art class, but then crossed her name out. Miss Arbor is covering the class now." He looked up. "Are you sure everything is okay, Detective McKenna?"

"Yes, yes…all is good," Grace said, scurrying to get some words to surface. "It's just that we live in a small town, ya know? When times are slow, I check in on the regular traffic offenders. Try to make Bridgeton a safer place to live.

"Makes sense. I have the utmost respect for your career, Detective McKenna."

Grace was well aware of Ray's admiration for her position at the town police department. The man dropped everything anytime she entered the school, catering to her like she was a celebrity. When Grace first met the man, she wondered about his innocence, since he sucked up to her like he was a criminal trying to escape his past.

"Well, thank you, Ray. I have the same respect for your career." Grace stood. "To be honest, I don't know how you put up with all these kids." She walked over to the wall just outside his office, Ray followed behind like a puppy dog. Various different pieces of art hung on the wall enclosed in a glass case, a hodgepodge from various grades and artistic levels. "Are these all done by the students?"

"Yep, for the most part." He rested his arms across the maroon sweater vest that sat on his small frame. "From over the years, of course." He pointed to an elegant flower colorfully painted on a canvas, a slight yellowing outlining the edges. "This one's old, though. Done by a student who graduated nearly four years ago. It's always been one of my favorites. Something about the colors." He wiped off a smudge on the glass, a leftover fingerprint. "Aiden McGilvary. One of the most promising students we've had here. The boy excelled in everything. Went off to New York to become a successful attorney. I guess I keep his artwork up because it's proof that what I do every day, even with all the crap I have to put up with, pays off in the long run—ya know? It's a good feeling when you see these kids go off and become successful members of society. Yeah, the majority stick around the town surrounded by the same people and the same small town mentality, never to spread their wings and fly. But every now and then, you get an Aiden."

"Do you have any Aiden's in school now?" Grace pressed, certain he was going to mention Mackenzie Waterford, an easy access point into a further conversation on the girl.

"I do have my favorites. I'm not gonna lie."

"Who are your favorites? You can tell me," Grace said, bumping his elbow like an old friend.

"These days, I think Taylor Ryder has a lot of promise." He nodded toward another piece of artwork that was hanging up. "Of course, another artist. I feel like all the kids who excel are naturally good at art, too. You can throw it on top of all their other subjects and they just get it. They absorb the lines and the colors like its math, English or science."

Grace looked at the painting of a stallion running through a field, its hair blowing in the wind as if any moment the animal could come to life and run right off the paper. "It's beautiful. Looks like another one with a lot of promise."

It was in that moment that Grace's eye caught the same sunflower painting she'd seen in Jenny's house staring back at her against a backdrop of white. It was darkened around the edges and wilted, its lifeless frame falling over and absent of vitality. The background was shaded in purple against a black cloud. It was a sullen, yet beautiful piece of art and depicted a loss of hope, if Grace had to translate it into something meaningful. "What about this one? That's an interesting piece."

"It's by Mackenzie Waterford. Gosh, I've seen that girl change over the years."

"How so?"

"Well, she used to be a very prim and proper well-liked girl. And then something changed, almost like a switch was flipped." Ray stopped, catching himself from revealing too much.

"Really? She's a smart kid, isn't she?" Grace pressed, her arms resting across her chest.

"She is a nice kid . . . or, I guess she used to be. I mean, this artwork is a perfect example. She used to be the type of kid to excel, but she was still likeable. Then, I started to see this dark side rise in her. And she started producing odd art work like this. I mean, maybe I just can't appreciate all that contorted art. I think they call it 'depression art.' But, Mackenzie used to be the type of girl who painted fields with butterflies, and now this mysterious warped sunflower appears out of nowhere. This piece wasn't my decision. In fact, I think Jenny Silva suggested we hang it up. And she started dressing different when she came to school. I'd see her show up in her regular clothes and by the third period, she'd be in all black with crazy jewelry. I guess she's going through a phase, trying to express her artistic side or something. Actually, now that I think of it . . ." he used two fingers to scratch his chin again, his eyes searching for an answer. "I noticed that she started spending a lot of time in Miss Silva's classroom, long after the school day ended. I never really thought much about it—just another overachiever trying to get ahead. Jenny Silva may be a bit spacy, but she's a good teacher. Always staying after hours to help her students—apparently, becoming quite the role model for Mackenzie Waterford."

"Is Jenny Silva usually on time for class? Does she show up every day?"

"As far as I know, she's on time . . . mostly because she rarely leaves her classroom. I can show you the teacher attendance records if you'd like." He started back in his office, but Grace stopped him.

"No need, Ray. I'll take your word for it." She felt the confidence swim through her as she said the words. In a career where she was trained to be skeptical of the average man, Grace felt comforted and confident that Ray Woeburn was telling the truth. The man had never proven to be anything other than an upstanding member of society and a passionate principal, someone who was out for the best interest of the students.

"I guess some students just get attached to their teachers," Grace said as she looked over at the image of the wilted flower, zipping up her jacket and trying to hide her excitement for the new details she had on Mackenzie Waterford. "I can remember the crush I had on my PE teacher, Mr. Martucci. I'm pretty sure I had high hopes of marrying him after I graduated." Grace giggled to herself, looking back on the crush that she remembered so vividly.

"And how did that work out for you?"

"I think by the time I graduated, I had moved on to another guy."

"That's the thing with these teenagers. They move on fast. That's why I never thought much about Mackenzie's art phase. I'm sure she'll be back to her normal self soon enough."

Grace shook hands with the principal and led herself down the hallway, pushing through the heavy glass doors. The sky had darkened; shades of gray and dark blue filled in the clouds, creating an eerie background to the small town that was about to get flipped upside down.

There was something off about the relationship between Mackenzie and Jenny. This wasn't a typical schoolgirl crush. Grace could feel it in the pit of her stomach.

As she tossed her bag into the passenger seat, the vibration of her phone broke into her thoughts. A Boston area code popped up on the screen, followed by a text message:

I KNOW that you are technically supposed to wait at least twenty-four hours, but I just wanted to say I had a great time chatting with you today . . . police work aside. If you ever want to experiment with some other vegetarian options, I'd like to take you out to some of my favorite "animal friendly" restaurants. ;)

GRACE FELT giddy for a second before getting angry with herself. She didn't have the time or energy to be stuck in the midst of something else to take up precious space in her mind. Mark was the type of guy that she crushed on back when she allowed herself to show interest in the opposite sex. After so much dating gone wrong, Grace had given up.

It had started as a New Year's resolution last year and with the exception of the so-called date she went on with Eric, it was probably the only resolution she actually stuck with. "You know what's going to happen, right?" Her mother had said through her smiling yellowed teeth. "Mr. Right is going to come around, just as you turn your back. Make as many resolutions as you want my dear, but there's nothing stopping fate from working its magic." It had been an annual New Year's tradition to write down negative thoughts on paper before throwing them into the fireplace and watching them go up in flames as they sipped on peppermint schnapps, counting down the hours until midnight. Of course, the tradition had been started by Ellen on one of her missions to "cleanse her soul," but Grace had found herself looking forward to the evening as early as Thanksgiving, just as the holiday season was commencing. She could hear her mother's voice bickering in her head now. Grace sighed. As much as she couldn't stand Ellen's flighty rituals and herbal teas, she was the one who Grace went to first every time something in her life shifted. Because surely, Ellen would have an answer that would always end up making Grace feel better, even if she didn't want to admit it. *There is no such thing as accident; it is fate misnamed.* Grace could hear her mother's words as she found herself pulling onto Jenny Silva's street.

She pulled into the farthest open spot from Jenny's house, right up against a pile of snow that had been plowed yesterday. Before she confronted the demons of Jenny Silva's past, she decided to do something for herself for once. She picked up her phone and typed back to Mark: *I'd love to join you for some animal friendly fare.*

Her boots crunched into the snow as she made her way toward Jenny's front steps, which were now three rectangular piles of snow. Winters could either help or hurt a police officer's work, and in this case they were helping. The lack of evident footprints was proof that no one had been to Jenny's house since at least yesterday.

Van Gogh came barreling toward her as she pushed the door open, but he stopped short when he saw the pile of snow that had collapsed into the entryway. If anything, Grace had convinced herself that if nothing came of this case, then at least she could give herself a pat on the back for feeding a hungry cat.

"Hey there, buddy." Grace stepped into the small kitchen and crouched down to let the cat wrap himself around her legs. "I bet you're hungry, huh?" she said as she scratched behind his ears. He was already starting to look malnourished. The line of his spine was showing, a bumpy arch that ran under her hand as he walked underneath. If Grace couldn't solve this case, or if it was too late to save Jenny Silva's life, at least she could rescue an animal in need. "You wanna come home with me, buddy?"

The cat let out a piercing meow as if he could understand her words.

"I'm not sure how Brody is going to feel about it, but he'll live." She walked toward the fridge and shoveled some of the homemade food into his bowl. "I'm not sure if you will dine quite as well at my house though . . . think you could settle for the store-bought stuff?"

The cat ignored her as he put his whole body into eating the bowl of food. The bell on his collar was hitting the bowl so fast it sounded like a pair of wind chimes.

Grace made her way back into the room she suspected was dedicated as Jenny's art space. Everything was laid out exactly as it was the day before, including the same pair of purple stockings that sat crumpled up on the floor.

Grace went to work going through the many small drawers in a hutch hidden behind a massive canvas painting of a girl with bright blonde hair and big blue eyes. It looked like Miss Silva had been painting a younger version of herself. Grace made sure to pull on a pair of gloves before she laid her prints on any of the woman's belongings. She delicately moved the canvas so she had full access to the multi-colored drawers that were lined in rows of five across the dresser.

"This is gonna take awhile," Grace said to herself as she shimmied open the drawer farthest to the left on the antique piece of furniture. She wondered if Jenny Silva was one of those women who spent their weekends scouting old antiques at consignment stores, taking them home to fix them up and give them a new life. Grace envied those women. She didn't have the patience to spend countless hours searching for the right piece, and she certainly didn't have the talent to turn a dusty old hutch into a masterpiece like this one.

The first row of drawers proved to be used as junk drawers, as she only found pens, pencils, a few random art erasers and some boring grocery store receipts. Grace wondered if the woman had been planning to return a bag of organic apples that she purchased nearly a year ago. It was never fun having a victim or a criminal who was a packrat, as it made for more evidence to sift through in order to get answers.

The routine of going through the drawers started to bore Grace, so she decided she would close her eyes and pick a random knob, making sure to leave it open after she had completed the search of the inside. She closed her eyes and reached level with her right hip. "Please be lucky drawer number one," she said to herself as she slid the drawer open.

A few pieces of paper fell out and fluttered to the floor. The floor creaked below her as she leaned down to pick up the fallen pieces of paper. Receipts from the local drug store reflecting a typical shopping trip to the nearby CVS for a woman her age: tampons, Burt's Bees hand lotion, L'Oreal eye cream, coconut water and a bag of Doritos.

"I guess Jenny Silva isn't the health nut I thought she was." Grace slid the receipts back into the drawer. As she mashed them in the tiny drawer, she heard something small roll from the back of the drawer to the front. She wrapped her hand around the tiny figure and pulled out a little stone Buddha. A necklace dangled from his neck, similar to the one that Grace saw in her visions of Jenny. His eyes were closed and his mouth open in a taunting laugh as if he were mocking her. Buddha was supposed to be a friendly, peace-loving little man, but he sent an eerie chill down her spine so she dropped him back into the drawer and slammed it shut.

She closed her eyes again and took her chances at lucky drawer number two. Her hand landed on the bottom right drawer and as she slid it open, she knew that she had opened a drawer that would lead her a little bit deeper into the depths of Jenny Silva's life.

A stack of photos looked up at her, their edges slightly tattered, some still with tape on the back from where she had secured them against a wall or another surface. Others were cut to apparently fit some type of collage or frame. Grace allowed her gloved hand to slide around the pile of photos as she backed her way into the nearby Papasan chair, the round pillow conforming to her body and the wood creaking as it gave way to her figure. The photos appeared to recount Jenny's life in one simplified pile. Jenny as a toddler, snuggled in her mother's arms, their matching blue eyes stare ahead at the camera as if caught daydreaming. Jenny as a little girl in the eighties on a beach sitting under an umbrella wearing one of those bathing suits with the hole cut out of the center, her hair resting on her shoulders in wet stringy clumps. In the background, even in the faded photo, Grace could still see the sun reflecting off the clean white sand with a backdrop of a clear blue-green ocean.

"Certainly not a beach around here," Grace said to herself, thinking about the tan sand and rocky layout that flanked the Massachusetts coastline. She picked up a class photo of Jenny with teased hair against a backdrop of fluorescent lighting, bringing Grace back to her own teen years. She recognized the baggy turtleneck sweater with brightly colored shapes as one that she herself would've worn back in those days.

As Grace sifted through the old photos boasting of typical experiences of an average girl growing up in the eighties and nineties, she had started to give up hope on finding anything that stood out in the art teacher's life, until her gloved fingers rested on a photo that was cut down to fit a tiny frame. Jenny's big blue eyes were still recognizable, even though they were turned down in a soft sadness as she looked down at a tiny pink bundle wrapped in her arms. The bulky hospital gown looked foreign on the woman who typically dressed in either black or something that embraced the fact that she was an artist. Grace imagined Jenny Silva would've despised having to slip into the pastel patterned gown that hung off her body like a sheet. Her hair was longer and a more natural shade with hints of brown and blonde blended together. Grace realized how naturally beautiful Jenny Silva was in the photos, free from the vast display of colors that canvassed her face in the more recent photos that she had seen. Her naturally young-looking face appeared to be even more childlike, with clusters of acne on her chin and forehead. Grace turned over the photo in her hand in search of a date. *March 1999* was glowing in red computerized font. While she seemed to get her hands on a deep-seated secret from Jenny's past, it was still not a valid reasoning why Jenny was missing and Mackenzie Waterford had embarked in some type of torture on the woman.

Grace looked at her watch, suddenly remembering that she had to prepare for a meeting she had scheduled with the Chief first thing the next morning. He had been urging her to apply for the promotion, a jump in the ranks that may not be a huge boost in her pay, but would be enough to keep her moving up and well-respected in the small town police department.

She tucked the photo into the inside pocket of her jacket and tried to avoid the creaks in the floor as she slid out of the room, making sure to keep the door slightly cracked like it was when she arrived. Just as her hand was on the knob, she was overcome with the feeling that someone was watching her and it sent an eerie chill down her spine. She turned to give the kitchen a once-over before turning the knob, and was greeted with two magnificent yellow eyes. The cat sat on the top of a cabinet, looking down at her like he was some type of higher power. He let out one loud meow, the force of it made the bell on his collar rattle.

"Oh, buddy, I know. You're all alone." She walked toward him in two giant steps. He jumped down to the counter before making his way to the floor and brushing up against her legs. "I tell ya what . . . you can come home with me for the night. But you gotta come back here tomorrow. I don't know where your owner is, but I'm going to try to find her, okay?" She spoke aloud to the cat as she picked him up, thinking about the slim possibility that Jenny Silva was even still alive. Grace couldn't turn her back on a hungry, lonely animal, though. She would take a room full of cats and dogs over a room full of humans. She never once had to approach a crime scene where a dog was the perpetrator, never once was a cat pulled into a courtroom because of murder. Animals could be trusted. People could not. Cradling the cat in one arm, Grace maneuvered her way down the stairs, using steady steps to walk through the snow.

Another round of snowflakes had started to make an appearance and Grace felt a few moist flakes land delicately on her eyelashes. The sky had turned to a somber gray, as nightfall descended on another day. Grace hoped her timing allowed her to slip into her car unnoticed with the kidnapped cat in her arms, but her hopes were quickly demolished when she saw Mark leaning against her car like a male model in a cologne ad. She faced him head-on, clearly busted from setting up her own secret mission to solve her own secret case. The cat was an added bonus.

"If I didn't know you so well, I would ask if you took up a side job as a cat detective, but—"

"What are you doing here?" Grace tried to sound mad, tried to scare him off, but it was a hard thing to do when she was a sucker for his hazel eyes. Something about the way he held her stare made Grace feel like they had one of those unexplainable connections. Something about Mark Connelly made sense to her.

"I didn't become a cop because I like carrying a gun or because I'm one of those guys who need to replace their insecurity with a power job," he said as he dug his hands deep into his jean pockets. "I became a cop because I love solving a case."

"Then why aren't you a detective?"

"Oh snap—that hurt," he said. "To be honest with you, I guess I just got comfortable in my position. But seeing you so passionate about a case that isn't even open, a case that essentially doesn't exist, makes me want to help you. Listen Grace, I don't know your reasons for being obsessed with this Mackenzie Waterford girl and I certainly don't know why you are walking out of a strange house with a cat in your hands. But, I know this isn't your house and I know that you're a good detective who hasn't really been given the opportunity to crack a big case mostly because of the small town boredom of where we both work. So, I'm guessing you're onto something." He pushed himself away from the car, standing closer to her. "And I want to help. You don't need to give me any credit if something comes of this." He waved a hand toward the house and then the cat. "I know you probably think I'm crazy, and you're probably the furthest thing from trusting me, but I promise you—I'm honest to a fault." His eyes darted back and forth, as if searching Grace's eyes for understanding, before they settled and held her stare.

"Get in the car." The words fell from her mouth as she opened the back door and gently set the cat on the blanket that had been placed on the seat for road trips with Brody. She wasn't sure how Brody was going to take the introduction to a cat. He had been her baby for the last seven years, and she wasn't sure how he'd manage with the new roommate. "Go on . . . get in the car," Grace said as Mark stood in a puddle of shock, snowflakes falling all around him like he was standing in the center of a snow globe. He made a mocking motion of surveying the area before sliding into the passenger seat, a paranoid suspect.

"Where did you park?" Grace asked as she flipped on her windshield wipers and eased onto the road that outlined the beach.

"I didn't. I walked. I'm a townie, remember?" Mark said as he turned up the volume on her radio. Much to Grace's embarrassment, a *Fifty Shades of Grey* audiobook had been in the CD player. Grace prided herself on despising books like this, always taking the high road with her subtle feminism, but she had to admit she was hooked. "Is this—"

"Let's listen to radio," Grace said as she frantically pushed the buttons on the dashboard.

"Well, I can't say I'm not shocked, Grace McKenna. First of all, I'm stunned that you still listen to CDs, let alone sex CDs."

"It's NOT a sex CD. It's a story. A really good plot."

"I bet." Mark gazed out the window, entranced in the view of the growing waves.

Grace pulled into the parking lot of the elementary school. With Christmas looming it was unlikely there would be any children or teachers on the property.

"Are you kidnapping me, too?"

"No, listen." Grace put the car in park and fumbled with her hands.

"I know that Mackenzie Waterford is guilty of harming Jenny Silva, the art teacher." She paused, raised her gaze so her eyes were locked on his. "I can't tell you how I know, but just trust me when I say that I know."

For the first time in her life, Grace felt a strong pull to spill her secret, to tell Mark Connolly about the visions that have been crippling her since she was three years old. But she couldn't risk it. After all, she still felt uneasy about the psychologist that she saw. She imagined him going home to his family sharing stories about his patient, the crazy girl who claimed to see visions of victims in the eyes of suspected murderers and criminals. She could hardly believe it herself, which is why she had never allowed herself to get close to a man. No way in hell would any man in his right mind believe her when she described the tortured eyes and fearful expressions that gripped her memories and thoughts.

"I trust you," Mark said, as nonchalant as if he were responding to a simple confession. She told him about her plan of attack, and watched Mark's reaction when he surveyed the photo that she had filched from the messy house.

"I don't get it. Is this Jenny as a baby? Her mom?"

"No, Jenny *is* the mom in the picture. Look at the eyes." Grace pulled out an image of Jenny that she had printed from online. "I don't know about you, but I can't say I've ever seen such giant blue eyes on a face before. No trace of the baby, though. Look at the date. She had the baby in March of 1999—that would make that baby seventeen years old."

A revelation passed over Mark's face. "You're not thinking Mackenzie's her kid, are you?"

"I've seen stranger things. But here's the thing . . . Jenny Silva only moved to Bridgeton four years ago. She's been a teacher at BHS for nearly three years. According to the records we have at the station, her past licenses hail from Florida and California."

"I wonder what would bring her to Bridgeton."

"My thoughts exactly. Now, if you truly want to help, I think the best thing to do would be to start out by finding anything you can online. Maybe pull up her old addresses. I can get them from Joe."

"Assertive and good-looking. I'm starting to like you, McKenna."

Grace rolled her eyes and laughed him off, but the butterflies in her stomach did a little dance to his words. "Now, shall I drop you off at home? I have to head back to the station to finish up some paperwork. Or do you plan on stalking me further tonight? Maybe I should just drop you off in front of my house so you can peek into my windows like the creeper that you are." She had quickly learned that she could joke with him and her comfort level seemed to increase every time she was around him.

"Very funny. No, I'll walk home from here," he said before an awkward moment thickened the silence between them.

"Are you one of those people who walks everywhere?"

"Just trying to get my ten thousand daily steps in." He held up his arm, showing off a sporty pedometer wrapped around his wrist, a few veins snaked their way down a tanned masculine hand.

"Oh boy, you really are obsessed with being fit."

"Can't deny that. I guess there could be worse addictions, right?" He opened the door and slid out of the car before placing one hand on the roof and leaning in. "I'll report back to you when I find something on her."

Mark pulled the hood of his gray ski jacket up, shielding him from the snowfall and making him appear mysterious and sexy. Grace knew that she was in trouble.

"Thanks. I'll get those addresses from Joe."

With that, Grace steered her Jeep out of the parking lot, crunching through the quickly accumulating snow and turning the volume up on her audiobook.

As soon as Grace walked through the front door of the station Barb looked up, clearly expecting someone else. Just as quickly, she looked away and gave Grace the cold shoulder that she thought she deserved.

"Hey, Barb," Grace said as she walked past acting as if nothing happened between them. In exchange, Barb punched the keys on her computer with such force, taking her anger out of the keyboard. While Grace was sad to lose a friend, and even missed Barb's boisterous personality always butting into her business, she knew that Barb couldn't be quiet for too long.

Grace busied herself with putting together a folder of all her achievements at the station, along with certificates for additional courses she had taken in hopes of being of more use in her position. She wanted to submit herself for the promotion before Chief Welch clued in on the fact that she was technically running a private case. She imagined him lecturing her on the importance of communication within the station and how all cases had to be run through the chain of command with daily check-ins and middle of the night updates if necessary. Grace had the communications training to prove her capability.

She slid the cert into the folder and prayed that the chief wouldn't get wind of this before the promotion was granted.

CHAPTER SEVENTEEN

JENNY

It started as a simple search on the Internet four years ago, and then I became obsessed. I even started dating a guy for the sole purpose of obtaining information from the national adoption agency where he worked.

Since that day in the hospital on March 13, 1999, I have longed to see her and to hold her in my arms again. I was only sixteen when I got pregnant. My parents had convinced me that I would be of no use to society if I had a child at such a young, inexperienced age and they had tried to convince me to have an abortion. But there was something about seeing that heart beating inside me that told me it wasn't my choice. Yes, my body was home to a growing baby and it was supporting it in all its efforts to come into this world, to leave its mark, but it wasn't up to me to tell that little heartbeat that she couldn't live just because of one stupid night of unprotected sex by two teens in love. If anything, maybe it was a chance for my line of DNA to take a turn for the better. So, as painful as it was, I gave her up for adoption. It was a good family, I was told. They had been trying to conceive for years with no luck. All they needed was this baby, my baby, and their world would be complete. They lived in a small town outside of Boston, where the father had planted some solid roots. I knew that they lived in a home that had been passed down generation after generation, its structure being altered to accom-

modate more modern rooms and additions to allow for the space that their new baby needed.

Like a ripped Band-Aid, I opted for a closed adoption, having the idea in my head that I would get over it. That with time, one day I would forget that I birthed a baby girl. And when the time came that I had moved on with my life, possibly even mothering a new child with a loving husband, I didn't want to give that baby girl the opportunity to contact me and send my life on a rollercoaster of emotions once again. I wanted to forget. I wanted to forget the feeling I had when I held her in my arms and I was encompassed with a love so strong that it literally scared me. In the brief moments that I was able to hold her, I felt as if I would kill for this baby and I would have no qualms about it. In just minutes of embracing her perfect little body, I felt a rush of emotions that, much to my chagrin, would last a lifetime. The memory of those moments sat within my heart for years, never fading or growing absent of the intricate details. I could still smell her; I could still feel how she fit into the crook of my arm as if we were designed to be two pieces of a puzzle. I waited patiently for that longing to go away. I saw shrink after shrink. I dated, and even got married once. But nothing could fill the void of that piece of me that was missing.

When I finally tracked her down, when I had decided to pack up and move to the same town where she had grown up, it was too late to turn around and pretend that this obsession had never formed in my mind and heart. It started with me blending in with the crowd at her soccer games but it slowly drew me to switching careers. My life as a whirlwind artist was no longer meaningful as my biggest accomplishment; the best piece of art that I had a hand in creating was her. So, I went back to school and got my teaching certificate. Apparently you really don't even have to be an artist to be an art teacher. You simply have to teach the basics in color and lines and a little bit of history about the famous artists before our time. I got lucky and got a job right away at Bridgeton High. While an artistic background hadn't really been required to fill the position, the principal understood my past life as an artist to be more beneficial to the students.

Mackenzie had been starting out as a freshmen at the time and I was teaching an upper-level art class. I'll never forget that first day of school that I saw her walking down the hallway. I had been standing outside my classroom greeting the students, like all the good teachers do, when she walked into the classroom next to mine for AP chemistry. At first I had been shocked that I could produce a child who was so smart that she was accepted in the advanced classes, and then I realized maybe it was the nature vs. nurture thing. Maybe her new family bathed her in the importance of good grades and finding a future. I couldn't help but wonder if I had raised Mackenzie, would she have been more like me? Artistic and disorganized and unable to understand such subjects as chemistry. Or had all of her natural genes been shed like a snake ridding its skin the day I handed her over in the hospital?

On that first day of school four years ago, I had been staring at her, but she didn't notice. She was so focused on finding her classroom and probably getting a front seat. She is that type of girl, so very different from me. It didn't take me long to butter up to her chemistry teacher, Mr. Davis. He was a little older than me but as luck would have it, he was single and happened to have a thing for girls like me: tattooed, heavy makeup, and utterly disorganized. Mike Davis was that classic nerdy chemistry teacher, the type who got so wrapped up in an experiment that he didn't realize his hair was in disarray and sticking up in the air from behind his massive goggles. But, maybe that's how we meshed for that brief moment in time; we were both passionate about something in life. Originally I had befriended Mike so it wouldn't look so odd when I snuck through the door of our adjoining classrooms to get a peek at Mackenzie. I wanted to watch her learn and absorb, even something as foreign to me as Chemistry. I missed out on teaching her the alphabet and counting her numbers, so I longed to see that focus in her eyes and that sparkle when she realized something in her brain clicked.

I wanted to know what her favorite food was, how she took her coffee—if kids her age even drank coffee. Was she a morning person, or a night owl like me? Was she lefty or righty? I wanted to know if she had a favorite stuffed animal or blanket as a toy. I wanted to know if she truly liked all those sports and activities that she did so well, or if she was just trying to please her parents. I wanted to know all those little details that you find out about a person when you truly get to know them and build a relationship. After all those years of staring at the hospital photo, it was surreal to see her in person. I would watch her as she talked to friends in the hallway and try to pick up *on any gestures that she had similar to mine. Naturally, I saw myself in every move she made.*

One night after all the faculty and staff left for the evening, I found a lonely custodian wandering the halls, sweeping up random balls of dust. I knew his type and I'd caught him staring at me on several occasions. It wasn't hard to miss the way he nervously pushed his long greasy hair out of his eyes when I walked by. I knew he had been a criminal in the past. Maybe it was in his shaky gestures or maybe it was the way that he always dropped his head when a student walked by, afraid that he'd get in trouble for looking at a minor, or made fun of by the athletic teenage boys who roamed the halls in gangs. I was one of the only ones who gave him the time of day. I never knew who would come in handy on my mission to getting closer to Mackenzie, so I was kind to everyone. He was a bit taken aback that first time I smiled at him, and he actually looked over his shoulder, assuming the sincere grin was meant for someone else. As a custodian, I knew he had access to the tools that could bust open locks and pry open doors. So, I did what I had to do to learn more about my daughter. I asked him if he could break open her locker and make it appear like some hoodlum had been on the prowl. All it took was a politely asked question and a smile. I threw in a couple of flirtatious gestures as a bonus.

Unfortunately there wasn't much to see in the locker, as Mackenzie was a compulsive neat freak. But there were a couple of hooded school sweatshirts hung up. I ran my finger over the neckline, feeling the part that was closest to my daughter's face. I tugged the material gently, like it was an invaluable article of clothing. I read the size on the tag. She was a size small, just like me. I couldn't help but be proud of the simplest little things that marked our similarities. The closer I got to things as mundane as her clothing, the more I longed to hold her in my arms.

It was an addiction, and she was my drug.

CHAPTER EIGHTEEN

CHRISTMAS WAS THREE DAYS AWAY, AND GRACE HAD A LOT TO DO before she and her mother celebrated the holiday together. It was typically just the two of them, but this year Ellen was on a mission to make the world a better place, so she had invited a few acquaintances who had no place to go. Grace hosted, as she preferred. Her mother had always opted to live in a tiny apartment that she could barely afford instead of moving into Grace's small but spacious-enough home. Ellen McKenna liked her own space and she didn't want to intrude on her daughter; besides that, she clearly had very high hopes that one day her daughter would have a husband and children to fill the home.

As Grace pushed her cart down the grocery aisle searching for ingredients for some new dish her mom wanted to try, she couldn't help but see Jenny Silva's image in the back of her head. When she picked up a bottle of shampoo in the beauty aisle, she saw Jenny's haunting big blue eyes on the model. Jenny Silva was everywhere, but nowhere at the same time. Grace had so badly wanted to corner Mackenzie and beg for answers, but knowing what little she knew of the girl, she wasn't someone who would back down or be easily bribed or threatened for answers.

Grace found herself in the cat food aisle. Having always preferred dogs over cats, she never had to make the decision between all the different canned cat food options. She selected a tuna-based mix and a bag of Friskies dried food that were in the shapes of little fish. Grace heard a gaggle of teenage girls in the next aisle over and before she knew it, her cart was pulled up right beside them, back in the hygiene aisle. She picked up a box of ultra-absorbent pads. If she wanted to get to know teenage girls, she had to learn them. Although, she didn't think Mackenzie Waterford was an average teenage girl.

"Personally I prefer the ones that fit into your wallet. I mean, do you really want to carry some big bulky tampon around? And pads are soooo gross." A girl with shoulder-length brown hair and excessive eye makeup had been counseling a younger, meek girl with strawberry blonde hair and small eyes that made her look like she was struggling to see. Grace certainly couldn't imagine Mackenzie getting counseled on something like this. No, the Mackenzie that she knew would march right into the store and purchase what she wanted, without a question in the world.

"Detective McKenna?" Grace heard the familiar voice and dropped the box of pads. The girls looked over and giggled as Grace bent over to pick up the box. She stood, and found herself face to face with Anthony Waterford. "I didn't know you shopped here."

"Mr. Waterford—Anthony. Hi." Grace rested the box back on the shelf. After all these years and she still got embarrassed when she was caught with a box of sanitary napkins in her hand. "Well, I just had to pick up a few things on my way home and I have to admit, the produce is way better here than where I live, in Cabotville. How are you?"

"Good, good," Anthony said. He looked a lot less angry than two days ago, on the day of Mackenzie's false alarm. His gestures were relaxed and calm, unlike the temper Grace had seen escape when he accidentally broke his phone "And you? I'm sorry, it seems my daughter has found a new friend. He peered over Grace's shoulder at his younger daughter, who appeared to be using her entire body to tell a story to a grocery clerk. "Penny! Penny, come back here, honey!"

"She's such an animated little girl, isn't she?" Grace said, her eyes fixed on Penny. It wasn't often that Grace dreamed about having a child, but if she did, she'd want her to be like Penny. Such a curious little girl, fearless and filled with personality. Grace imagined the entertainment value alone in having a child like that.

"Oh she certainly is, aren't you, Penny?" Anthony said as Penny sidled up to her.

"Hey you're that pretty girl police officer that came to our house!" Penny said, recognizing Grace.

"Why, thank you," Grace said.

"You're very welcome." Penny accompanied her polite words with a little curtsy. "Hey, guess what?" She tilted her head toward Grace as her two eyes widened, eager for her to answer.

"What?"

"My birthday is in two days!"

"No way! But isn't it Christmas Eve in two days?"

"Yes, but daddy says that I'm extra special because I was born on the day that Santa and his elves make all the presents." She pushed a strand of hair out of her eyes. "Maybe I'm one of the presents that Santa made for mommy and daddy?" Penny looked at Grace, searching for an answer.

"Well, you are definitely a treat, Penny, so I don't doubt that."

"Yes, that was certainly a memorable night in the hospital." Anthony winked at Grace and ran a hand down Penny's blonde hair.

"And do you know when your mommy and daddy's birthdays are?" Grace couldn't pass up an opportunity to find out when Mackenzie was born.

"Ummm . . . daddy's birthday is in the summer. I know because I always get to pick out his ice cream cake. I think it's August."

"Close, honey—it's July. You were one month off."

"I know Kenzie's birthday, though! It's March thirteenth, right around when that scary green leprechaun comes out."

Grace tried not to look too happy about receiving the exact answer she wanted, but couldn't help the smile that spread from ear to ear. "And when is your mommy's birthday?"

"Ummm . . . Daddy, isn't mommy's birthday when I get dressed up and go treating?"

"That's right, honey. Mommy's birthday is October thirteenth, two weeks before Halloween, and the same day of the month as Kenzie's."

"Oh yeah! Miss police officer, when's your birthday?"

"My birthday is February ninth."

"Penny, do you know what holiday is close to February ninth?" Anthony asked as if he was asking an important history question.

"Ummm, no, wait . . . is that when the Easter bunny comes?"

"Nope, February is the month when you make daddy and your classmates Valentine cards."

"Ohhhh! And it's when you get mommy all those flowers. Hey, Miss police officer, when can you come back to our house to play? Mommy and daddy have been fighting a lot."

"Penny! What did daddy tell you about spreading rumors?"

"It's bad."

"Yes, spreading rumors hurts people's feelings. Now why don't you go pick out a cereal in the next aisle, okay?" And just like that, Penny was skipping down the aisle singing about which cereal she was going to pick.

"Sorry about that. She's right, we have been fighting a lot," Anthony straightened his chin and looked Grace directly in the eye. "Well, I should say, we *had* been. We're better now. Just a lot of miscommunication and typical marital things. And of course, the stress of Mackenzie going off to college. Mackenzie's just so fixated on it which, personally, I think is good. But, Beth feels like she's been so focused on school all these years, she never got to be a kid."

"I can imagine. She seems like quite the perfectionist," Grace said, the nerves in her body romping around. She was practically dancing with her grocery cart, pushing it forward and back in tiny movements.

"Vanilla Blast Teddie Bear cereal!" Penny said as she raced toward them and tossed the box into the cart.

"Well, we better get going. Lots of prep for Santa's big visit." Anthony winked as he turned his cart.

"If you ever want to talk—I mean off the record and all, I'd be happy to listen." Grace couldn't believe she was saying this to the parent of someone she was investigating, but there was something about Anthony Waterford, and his wife seemed skeptical of Mackenzie, even though she'd raised her. Maybe Beth had doubts about her DNA, Grace thought. There were so many things that she wanted to ask the two of them, but she had to stop herself when the words came to the surface. She reached into her pocket, pulled out the cardholder that her mother had made her so many years ago, and handed a card over to Anthony. "Where is Beth today, anyway?"

"Oh, she's home getting prepped for Christmas dinner." Anthony gave an exasperated smile. "Thanks, Detective McKenna." He took the card delicately and gave her a close-lipped smile before turning down the aisle.

Grace looked at the list that her mother had emailed her for the required food for Christmas day. Under the long list of food, she wrote *Carl is a vegetarian so we'll have to make some sort of veggie casserole or pie?* Grace couldn't help but smile, thinking about Mark and how he loved his baby sister so much he converted to vegetarianism.

Every year, Grace was responsible for doing the grocery shopping and hosting the Christmas gathering and her mother was responsible for doing the majority of the cooking, at least the difficult stuff. Grace could throw together a green bean casserole but that was about it.

A calendar alert rang on her phone as she pulled out of the parking lot, stealing her from her shopping trance.

Reminder: station Christmas party in one hour.

"Shit!" Grace accidentally said the word out loud. She had completely forgotten about the department's party and missed all those in-office reminders because he had been spending so much time on the road gathering information on Jenny Silva. If she was fast enough, she could get to her house and drop everything off, freshen up a bit and slip on some jeans, then get back to the station.

Unlike most work Christmas parties that were held in hotel ballrooms and high class venues, Bridgeton Police Department didn't have the funds nor did most of the staff care for getting dressed up to go out on the town. Instead, they celebrated creatively, with a few appetizers, limited drinks, and a gift swap. And if things got really wild, select officers would hit up the local pub after the party died down. Grace considered herself lucky that she could show up in jeans with a used gift and store-bought cupcakes.

She decided to put a little more effort into her appearance this year, knowing that Mark would be there. After she put away the groceries she ran up the stairs, in a hurry to get ready for the party. Opting for a slightly darker shadow and gray eyeliner, as opposed to her usual light brown pencil, she went to work accentuating her lips with a raspberry color instead of the usual clear gloss. She wore her best-fitting pair of jeans with knee-high black boots and a dark green sweater that drooped slightly off one shoulder if she moved the right way. She pulled out her ponytail and ran the hair straightener through her hair for a quick touchup. It didn't take much to pull out Grace McKenna's natural beauty and transform her from cute detective to bombshell.

As Grace made her way to the station, she rehearsed how she would act in front of Mark, throwing random scenarios at herself. She wasn't sure if he would be openly friendly in front of their colleagues, or if he would hide his feelings.

She balanced the plastic container of cupcakes in one arm and slid the gift bag over her other wrist before using a free hand to pull open the station door. Even the front office had been transformed into a cheesy Christmas wonderland with tinsel strung from the console to the top of the cubes and continuing to the shelf that housed the standard operating procedure manuals. Grace was nearly blinded by the glistening of different colored tinsel and the blinking lights that were strung on the Charlie Brown tree that stood on top of a little table in the corner of the entryway. "Wow . . . this certainly looks like Christmas," said Grace to the two newbies who were stuck working during the party and probably the rest of the week.

"A Griswald Christmas, maybe." The newbie rolled his eyes and swiveled around in the chair.

"Here's something for you guys. I know it's no fun working the holidays for your first few years, so maybe this will help cheer you up. *Off duty*, of course." Grace pulled a bottle of Bourbon out of her bag and leaned over to set it on the console. "Shhh, don't tell anyone." Grace held a finger to her lips. She slid the bag of wines that she promised Joe into his cubby.

"Aw, thanks, Detective McKenna. You rock."

"*OFF* duty." She transformed her voice from friendly to stern as she turned on her heel and walked back to breakroom where the noise was coming from.

As to be expected, Barb was standing in the middle of a group telling some joke about a guy in a bar, her Boston accent heightened, probably because of the cup of cheer she had in her hand. She grew quiet and her eyes lifted off her audience and turned toward Grace as she entered the room. She was not going to let this Eric thing go. It had been nearly three days since they had spoken, and Grace wanted her friend back. She longed to be in cahoots with Barb and hear her daily jokes. Mark stood out from across the room, his hazel eyes standing out against the deep green shirt he was wearing. As soon as Mark saw her, he left the huddle and marched toward her, a beer in one hand.

"Hey, can I get you anything from the elaborate bar?" Mark waved a hand toward the two lunch tables that were pushed together to make a mock bar. The recycled high school lunch tables were covered in a shiny red plastic tablecloth, the awkward rectangle shape of the table made the cover dip and rise in certain spots, revealing a stash of cardboard wine boxes underneath.

"I'm assuming we aren't serving martinis at this year's party?" Grace joked.

"I wouldn't be so sure; I think Barb brought a couple flasks of something. I'm sure she could whip one up for you."

"I'll take a glass of the boxed wine," Grace said, surveying her options. Bud Light, boxed white zinfandel, or Bud heavy for the cops who didn't believe in light drinking. She wasn't sure how she was going to avoid anyone noticing the strife between her and Barb, but she certainly wasn't about to ask the woman to make her a cocktail.

Barb had deep Boston connections, and there was a good chance she was armed with some type of drug that she could easily slip into Grace's drink. The woman was ruthless when she was angry with someone, and unfortunately Grace could already feel her former friend's eyes looking her up and down like she was about to ask for a face-off.

Mark sauntered toward the display and slid a small plastic cup off the stack, filling it with the pink liquid. He turned on a heel and brought it back to her, maintaining eye contact the entire time.

"Are you trying to take advantage of me?" Grace asked, analyzing the wine cup that was filled to the brim.

"Are you saying that you need wine for that?" Mark said under his breath as he looked out at their colleagues, cautious of keeping the flirting between the two of them. Grace giggled, smitten like a schoolgirl. She was kicking herself for falling for this guy. Dating co-workers had been on her list of things not to do since she was old enough to work. She had made it this far in life passing up opportunities to date those who she punched the clock with, surely she could keep her record going. She wouldn't even give in to Jeffrey Owens, her super cute co-worker at the ice cream shop when she was fifteen. She remembered that crush like it was yesterday. She would never forget the time that Jeffrey cornered her in the walk-in freezer while she was taking inventory. He leaned in to kiss her, his cold breath creating a cloud of smoke between them, his blonde hair overgrown and curled up on the ends underneath the red Moo Cow Ice Cream baseball hats that they had to wear as part of their uniform. As soon as he leaned into her, she pushed him so hard he fell backwards and his sinewy body was wedged in between two tubs of mint chocolate chip ice cream. She'd stepped out into the warm air and went back to work scooping ice cream for the line of patrons at the carry-out window, never to speak to Jeffrey Owens about anything non-work related again. Nearly twenty-one years later, she was surprised to find herself confiding in a co-worker. She had known other cop couples that met while on duty and went on to get married and start families, but the women typically ended up quitting the force to avoid having both parents in strenuous careers with hours that interfered with family time. Grace was not willing to leave her position, so if she opted for a man who was a public servant, he'd need to be willing to stay home with the children. And she couldn't imagine any male police officer giving up their pride to stay home with babies.

"Well, you two look awful cozy over here," Officer Jeffries said as he ambled toward the two of them, his arms held away from his sides like he had so much muscle he couldn't possibly allow them to relax like a normal person.

"Did mommy press that shirt for you, Curtis?" Mark asked, stepping in and changing the subject.

"Very funny! Hey guys, I got a joke for you." Curtis positioned himself in front of them, setting himself up like he was about to give the most enlightening presentation in the world. "What comes before part B?" he said, a big goofy grin spreading across his overly whitened teeth.

"Gee, I don't know Curtis." Mark elbowed Grace in the side. "This should be good."

"Part-AYYY!" Curtis raised his hands in the air and did a little spin, spilling liquid out of his cup. Grace guessed that the liquid was from one of the flasks that were circulating around.

"You're such a cheese ball, dude," Mark said, but he couldn't help but release a small giggle.

"For real, though. You guys wanna go out and get wild after? The rest of us are gonna hit up Amendment, in da city." Curtis's eyes were so big, they looked like they were going to pop out of his head.

"Wow, well as tempting as that sounds, we may have to pass. I mean, *I* may have to pass." Mark stumbled across his words before catching himself. "Grace here has her own mind, I'm sure she'd love to join you."

"Well thank you, Mark, for speaking on my behalf," Grace joked, starting to have fun with the little exchange and secret between the two of them. "But, I think I have to feed my dog tonight."

"Whatever, lame-o's. If you change your mind I'll be over there getting crunked!" Curtis danced his way back to the rest of the staff who were getting louder by the minute.

"Hey, need any help feeding that dog later?" Mark winked at her. "Then again, you gotta admit—it might be kinda fun to watch that doofus hit on girls in the city."

"I'm sure we'd get a few laughs, but I'm pretty sure I could stand right here for the next hour and get just as many laughs." Grace looked ahead, her eyes focused on Curtis, who was now attempting to do some type of rapper dance move in the middle of the other officers. "He does realize we're in an old lunch room and not a dance club, right?"

"You can't always be sure with that one." Mark leaned into her side.

Just as Grace was starting to feel settled at the Christmas party, Barb came stumbling toward her. As soon as Grace saw the pointed finger waggling in her direction, she knew things weren't going to end well.

"Hey, everybody! I have an announcement to make," Barb slurred, the entire sentence blending together in one long word. It was typical for Barb to get sloshed at the annual Christmas party, but it was mostly harmless. Usually she would just be overly flirtatious with a younger officer while everyone laughed with her. Grace had always been the one to drive her home in the past, but she assumed she'd convince someone else to do the driving this year. "Grace . . . tsss . . . Detective McKenna . . . is a liar."

Grace could feel the heat in her face funnel its way up from her neck. She suddenly cared a lot about what Mark thought about her, and she certainly didn't want him thinking she was a liar.

"Barb, come on. Let's go talk—in private." Grace tried to put an arm around Barb's wide-set shoulders, but the woman moved surprisingly fast for someone who was drunk and she shrugged the arm off of her while giving Grace a shove that was packed with anger.

"Hey, hey. What is this all about? Barb, maybe it's time to go home?" Mark interjected.

"I got this, Mark," Grace said, trying to steer him away.

"No you don't GOT this, Grace." Barb's face exploded with anger, her drink unsteady in her hand. "How dare you make up lies about Eric . . . how dare you? I always thought you were a good kid, but you're just like all the others. A fake and a liar."

Barb stormed out the door, leaving Grace to feel the sting of her words. Mark had heard the whole thing, and now she would have to figure out how to explain herself. Maybe Barb was right, because her life was starting to feel like a tangled web of lies. Trying to conceal her visions was like having a deep dark secret.

CHAPTER NINETEEN

GRACE CLENCHED THE STEERING WHEEL AS SHE GUIDED HER JEEP around the tight turns that cut through Cabotville. After making her rounds at the Christmas party and making sure that she said hi to Joe and the chief, Grace got out of there as fast as she could, thankful that only Mark was in earshot to witness the scene that played out between her and Barb. Nobody seemed to notice, as they were all caught up in eating and drinking and focused on Curtis' antics. For the first time, she was grateful for the boy's presence. She couldn't worry about Barb now though, she had to focus on getting her house straightened up before Mark arrived. As her emotions were flying from the pain of Barb's words, she had invited Mark over to her house. She was already regretting the decision and had made a promise to herself to keep it innocent, a casual meeting between two friends. Grace was up against a big challenge, as she felt herself sinking deeper into Mark's allure.

The tires crunched through the snow, leaving a fresh path of tire treads in the driveway. She still hadn't shoveled and she nearly slipped on the ice as she raced to her front door, counting off how many minutes she had before Mark arrived. He had agreed to take the boys into the city so they could continue the party well into the night.

As expected, Brody was lying by the front door, his one-hundred-fifty pound body curled up into a big black ball of fur. As she pushed the door open, his body moved with it like a carpet, before he looked up and saw her, his ears perking as he used all his strength to slide his body up off the slippery tiled flooring. He bounded from side to side, finally settling his head up against her hip to receive pets.

"Hey, Brody bear, how's my boy?" She bent down in front of him, his big head towering over her. "Don't be mad, but a boy is coming over." She looked down at him as if she were having an everyday conversation with a friend. "But, he's really nice, and I'm sure you two will get along great." Grace thought about Mark's commitment to being a vegetarian and while Brody never seemed to come up in conversation, she imagined they would get along just fine. He may even end up falling in love with the dog.

Grace went to work clearing countertops and tables and shoving miscellaneous items into drawers and cabinets. She scoured her fridge, but all she had was the ingredients for Christmas day and a half bottle of Cabernet, three yogurts, and a lonely apple. There was no shortage of condiments, but she certainly couldn't offer Mark a bowl of mustard.

"Shit!" she said loud enough to startle Brody, who was back in his ball on the floor. He raised his eyebrows at her, as if reprimanding her for the foul language. She raced up the stairs to assess her face and give her outfit a once over. The full-length mirror that hung from the back of her bedroom door reflected a slight weight loss in her already small frame. She had been so busy consumed with Jenny Silva that there had been days that week where she had forgotten to eat meals entirely. She pulled her jeans slightly outward and observed the additional space and a slightly jutting hipbone. Her face even showed signs of caving in near the cheekbone region, making her look a little malnourished. *This shouldn't be hard: Eat more and obsess over crimes less*, she thought to herself. Just as she was fluffing the comforter on her bed for some unknown reason, there was a knock on the door and she could hear Brody's legs slide to a standing position and his paws tap along the hardwood floor. She drew in one strong, deep breath and held it in for as long as she could before releasing it.

"Here goes nothing," she said out loud.

The front door met the landing at the bottom of the staircase and there was a narrow window the length of the doorway where the visitor could see in if interested. She made sure that her walk down the stairs didn't give way to any kind of embarrassing slip or nose pick, because she wasn't sure if Mark was the type to peek in or stand in front of the door like a proper gentleman. She was guessing the latter. As she pulled the door open, a lump of soft white snow fell into the entryway, leftover from the few footprints that she had created from going in and out of the house in the past few days.

"Hey, you really do live out here," Mark said with a giggle, balancing a pizza box in one hand while slipping his snowy boots off with the other.

"Oh, please. Just because I don't live in Bridgeton doesn't mean I'm in some kind of foreign land. I know this seems far to you Bridgeton townies, but I'm technically only twelve miles from the station," Grace joked as she led him in the house while holding onto Brody's collar. It had been awhile since the dog had an opportunity to sniff and scrutinize a new visitor, so he was on high alert, ready to either give Mark the cold shoulder or befriend him. The dog was a snuggle bear, but every now and then he had a tendency to just not like someone, for reasons Grace really couldn't understand. She could hear her mother's words now. *That dog is going to ruin your love life, Gracie.*

"Is this the infamous Brody who you spend every Friday night with?" Mark didn't hesitate as he set the pizza box on the table in the entryway and got down on his knees, grabbing Brody's head between his two hands. "Brody, I see why your mommy would rather stay home with you than go on a date with me." And that's all it took for Brody to lean into Mark, resting his snout on his shoulder and letting out a loud sigh. It didn't help that Mark brought with him delicious scents of pizza.

"Hey, Brody bear, do you want to actually let Mark in the house?"

Grace said, leading the dog into the living room, Mark following behind. "I'd offer you something to eat, but—"

"I've got it covered." Mark retrieved the pizza box from the table. The guy certainly knew the ways to her heart: pizza and dog-loving.

"I'm pretty sure you saved the day. All I have in my fridge is a half-bottle of Cabernet and the untouchable Christmas day ingredients."

"Cabernet is a lovely pizza pairing."

"I'll get us some plates and napkins . . . and wine. Take a seat." Grace pointed to the couch, where Brody was already snuggled up in the center, clearly doing his best to keep them separate from one another. She made her way to the kitchen before turning around quickly. "Oh, but just be careful—he has a tendency to sneak food," Grace said as she peeked back in the room to see Brody's snout pulsating as he leaned his big head off the couch and hovered over the box.

"Oh, he's just fine, aren't you Brody," Mark said as he leaned into him and scratched behind his ears.

Grace popped the cork out of the wine bottle, took a sniff and when she decided the wine smelled acceptable, she poured them each a glass, finishing off the bottle. Under one arm, she balanced some paper plates and napkins and made her way back into the living room.

"Thank you," Mark said taking a sip from the wine glass before opening the box of pizza. "I know that you love your meat, so I ordered half with pepperoni and half with veggies. I mean, you're certainly welcome to my 'animal free' half of the pizza but, I didn't want to force any healthy habits on you." He winked as he slid a very green slice of pizza onto a plate.

"Wow, I'm actually surprised that you allowed the meat to touch the same pizza."

"Well, technically it's not touching my half of the pizza, so I think I'm pretty safe. Just keep your pepperonis away from my broccoli, got it?"

"Got it. No veggie-meat intermingling. That could turn out to be a disaster," she said with a giggle.

"So, are you gonna tell me what was up Barb's ass tonight? Surely that wasn't just typical drunk Barb. You guys are always so close. What's going on?"

Grace took her time chewing the pizza, trying to think of a way to explain this to him without sounding like a wacko. She used the back of her hand to wipe away the sauce that escaped her lips.

"Well . . ." The hesitation was evident in her voice. "It all started with a stupid blind date she set me up on with her nephew. I didn't want to go, but you know Barb—she's pushy, and I wanted to pay her back for all the favors she does for me at the station."

"She does do a lot of extra work she's not required to do." Mark nodded, not showing any signs of strain about the blind date.

"Exactly. And she said her nephew was a good guy going through a divorce who deserved a chance. She assured me I'd only have to go on one date and then she'd leave me alone."

Mark raised his eyebrows, well aware of Barb's pushiness.

"And. . ." she continued.

"And?"

"Well, do you ever just get a gut feeling about someone?"

"All the time. It's one of the many reasons I became a cop."

Grace sipped her wine, an attempt to kill time while she figured out how she was going to explain it to him. She thought about how good it would feel to let it all out, to let Mark know about her visions, her gift. She pictured him running away as fast as he could.

"So, what happened?"

"There's something I have to tell you, Mark."

"I don't care about your past—what happened with you and him has nothing to do with us. I get it, I know what it's like to be single, but then I found you—"

"Wait, what?" Grace was clearly driving him down the wrong path.

"Grace, I like you. A lot. And I know we work together and I know that's weird, but stranger things have happened. I'm not a jealous guy, so if something happened between you and that guy, it was before us, so I don't care."

Grace wasn't sure if she should laugh or kiss him. He was reading this conversation all wrong, but she was giddy like a school girl, smitten by him and his sudden openness. And suddenly she felt a strong urge to be open and honest with him.

"Mark, I like you too. I really do. But there is something I need to tell you and it's not about something that necessarily happened with Barb's nephew. It's something about me."

"Oh God, did I read this all wrong?" He buried his head in his hands. "You don't like guys? Or, wait . . . you're dating someone else? Wow, I feel like a total ass."

"No no! Wrong again. Follow me."

Grace led Mark back to the small room that she used as an office and told him to sit down as she hit a few buttons on her laptop, bringing it to life. She felt the only way to do this was to show him written proof, doctors' notes, and the letter sent by the priest so many years ago. All the paperwork had been scanned and saved in a folder labeled "Grace," hidden deep within the files on her computer.

"Read this," she said as he leaned in to see the messy scrawl on the screen.

BASED ON GRACE MCKENNA'S *descriptions, she has the classic signs of having the capability of seeing visions that are outside the realm of a reality that the normal person can see. –Dr. Schwartz*

GRACE'S SYMPTOMS *show that she was born as a visionary, having the power to see certain visions when she is triggered, leading to a heightened experience. –Dr. Edmonton*

THE LIST WENT ON, accompanied by photos of Grace at the various ages when she had visited the doctors. Mark sat there, scrolling down the long line of scanned documents, the expression on his face blank. He stared ahead even as he took sips of wine. Grace felt her heart building heat in her chest. She was frightened by what he would think of her. Would he drop his glass of wine and run as fast as he could? Or would he be nice and understanding and then make an excuse to leave and never come back? The questions circled within Grace, a tornado of anxiety whirling in her head.

When Mark was done reading, he sat back in the chair and swiveled in a full circle. Just when Grace thought he would keep his back to her, get up and walk away, he settled in the chair facing her with his hand wrapped around the stemless wine glass.

"So, you think I'm some type of freak?" Grace asked, hesitant for the answer.

Mark set his glass down on the desk gently and leaned forward with outstretched arms. "Come here." He pulled her into a hug, embracing all of her fear and anxiety with the strengths of his arms. "Listen, I'm not going to say I'm not completely shocked and flabbergasted, but I've seen a lot in my lifetime and I believe that there is more out there than what we see. I believe some people have certain gifts for a reason, I believe in some type of an afterlife, whether it's reincarnation or us floating around with wings . . . hell, I even believe in ghosts." He kissed the side of her head, his mouth pressed against her hair. "Who else knows about this?"

"Besides the oodles of doctors and professionals who have attempted to diagnose me, just my mom," she said. "So please—not a word to anyone."

After Mark was sworn to secrecy, she divulged nearly all the visions she had seen, or at least remembered. She told him why Barb currently despised her and she confirmed his suspicions as to why she was working the Jenny Silva case, a case that was technically nonexistent as far as the police department was concerned. He agreed to help her in any way he could in tracking the woman down and verifying that Mackenzie Waterford was a suspect.

Grace said, "I just don't get it. Mackenzie, who has or had everything going for her—why would she do anything to jeopardize her life? Maybe it was jealousy over another over-achieving student? I mean, her mom even seemed a bit concerned about Mackenzie's obsessive need for perfection."

"The only problem now is that the schools are closed for holiday break, so her colleagues won't think anything is odd if she isn't there. No one will go over to check in on her. Did the principal mention any close friends that she chummed with on the school grounds?"

"No. From everything I've heard, the woman kept to herself. But I know from snooping in her house that she had a budding relationship with Mackenzie, who could very well be her daughter. I mean, all the dates match up. Same birth month as the photo I found."

"But why would she hurt her biological mother. Wait—does Mackenzie know that she is adopted?"

"That's a very good question. How do I go about asking that without sounding like a stalker?"

"Maybe I could get Rain to find out?"

"Think she could keep it on the down low, not make it look too obvious?"

"She learned from the best." Mark smiled as he leaned down to pet Brody, who had followed them into the office. The dog was like a leech; he had to be around his people at all times. "I'll start working on her tomorrow."

"Think she can have an answer for us soon? Time is precious when a person is missing with no family to track them down and report their absence."

"She's a creative kid. She'll figure it out. I know that she has some activities scheduled for the Christmas break. Knowing how involved Mackenzie is, I'm sure she'll be around. I think there's a bonfire on the beach one night. And no, we aren't supposed to know about this."

"Is it bad we're using your teenage sister as a secret spy?"

"Nah. Who knows, maybe it will inspire her to be a detective like you."

Mark pulled her on his lap, leaning in for a kiss that was just deep enough to unleash butterflies in her stomach, but coated in a delicacy that made her feel protected and safe. When they swiveled around in the chair, Brody sat by the door, his head tilted to the side and his ears perked up.

"You think he's jealous?" Mark asked.

"Possibly. But it doesn't take him long to welcome new friends into his life. I'm pretty sure that if a burglar broke into my house, he'd roll over and let them in as long as they gave belly rubs."

They settled on the couch, with Brody nestled between them. The bear of a dog made it difficult for the two of them to take it to the next level, his body a permanent fixture on the old couch. They watched some mindless nineties sitcoms in silence, every now and then one of them would make a comment about the show making them forget they weren't alone. For a brief moment, Grace imagined this is what it would be like as part of a married couple. Nights on the couch in the comfort of a shared home, splitting a pizza and being a permanent half of the whole. Just as Grace's eyes were getting heavy, Mark leaned over Brody and grabbed her hand.

"I better head home. It's late and I've got an early morning," he said, his voice low and scratchy from the fatigue that was settling in.

"Of course." Grace squeezed his hand, feeling a steady comfort fall over her. She didn't want him to leave, and she scolded herself for the freeing of independence that was building up inside her. "Thanks for coming by, and thanks for the pizza. And of course thanks for being understanding about my meat-loving ways."

Mark stood before her and reached a hand out to pull her up off the couch. He embraced her as she fell into him from the force of his pull.

"I won't say a word, don't worry." He cupped her head in between his hands and angled her eyes up to his.

"So, you don't think I'm a freak?"

"Far from it." He leaned in and gave her a soft gentle kiss, reassuring her that she had made the right decision to tell him the truth about her visions. "I'll give you a call tomorrow." He paused. "Or better yet, I'll see you at the office."

"Oh boy, that's not the best goodbye. Can we at least keep this our little secret in the workplace," she used a finger to indicate the two of them and the budding relationship.

"Yes. Don't worry, I have a rule against dating my colleagues, too. Except it's a lot easier for a guy, when the ratio is ten males to every female. I just happened to be at the right station and score a hottie like you."

"Oh boy. Go home now, you have officially lost your mind." She led him to the door.

"Bye, Brody. I'll see you soon." Mark gave Brody a wave on his way out.

Grace couldn't help but feel her insides bursting with butterflies at his indirect promise to come back.

CHAPTER TWENTY

GRACE HAD A RESTLESS NIGHT OF SLEEP, FILLED WITH VISIONS OF JENNY Silva. Several times she jumped awake, startled by the bits and pieces of Jenny's face that appeared as frightening images, as if she was trying to lead Grace to answers. In one of the delusions, Jenny looked peaceful as she reached her delicate hand toward Grace, leading her through a wooded terrain. As Grace began to follow the ghost-like woman, reaching for her outstretched hand, Jenny's face transformed into a skeleton, her eyes disappearing into the deep-set hollows of her bone structure, her body melting away from the white dress she was wearing. Even in the dream-state, Grace had thought the dress was unlike something Jenny Silva would wear, its feminine flair replacing the black and in-your-face accessories that Jenny wore to express her art. She woke feeling confined, the sheets tangled around her legs and damp from sweat. She slid her phone off the nightstand and flipped it over: It was five forty-five.

"Shit!"

She struggled to untangle the sheets while rolling Brody over from his outstretched position. "Move over buddy, mommy's stuck here." He used a paw to scratch his snout, before rolling over and looking up at her, blinking the sleep from his eyes.

After she slid into her boots and donned the layer of winter apparel needed to stay warm, she walked the pup around the block, giving in to his need to stop every thirty seconds to most likely sniff his own pee from the day before. She paused in front of her house to admire the Christmas lights that were still on from the night before, and felt her body warm as she remembered Mark saying he would be over sometime this weekend with his staple gun to secure some of the loose strands. She wasn't used to having a man around, let alone one who offered to fix things up around the house. Even as a child, Grace and her mom had managed to get by without a man in the household, with the exception of the local handyman coming by every now and then.

As Grace did every day, she chose an outfit that reflected professionalism, as if she was going to a corporate job in an office. The only difference was that she had a gun, handcuffs and a badge attached to her body. She kept her gun hidden under a longer blouse that covered her rear and concealed her badge inside of her black jacket. She pulled on a pair of high black boots, with a wedged heel that allowed her to maneuver her way through inclement weather while giving her a little lift. Brody lay beside her on the hardwood floor, following her every movement with the squinty eyes that sat on his massive head like two little peanuts. For such a large dog, he had awfully small eyes.

She threw her bag over her shoulder and raced down the stairs, scolding herself for sleeping through her alarm and missing her morning run on the treadmill that was currently being used as a drying rack in the basement.

Immerse yourself in the atmosphere. Grace could hear her mentor's mantra repeating itself in her head as she drove into Bridgeton, passing by the barren beach on one side and the hardware's sign highlighting the upcoming winter carnival.

John Youstra had taught one of Grace's forensic courses at the academy and for whatever reason, he took her under his wing, meeting with her after class to discuss their passion for forensic science. Having been a detective for several years before retiring and becoming a teacher of the subject, John gave her his most valuable piece of advice that a detective could have. He pressed the importance of immersing yourself in the suspect's life and the everyday life and location that surrounded the victim.

Grace pulled up in front of Bridgeton Coffee Depot, where the townies came to gather and the students came to get their caffeine fix between and after classes. The coffee was good, the staff was friendly and if Grace was lucky, she just might be able to pick up on some clues that led her to Jenny Silva's whereabouts.

Pulling the door open to the shop, she was greeted with scents of freshly roasted coffee beans and buttery bagel smells. A group of woman gathered in the corner chattering intensely about a longtime friend who had recently passed. A man sat nearby, offering his opinion every now and then between bites of a bagel smothered with cream cheese. A dollop of the cheese sat leftover on the corner of his mouth.

"What can I get you?" The girl behind the counter greeted Grace by getting right to the point. She wore all black and had a dove tattoo on each wrist. A chalkboard nametag rested on her shirt pocket, inscribed with *Suzanne* in messy scrawl.

"Ummm . . ."

"We have a list of flavored coffees here." The girl turned a home-made sign toward her. "If you're into that type of thing."

"Hmmm, how about a snickerdoodle?"

"You got it. That tends to be a favorite around here, especially with the kids." The girl went to work assembling the coffee. "How do you take it?"

"Just skim milk and sugar."

"Here you go." The girl slid the coffee across the counter and proceeded to help the person behind her in the line that was now forming.

"Thanks." Grace slid into a table up against a wall covered in artwork and pretended to stir her coffee as she felt the group of ladies eyeing her.

She watched how as the line grew, people stood and chatted with one another, bundled in their winter gear. Everyone seemed to know each other. It made Grace wonder how Jenny Silva felt when she first moved to Bridgeton, and how she had stumbled across the hidden gem of a town. Was she following the young girl who she had given up for adoption so many years ago? Just as the wheels were turning in her head, she heard a tapping on the glass window and staring back at her was Anthony Waterford. A big white smile stood out against his tan skin and his kind blue eyes were accentuated against the navy blue ski hat he was wearing. He had a brown leather messenger bag slung across his chest making him look like a professor on his way to teach a class. As if they were old friends, Anthony opened the coffee shop door, surpassed the line and stood before her.

"It's so good to see you again, Grace."

"Seeing an awful lot of you these days. Guess it's a small town thing, huh? Anything new since the grocery store?"

"Not much. Busy with work." A flicker of nerves seemed to move in his eyes. "You know, I've been wanting to apologize about wasting your time when Mackenzie was just being a typical teenager with a dead phone. It kinda slipped my mind at the grocery store. I'm really sorry, I'm sure you have much more important things to deal with," he said as he adjusted his bag on his shoulder.

"Oh, it's the nature of the job," said Grace. "Any big family activities planned for winter break?"

"Well, Mackenzie's been so busy with her senior project and she's probably too absorbed with her friends to hang with her family, but I did promise Penny I'd take her to that new cartoon movie with the panda."

"That sounds nice. Hey, do you want to sit down and have a coffee?" Grace motioned to the empty chair across from her.

"Sure. No coffee for me, but are you sure you're not meeting anyone?"

"Nope, just me. Just stopped in for a coffee on my way into work. You're not a coffee drinker?"

"Nah, I tend to get bad ulcers. The acidity gets to me." He unbuttoned the flap on his bag and started rummaging through its contents.

"Ahhh, there it is," he said as he dug deeper. Grace's eyes caught onto something in his bag: a sketch pad.

"Are you an artist?" She pointed to the pad that was now sticking out from behind the leather flap.

"Um, no . . . God, no." He stumbled, and for the first time Grace saw his eyes divert away from her, as if searching for an answer. "I took an art class. I guess I was trying to be an artist. I've since given up though; opted to stick with my talent as a card trick master," he joked.

"Can I see?" Grace asked, pointing toward the pad. "It might make me feel better about my own attempt at being an artist." The statement was a flat out lie. She never even had the slightest inclination to attempt drawing a circle, let alone take an art class.

"Oh, um . . . really, it's quite embarrassing."

"Trust me, I won't laugh."

Reluctantly, he slid the pad across the table, locking eyes with her before pulling a thermos out of his bag. "I made a resolution to be more environmentally friendly," he said, holding up the cup. "Guess I'll start early. I'll be back." He got up and stood in the diminishing line, appearing far more on edge than when he first walked in.

Hesitantly, Grace started to flip through the pad, bracing herself for some really bad art. Sketches of squares and three-dimensional images filled the pages, the pencil smudges forming a twin version of the pages they were pressed against. When Grace was halfway through the pad, she nearly lost her breath when she saw a colorful drawing of Anthony's eye staring back at her. It was the match to the one that she had seen at Jenny's house, the same color with brown flecks against the pale blue, an image that you would only notice if you were close up to someone's face. She tried not to look too alarmed, and continued making her way through the pad. Several colorful sketches of sunflowers brightened up the pages. Each sunflower was in a different position. One was standing erect and reaching for a sun that was hidden between a huddle of gray clouds, another was bent over as if drained of water and life, nearly a replica of the one hanging outside the principal's office. The one that stood out the most was the one of the little blonde girl, clenching the sunflower with two chubby fists. Her head was tilted forward. She sniffed the flower, her lips concealed by the big yellow blossom as a pair of deep-brown eyes looked up. The eyes looked hesitant but confident, timid but fierce. The little pools of water at the bottom of the eyes reflected a sadness that was unsettling to Grace. Whoever had drawn this had to be feeling pulled and compelled by this little girl. It was the first piece of artwork Grace had ever seen that was as close to real life as art could get. After she made sure Anthony was in a heavy conversation with another man in line, she tugged at the bottom of the paper until the binding released the picture. She folded it under the table and slid it into her inside coat pocket.

"Hey, so what do you think? I can draw one hell of a 3-D cube, huh?" Anthony slid into the seat, covering the top of his thermos with a hand, while flicking the tea bag string with his thumb.

"Actually, these are pretty good, Anthony. I can't say I've ever seen such beautiful colors and lines," Grace said as she flipped back to one of the sunflowers.

"The teacher did that one as an example, and I was so frustrated, I had planned on taking it home to trace."

"Where did you take these classes? I'd like to take one sometime. It's kinda been on my bucket list."

"Oh, they don't have them anymore. It was a onetime thing they were trying out at the library."

Grace had to admit, Anthony was quick on his feet for someone who was lying through his teeth.

"Well, I better get going. Gotta hit the office." He closed the sketch pad and shoved it back into his messenger bag.

"It was nice seeing you, Anthony. Keep in touch."

"Sure thing, detective." He gave a curt smile, before nearly slamming into the barista who was delivering a coffee to the table next to them.

Grace waited until he was halfway to the door. "Anthony, one more thing. When was that class at the library?"

"You know, I can't remember exactly. It was a few months ago. Sometime at the end of summer or beginning of fall. Sorry."

Grace gave him her best smile and nodded. As soon as he was out of sight, she swept her coffee cup off the table and raced out of the café, aware of the group of ladies eyes on her. She could only imagine what they were saying.

~

GRACE FELT a sense of relief when she saw Mark's car in the station's parking lot. He was probably finishing up his workout with the newbies. She couldn't wait to tell him about the new detail she'd found.

She whipped the door open and raced by Barb's desk and the console. After the incident at the Christmas party, she didn't even bother making an effort with Barb.

"McKenna!" Barb's voice stopped her in her tracks. Was she hearing things?

"Listen, Barb, I don't want to fight with you, so I'll just mind my own business and stay away from you, but remember we still work together and I have to walk by your desk to get to my office so if you don't like it—"

"McKenna, stop." Barb stood at her desk, grabbed Grace's arm and ushered her to the small conference room. "Sit." She pointed to the nearest seat and slid into the one on the opposite side. Grace ran her hands over the wooden table, feeling the leftover muffin or donut crumbs from the last meeting. "You were right."

"What are you talking about, Barb?"

"You were right about Eric. I did a little recon. Turns out that his wife left him because of an incident that happened with the babysitter. I didn't want to get too many details, because I was so disgusted. His wife—ex, was taking the high road and didn't want his family and work to turn on him. God knows how people feel about child molesters."

Grace couldn't help but be proud of Eric for being honest with his wife, assuming he ended up sharing his side of the story. And a piece of Grace couldn't help but think that maybe she had led him to spilling his demons.

"So, you actually trusted my word enough to investigate the situation?"

"Yeah, you're not all that bad, Princess."

"But, what about if it happens again, and his wife doesn't want to press charges. I know there isn't any tangible proof but—"

"I already took care of that. I cornered him and threatened to report him. He told me to talk to the girl. So, of course I did that—you know me."

"And?"

"She admitted that while she was far younger than Eric, she had agreed to the sexual *relation*." Barb held up her fingers to signify quotes around the word relation. "Eric admits it was a mistake and she was too young, but he didn't force himself on her. He's in a black hole. His wife won't give him a second chance, and who can blame her. I'd twist that rat bastard's balls off if he was my husband."

"So, where does that leave you and Eric?"

"Well, I'm absolutely disgusted with him, but he is family. I don't turn my back on blood." Barb cracked her knuckles as dampness formed a layer over her hazel eyes, creating a sparkle that made her appear vulnerable and sad. "It's just those girls . . . his daughters. I know how much he loves them. He really does. As someone who never had a father, I can really appreciate how present he is with them. He's never once missed a life event, never wasn't there to tuck them in . . . until now. His ex won't let him see them since she found out. So, I approached her and made a deal. If I supervise the visits, she has agreed to let him spend a few hours once a week with the girls. It's a start. I just can't believe that he would be so stupid. And here I am picking up the pieces." Barb's face was covered in tears now, salty droplets of emotions cascading down her pink cheeks.

"Well, that's because you know he's a good person overall. A good dad, at least. It's okay to have a heart. Barb. If there were more people in the world who had half the heart you have . . . well, this world would be a hell of a lot better."

"But . . . how did you know about any of this? Why would he tell you? I mean, he's pretty dumb, but I didn't think he'd be that dumb."

"I just knew. I can't really explain it. At least not now," Grace said, suddenly feeling nervous about having told Mark about her gift. "Just do me a favor, Barb: Stop worrying about it and just focus on helping him."

"Whatever you say, Princess." Barb got up and walked around the table toward the door, her hips still swaying side to side even in the midst of her sadness. Grace pushed herself from the table and stood, nearly bumping into Barb. "One more thing," she said as she pulled Grace into a hug. "I'm sorry. About not trusting you. About the not-so-nice things I said to you at the party. I'm really sorry. And you know how hard that is for me to say, right?" Barb hid her face in Grace's shoulder.

"Yes, I know how hard it is for you to give up your stubbornness," Grace joked, pulling Barb into a tight hug and feeling elated at their rekindled friendship.

"Oh, and on another note . . . I'm just gonna ask you once and I'll never mention it outside of this conference room. What's up with Mark?"

"What do you mean?" Grace couldn't help but reveal a faint smile ripple across her face.

"You little devil, Princess! I friggin' knew it."

"It's not what you think . . . *yet*, at least." She winked and turned on a heel, leaving Barb in a pool of questions.

Grace made her way downstairs to the gym, hoping to catch Mark before he signed in for patrol. She used the wobbly railing to guide her down the dark staircase that led to a room that held a row of small jail cells used as a holding place until criminals were released or sent off to a jail that was better equipped to house prisoners. Down the long narrow hallway outside the cells was a room just big enough to hold a punching bag, a treadmill, a bench and a set of old rusty weights. A shelf of donated equipment, including a jump rope, kettle-bells, a rack of weight plates and a few old *Men's Fitness* magazines sat along one side of the boxy, dank room. Rap music blasted from a small CD player that sat on the floor. The music came out fuzzy as it ricocheted off the four walls, penetrating Grace's tender ears that were used to lighter more calming music like Norah Jones and Jack Johnson. A couple of full-length mirrors were hung side by side, for the purpose of checking one's form.

Mark was engrossed in training the rookie, his hands guiding the guy's forearms in a bicep curl. The guy's face looked like it was about to explode as Mark serenaded him with motivational words like "breathe," "you got this," and "one more." As cheesy as Grace thought it was to see two men guiding each other through heavy lifting intended to bulk up, she couldn't help but be inspired by Mark's undying motivation for everything he did in life. It made her wonder why he didn't go for detective and why he seemed intent on staying as a patrol officer. Grace took a seat on the weight bench that was moved to the corner of the room as Mark's eyes flashed in her direction, noticing her presence.

"You're all set, kid. Good job." He grabbed the weights from the rookie, dropped them on the rack and bent down to lower the blasting music. "Remember what I said about protein. Recovering the muscles is the most important part of working out."

"Yes, sir." The rookie gave a mock salute before scanning Grace's body on his way to the showers.

"Do you always listen to obnoxious rap music when training?" Grace teased.

"Shut it," Mark joked as he wiped down some droplets of sweat that had landed on the floor. Then he surprised Grace and wheeled the bench she was sitting on to the middle of the room, her hands gripping the sides as she went along for the ride. "What's up?" He asked as he settled the bench and crouched down so he was eye level with her. She wasn't sure if it was the rippling of his abs visible through his sweat-drenched shirt or the way he paused and gave her his undivided attention, but she felt heat move through her body like a wave coming to its peak.

"I got something." She opened her black jacket and plucked her newfound evidence out. "Check it out."

"A little girl sniffing a flower?" Mark looked confused.

"A little girl that looks just like Mackenzie. Brown eyes, light hair and sniffing Jenny Silva's favorite flower. And that's not all— remember the sketch of the eye that I told you about?"

"Anthony's eye?"

"Yes. There was another drawing in this sketch pad of Anthony's eye. It was the opposite one of the one I saw in her apartment."

"First of all, how do you remember which eye and second of all, what sketch pad?"

"I took a picture on my phone when I was at her house." Grace went on to tell him about the accidental meeting with Anthony at the coffee shop that morning and how awkward he got about the art class. "Anthony and Mackenzie are somehow connected to Jenny Silva. Do you think he knows that she's the biological mother? Do you think he tracked her down?"

"Wow. This is getting a bit freaky." Mark swiped a hand over his face before resting it on her knee. The gesture came so natural to him, like they were one of those couples who had been together so long that their bodies just clicked into place.

"I know. First things first. I need to find out if there was ever an art class hosted at the library."

"Okay. What can I do?"

"Any updates from Rain?"

"She's working on finding out who at the school is adopted, or knows who is adopted, for that matter. She has a friend who is adopted and pretty open about it, and even tried to track down his biological mother. In fact, she's taking the task so seriously that she is thinking about having the topic of her senior project be nature versus nurture or something like that. She's sent out an announcement on social media to anyone who is interested in being interviewed. Of course, they would have to be aware that they're adopted. That's the tricky part. Not sure if it will work, but it's worth a try, right?"

"Worth a try. Thank you so much. And please thank Rain for me. What does she like? I need to get her a thank you gift."

"She likes sugar . . . and animals."

"Hmmm . . . is a chocolate reindeer off limits?" Grace was half-joking.

"The girl is so dedicated to being a vegetarian, she probably wouldn't even eat a chocolate version of a furry creature."

"Okay, I'll work on something else. In the meantime, Jenny is still missing. Doesn't seem like she has any concerned family members out looking for her. And it's Christmas break, so it's not like it's weird that she isn't at school."

"Speaking of Christmas, what are your plans?"

"Um, it's usually just me and my mom, but apparently she has invited a bunch of strangers over. You?"

"Sounds fun. I have breakfast with Rain and my mom, then we all go our separate ways. Rain goes to her dad's house and their family and my mom and stepdad are having dinner with his kids."

"And you're not invited to join them?"

"Oh, I am, I just choose not to go. It's not my scene. I guess I'm kinda the black sheep of the family. Me and Rain get each other; we click. But the rest of the family . . . eh, not so much."

"Well, would you like to come to my place?" Grace was feeling impulsive and the invite exploded from her without a thought. "I mean, it's pretty chaotic and my mom is always trying to get us to participate in some type of yoga chant with essential oils, and God knows who she's invited to my house, but—"

"I'd love to." Mark cut her off and leaned in to give her a gentle kiss on her forehead. She could feel his sweaty kiss leftover as she walked back up the stairs and to her office, giddy with excitement.

GRACE NEEDED SOME FRESH AIR, so she decided to walk the short distance to the library. It was evident that it was school vacation, by the number of kids wandering all over town. Grace passed a cluster of elementary-aged kids standing outside the convenience store, enjoying a serious sugar high, all bundled up in their fresh winter gear. The high school parking lot to the left of the library was deserted, except for a few lonely cars, one of which belonged to Principal Woeburn. The stairs to the library were freshly salted, prepared for the masses of children who would be entering the building over the next few days for the scheduled magic and storytelling performances. Every now and then Grace offered her help at the local events, greeting and directing families where to go. Last year, she had made the mistake of volunteering for a magic show at the senior center. Instead of impressing the kids with his magical talent, the magician actually made them cry and Grace had to be the one to ask him to stop the show, right in the midst of the bunny disappearing act. The scheduled activities at the library didn't start until the week after the holiday, so when she opened the old wooden doors, she was greeted by a calming silence. Just a few college students home from break, whispering to one another in the corner and a couple of older ladies knitting and discussing their latest read.

"Good morning, Detective and how are you doing on this fine day?" Mr. Willis looked up from organizing some files and straightened the glasses that had slipped down his nose. The man had been the head librarian for as long as anyone could remember. When Grace had inquired about his length there, none of the townie officers could give her an answer as to what year he started. All they could tell her was that he was ancient, and he never had a bad word to say about anybody.

"I'm good. How are you, Mr. Willis? Getting ready for the rush of kids?"

"Oh, yeah. It's always such a pleasure working with the youngsters. Do you have children who will be attending the events? Here, I can give you a handy activity calendar." He reached for a bright orange sheet that lay in a stack on the desk.

"I would love one," she said, not having the energy to explain that she didn't have children. It was a harder path to cross with older people. They assumed every woman had a child and that at Grace's age, she should have a house full of teenagers. "But, I was wondering about taking an art class. Does the library happen to offer anything for someone like me?" She was getting good at acting.

"Oh my, why no, I can't say we do. It sounds like a lovely idea, though. Maybe we could get one of the local artists to teach a class. I probably wouldn't be able to pay them, but maybe they would be willing to volunteer their time." He rubbed his chin as his eyes followed the idea that he was concocting in his head.

"So, you've never offered an art class here? Never?"

"I'm sorry to say, but no. I've been here for . . . oh, how many years now?" He slapped a hand on the desk, and let out a loud laugh. "By golly, I can't even remember! Never get old, Grace. Enjoy your youth while you have it, my dear."

"Thanks, Mr. Willis," Grace started to walk to the door, content with her confirmed answer. While Mr. Willis could be accused of losing his memory, she was pretty sure that she'd take his answer over Anthony's.

"You're welcome, dear. Oh and you're not going to leave without checking out a book now, are you?" He walked out from behind the counter and motioned to a display that appeared to contain all holiday romances. "The ladies love these romance books. They've been flying off the shelves." And because Grace didn't have the heart to deny Mr. Willis, she ended up checking out a book titled "The Christmas Date." Grace was certain that by the cover, she would end up returning the book at its two-week deadline. The cleavage that was peeking out from behind a red dress was enough to cause Grace to throw it in the trash, but she couldn't turn the old man down. Grace wondered if he was the one who was actually reading the naughty Christmas books.

CHAPTER TWENTY-ONE

T HE BEACH WAS ALREADY SCATTERED WITH TEENAGERS BY THE TIME Mackenzie pulled into the only remaining spot on the narrow sandy side street that flanked the beach.

Taylor turned to Mackenzie, holding her cell phone up to her mouth, the flashlight lighting up her face against her dark hair. "Do I have anything in my teeth?"

"No, goofball, you're in the clear. But I think you're going to have a lot more to worry about than a few pieces of cilantro stuck in your teeth if Jake's girlfriend comes tonight."

"Whatever. You still haven't told me—where did you score a VW Bug, anyway? I can see your dad caving and buying it for you, but I find it hard to believe your mom agreed. She's beyond strict."

"Yeah, well, I guess the perfect grades finally paid off." Mackenzie reached into the small backseat of the Bug and pulled her purse to the front, the wine coolers clanking against one another.

"You little devil. Well, she's a beauty," Taylor said as she slipped out of the car and slid a hand along the rounded edges of the pale blue framework. "I hope you realize you will be carting me around until I head out to Cali for school."

"Well who knows, maybe I'll be joining you in Cali," Mackenzie said as she sidled up to her best friend.

"Still haven't heard back from Harvard yet?" Taylor normally hesitated to ask Mackenzie such questions, but the shot of peppermint schnapps earlier had helped her loosen up a bit.

"Nope." The single word came out of Mackenzie's mouth clipped and emotionless.

The two girls braced each other as they trudged through the thickening snow-covered sand beyond the seawall. The bonfire flame sprouted out from a thick circle of high school seniors, some huddled together braving the cold and others sitting on pieces of driftwood with blankets draped across their laps.

"TaylZEEE!" A group of male voices called out the nickname of the two girls. It had been well-earned, as the two of them spent so much time together. They were one of the many female duos that infiltrated the halls of Bridgeton High.

Taylor bolted to the voices and jumped into the arms of Liam Donovan as Mackenzie eased into the crowd more cautiously. Having been involved in so many school activities, she naturally had to be outgoing, but the past few weeks had left her feeling a bit unlike herself. Ever since the accident, Mackenzie hadn't been able to free her mind from thoughts of Jenny.

"Hey Mackenzie, how's it going?" Rain Hildebrant stood over her as she bent down to retrieve a wine cooler out of her bag.

"Good, how are you, Rain? Got any big plans for break?" As badly as Mackenzie wanted to ask the status of Rain's college acceptances, she was afraid she would have to admit that she herself hadn't heard back from Harvard.

"Nah, just catching up on essays and stuff."

"Want one?" Mackenzie tilted her bottle of Jack Daniels Downhome Punch toward the girl.

"Sure," Rain said as she twisted the top off the bottle of pink liquid and took a tiny sip. Her eyes danced around like she was afraid of being caught.

"Hey Rain, what's up?" Taylor sidled up to the two of them,

forming a small circle. "Oh my God did Kenzie tell you about the new ride her dad bought her? It's—"

"Taylor! Stop. It's not a big deal." Mackenzie cut her off, the heat rising through her body as she realized that Rain could very well be aware that Miss Silva drove the same kind of car. Maybe she would just think it was a coincidence, blaming it on chance that the two of them had pale-blue VW Bugs.

"What? You should be happy that your dad was so proud of his little girl that he bought her one of the coolest cars ever." Taylor pulled her into a side hug, grabbing her cheek like she was a little girl. "You look so California in it. Oh my gosh, imagine if we both go to Cali and we can cruise around with the top down!"

"What kinda car did you get?"

"A PALE-BLUE VW BUG! It's soooo adorable!" Taylor answered before Mackenzie could stop her. She could feel Rain's eyes suddenly heavy on hers. Mackenzie had always been uneasy around the girl; there was always a mysterious layer hovering around her. The way she could feel Rain's gaze on her in art class, and the way she was so eerily quiet, always having her nose buried in a book. Mackenzie wondered why she was there. A beach bonfire party wasn't exactly Rain Hildebrant's scene.

"Wow, that's pretty cool. I've always wanted a Bug. Wait, doesn't Miss Silva drive a pale-blue Bug?" Rain's eyebrows danced on her forehead, eagerly awaiting an answer to the question.

"Does she? I didn't know that. I guess I'll have to ask her where she gets it serviced." Mackenzie was at a loss for words, and well aware that she sounded like a complete idiot. She was regretting taking the car. She was feeling the fluidity of her well-thought out plan start to slip like it was sliding down a funnel. But, she wanted one night to live. To feel like she was Jenny herself.

"Ohmygod, Kenz. You have the same car as your art teacher. I knew you were oddly obsessed with that class but seriously . . . you got the same car?" Taylor poked fun, bumping against Mackenzie's shoulders and giggling between sips from a red cup.

"Well, congrats on the car. Good seeing you girls. Thanks for the drink." Rain tipped her bottle toward the two girls and walked toward a group that was seated around a long-haired guy playing an acoustic guitar.

"Dude, what's your deal . . . you got a crush on her or something?" Taylor asked, as she used a hand to lift Mackenzie's chin, closing her mouth. "You're acting weird."

"You're just drunk. Let's go find Dana," Mackenzie said as she draped an arm around her friend's shoulders and tried to change the subject. A wave of heat passed through her body, even in the midst of the cold winter night. She felt her insides twisting into a combination of nerves and fear. She could feel Rain's eyes on her from across the way. "Give me your cup." She wrapped her hand around Taylor's red cup, rested her lips on the rim and tipped her head back. She felt the liquid burn down her throat, swimming amongst the unsettling nerves in her stomach.

CHAPTER TWENTY-TWO

"THERE'S NO ART CLASS OFFERED AT THE LIBRARY. NEVER HAS BEEN," Grace said into her phone as she opened the glass door to Rizzo's. The handprints on the door were enough to send any newcomer away, but the food was worth the scary germs.

"Shit, well I guess that doesn't surprise me. Sounds a bit advanced for Bridgeton."

"You want anything from Rizzo's?"

"Ummm, sure . . ."

"Don't worry, they have salads. And veggie burgers. I won't make fun of you if you ask me for something animal-free."

"Thanks. Surprise me."

"Okay. Meet me in my office in five minutes. Don't make it obvious."

After spending the day catching up on paperwork and meeting with the Chief to hand in her promo packet, Grace finally had the opportunity to focus on the Jenny Silva case. The night shift had started, so she was hoping the day staff wouldn't notice her ruthless dedication to hours spent at the office these days. Inquiring cop minds would surely want to know what she was so focused on.

"You said five minutes?" Mark greeted her outside her office, the door closed and locked.

"Sorry, there was a line of high school kids filling themselves up on fried food before going home and being forced to eat a healthy home-cooked meal."

"And you're any better?" Mark took the takeout bag out of her arms so she could unlock the door. A large order of fries was spilling over the top of the bag, grease decorating the outside of the paper bag in big blotchy spots.

"Hey, nothing wrong with a little grease every now and then. You could use some to balance out all those tasteless vegetables," Grace said as she used a foot to guide the door open while sipping the fountain soda in her hand. He followed her into the office, setting the bag down on her desk as she slid into her chair, the door slamming behind her.

"So, what's the deal?" Mark asked, trying to spear at his salad with a flimsy plastic fork.

"Everyone's gone, right? I mean Barb and the day shift?"

"Yeah, why?"

"Just don't want them catching on to the secret case we've got going on here."

"Is that what this is?" Half-joking, he tore into a piece of bread, the muscles in his jaw working hard to shrink the chewy carbohydrate.

"You know what I mean." Grace plucked a fry out of the bag, drenching it in a pool of ketchup before popping it into her mouth.

"Hold that thought." Mark picked up his vibrating phone from the desk. Grace could make out a picture of Rain lighting up the screen and suddenly remembered the bonfire.

"Sup, kid?" He balanced the phone between his ear and shoulder while stabbing at the lettuce. "Okay. Are you sure? Hold on." Moving only his eyes, he looked toward Grace. "Did Jenny Silva drive a pale-blue VW Bug?"

"Yep."

"Yep. Okay. We're on our way."

"What's she got?" Grace said the words between bites of her

burger."Mackenzie is driving what Rain thinks is Jenny Silva's car. She drove it to the bonfire. It's parked on First Street, by the beach entrance. Rain remembered a bumper sticker on the right side of the back window. Something about coexisting. But it looks like the sticker has been peeled off."

"Did she get the plate numbers?"

"Yep. She said she's gonna text them to me."

"Damn, that girl doesn't miss a beat." Grace dropped the remaining half of her burger in the bag, a smattering of ketchup was left behind on her lower lip.

"I trained her well." He looked up from his salad. "Wipe your mouth. You looked like you just kissed a vampire."

Slightly embarrassed, Grace used a napkin to dab at the leftover ketchup. She wasn't far enough into this relationship or whatever it was to feel comfortable leaving food on her face. He still hadn't seen her completely free of makeup, as she was always sure to put a stroke of blush on her cheeks and a coat of mascara on her lashes before she knew she'd see him. That's how Grace knew she was in deep trouble. She was rolling out the red carpet for a guy.

She stood from the chair and slid the file that held all of Jenny Silva's info into her bag. The file was purple, camouflaged from the normal bland manila folders that the station used. "Shall we?"

"We shall." Mark stood, dropping her greasy bag and his plastic salad container into the trash that sat beside her desk, before he followed her out the door. "I know you're into girl power and all that stuff, but do you mind if I drive? I know this town like the back of my hand and I'd prefer—"

"Go for it."

"Thanks." He aimed his keys at a gray minivan.

"Seriously?"

"Hey, I've had to cart my sister around for years and I just got comfortable with the ease of a convenient vehicle, equipped to hold the necessities while ensuring my family is kept safe."

"You sound like a frickin' commercial!"

"Well, that was actually one of the lines that was used on me when I was car shopping. So I guess commercials work."

"How the hell do I get into this contraption?" She stood by the passenger door, confused by the additional door handles.

"Here, you can put your bag in the back seat." He pressed a button on the back door, and the door opened and slid backwards in one fluid motion, revealing a plush backseat complete with a television in the headrest of the driver's seat.

"Do you have like, five kids that I don't know about yet?"

"Not yet." He glided over to the driver's side and slid into the seat.

"So, you want kids?" The words slipped from her mouth.

"Woah, slow down there, cowgirl. Just because I drive a minivan doesn't mean I'm ready to be a father."

"Sorry, I didn't mean to—"

"I'm just messing with you." He rested one hand on the steering wheel and leaned back, managing to look seductive in a car that was typically designed for soccer moms. "But, yeah, I'd love kids someday." He paused. "Be the father that mine wasn't," he said before turning up the volume on the console. Suddenly the innocence of the vehicle was lost as rap music boomed from the speakers.

"Hey!" Grace yelled over the bass. Her eye was pulled to the phone buzzing in the perfectly sized compartment on the console. "You got a message."

"Oh, can you check that?" He asked, turning the volume down. "Another perk on my driving resume is that I refuse to text, check or talk on the phone and drive."

"It's Rain." Grace turned the phone sideways so she could see the full picture fill the screen. "She got the number." Grace reached back and pulled Jenny's purple folder out of the bag in the back seat. She compared the printed piece of paper to the text message. "Shit. They match."

"That's a good thing."

"I know, but . . . I just don't get it. Why would she drive around her missing teacher's car?"

"You have to remember that so far, you and I are the only ones who know that Jenny Silva is missing."

"And possibly Anthony Waterford."

"True."

"Surely she's not driving the car home and parking it in the Waterford's driveway. The girl is supposed to be some neurotic genius."

"Genius doesn't always mean good decision making. Sometimes genius means crazy."

"Hmmm. True."

"So, what's your plan of attack once we see the vehicle?" Mark used professional driving skills to back into a driveway across from the line of parked cars.

"Is this your house?"

"God, no. I don't live beachside. This is my buddy's house."

"And he doesn't mind you parking in his driveway without stopping in to say hi?" Grace turned around to look at the high narrow red house with a white deck on the second level that was sure to catch some beautiful sunrises in the summer months.

"He's in Florida for the week. Has two kids and his wife is a teacher, so they go to Disney for Christmas every other year."

"That must cost a fortune."

"Yeah, but I guess money doesn't matter much when you come from ancestors who basically built half the properties on this beach."

"Wow," Grace said under her breath.

"Hey is that—"

"Yep," Grace said, looking straight ahead at Mackenzie Waterford, who appeared to be stumbling up the sand dunes. They watched as she struggled to find her car, then nearly missed the curb that dropped down to the VW Bug, catching herself on the rounded roof. She fumbled to dig the keys out of her purse before sliding into the driver's seat and pulling out into the street without even looking.

CHAPTER TWENTY-THREE

THE WINE COOLERS AND SHOT OF PEPPERMINT SCHNAPPS GAVE Mackenzie the confidence to round the corners along the seawall with her foot heavy on the gas. She had planned to head straight home and face the wrath of her waiting mother, but instead, decided to stop off at Alebury Avenue first, using every last minute up before her curfew. It was still early, she had time to waste.

All she wanted was to talk to Jenny, to tell her how much of a drunk bitch Taylor was being tonight. She was so sick of being associated with the overly flirtatious girl, always standing in the background as Taylor threw herself all over guys. It was embarrassing and so below her. She was too mature to be spending time with Taylor, whose only goal was to go off to college to be passed around and used at frat parties. That's why Mackenzie liked spending time with Jenny. She got Mackenzie, and she didn't judge her for being more interested in school than parties, more excited about learning than losing her virginity. If Jenny hadn't fucked up, she would be here to console her with a cup of tea and listen to her vent. But Mackenzie couldn't vent to a woman who had become her father's mistress.

Questions still swirled around in her mind. Had Jenny been using her to get close to her father? Her father was okay-looking for an older guy, but surely Jenny could find someone better, someone bold and artistic like her. Why had Jenny chosen her boring father, and why would she jeopardize their friendship?

Mackenzie released her grip on the steering wheel as she pulled into the driveway that greeted the little purple house. She rested her head on the steering wheel, completely oblivious to anyone around her, fully caught up in the tangle of her own wants and desires. She didn't want to go home and see her father; she was disgusted with him. Disgusted that he would stoop so low as to cheat on her mother, and even more disgusted that he would do the deed with her teacher. As far as Anthony Waterford knew, Jenny Silva was just a teacher to Mackenzie, not a friend. Did he really think his daughter wouldn't find out he was going behind both her and her mother's back and breaking up their family? Maybe her mother was dumb enough to not see the signs of a husband having an affair, but Mackenzie wasn't. The more she pondered the questions, the more they stung and pinched her self-confidence.

"Pull yourself together," she said as she got out of the car and walked up the steps, holding onto the ragged wooden railing for balance.

She wasn't surprised that the door was unlocked. Jenny had been far too trusting. The last time she had left the house, she thought she was simply going for a winter wonderland hike with Mackenzie. She had told Jenny about the beautiful views at Donovan Cliff, knowing her teacher wouldn't be able to resist the opportunity to paint the landscape.

Mackenzie could smell the lavender oil that Jenny used to promote calmness. It lingered in the air, leftover like a haunting ghost. She felt the tears well up in her eyes as she thought about Jenny's peace-loving ways. That was one of the things that she loved about her—Jenny was so different from her own family, so carefree and unlimited in her beliefs and desires. Mackenzie had felt an instant connection with her and often wondered if they were long-lost soul mates. She could talk to Jenny about things she couldn't imagine talking to her own parents about. They would look at her like she was crazy, but Jenny just accepted her and on more than one occasion, Mackenzie caught Jenny staring at her with a look of adoration in her eyes that made her feel utterly loved.

It had all started when she was struggling with her first art project. It had been a flower, and Mackenzie, aiming for perfection, had been in tears at the end of the class. She could tackle and conquer high-level equations, write essays that floored her English teachers and never struggled with regurgitating a historical or geographical fact, but when it came to art, she couldn't find herself.

"It's about seeing what's not there," Jenny would tell her as she used a delicate hand to guide her paintbrush along the canvas. "Close your eyes and picture the sunflower in a field of lush green grass," Jenny said with such passion that Mackenzie thought it was contagious.

Soon enough, Mackenzie developed the ability to conjure images in her mind and transfer them to the canvas. It had been more of a life lesson than learning the art itself, as she soon felt like anything she imagined could come true. She felt powerful in Jenny's presence, and the two soon formed the rare bond between teacher and apprentice, Mackenzie absorbing all of the life lessons that Jenny passed along. They were simple things that Mackenzie didn't learn in any other classroom, things that could catapult her through life without having to memorize facts or statistics in a book. Jenny would tell her about the California sun and its endless warmth, or she'd describe the Pacific Ocean in ways that made Mackenzie feel like she was immersed in the sea water. She would teach her lessons about kindness and the importance of paying it forward; she'd teach her about forgiveness, and how it feels to let go.

Mackenzie wondered what advice Jenny would give her now, as she sat at the small round table that the two had conversed at so many times over herbal teas and organic coffee concoctions. Surely, she would tell Mackenzie to offer up some patience toward Taylor, to accept her for who she was. As Mackenzie thought about the loss of her mentor, her sadness spread into anger as an image of her father presented itself again. She started to feel a wave of nausea pass over her, as the leftover taste of wine coolers grew stale in her mouth.

Mackenzie pushed herself up from the table and the movement made the queasiness grow, leaving her struggling to reach the bathroom in time. She fell to her knees in front of the toilet, her hands melted into the squishy 1980s toilet seat as a barrage of pink liquid plunged to the outside of her mouth, splashing into the bowl. A few little splashes of liquid splashed up and hit her on the face. When she was sure she had rid herself of the sick feeling and released all the vomit, she fell back against the bathtub, knocking over a bottle of shampoo. The hard sound of the bottle hitting the ceramic sent a pain straight through her temples, as if an earthquake was shifting through her head.

Mackenzie spotted a few lose pieces of kitty litter in the small hallway outside the bathroom and she was hit by a realization: *Van Gogh.*

"Here, kitty kitty . . ." She rose to her feet and flushed the toilet as she yelled to the cat. When Jenny was here, Van Gogh always made herself present, constantly hopping into Jenny's lap or slithering up against her legs. "Van Gogh!" Mackenzie got louder, opening doors and closets as she made her way through the house.

She ended her search when she opened the last door that led to Jenny's art room. A couple of half-burned incense sticks were sprouting up from a ceramic holder set on a plate that was filled with clumps of ashes. She could still smell the spicy scent, leftover from when she was here last week and Jenny had taught her how to make vegan chili. That was the last time that Mackenzie was in her presence before she discovered the affair and before she would be changed forever.

It was the day after their vegan chili experiment when Mackenzie accidentally saw Jenny and her dad kissing up against the school building like they were two teenagers themselves. She had been on her way to an evening student council meeting, and had wanted to run her speech by Jenny, always trusting her to be honest. She watched for longer than she would like to admit, but couldn't take her eyes off the two of them as she saw heightened emotion in Jenny's movements, her arms began to point and her face turned into a scowl as Anthony grabbed her arms and tried to calm her down. It was like watching an accident unfold, and then the two walked in different directions, clueless that Mackenzie witnessed the entire episode. She had been walking past one of the trailers that were used for additional classroom space, when she caught a glimpse between the cracks in the trailer of the bright red hat that Jenny always wore.

As she looked at the canvas leaning against the easel, she felt the same anger that she felt that day building within her, heating up her body into a rapid boil. It was in that moment that she recognized the painting of the blue eye that was staring back at her. Why had it taken her so long to figure out they were having an affair? How long had the painting of her dad's eye been buried in the sketches?

"WHAT THE HELL is she doing in there?"

Grace was growing impatient. She so badly wanted to follow the girl into the house and demand answers.

"Studying? Who knows. The girl is obviously crazy. She's probably doing some voodoo shit," Mark said, his eyes never leaving the house. "So, what's your plan, Detective?"

"I don't know. Technically we could've pulled her over for DUI and being underage, but you didn't want to."

"Considering we're both off duty and driving my personal mini-van, I apologize for not thinking that was the best idea in the world."

"Oh boy . . . look! It's the neighbor!" Grace leaned the seat back, trying to conceal her face from the window.

"Relax, you're in a minivan and the windows are tinted." Mark pressed a button and Grace was flung forward in the chair, her face in shock like she had just ridden an upside down rollercoaster. "Safety feature." He smirked. "So, what's up with the neighbor?"

"Last I saw him, he hadn't seen Jenny, so maybe he'll clue into the fact that her car is there and go knock on the door to check in."

"Doesn't look like it," Mark said, his eyes following Walt Brennan's figure as he slipped into the car parked in his driveway.

"How are people so damn unaware of their surroundings?"

"Well, not everyone is looking to crack the next big case. Unlike us, some people have lives that involve families, friends, entertainment and hobbies."

"That's it, I'm going in," Grace said once she was sure Walt's car was out of view.

"Wait, wait." Mark grabbed her thigh, then stopped himself when she caught his eye. "Sorry. But, what's your plan? You need to figure that out before you go busting in there and arresting an innocent teenager."

"She's not innocent!"

"I know, I know. You know what I mean. You need a reason, and she knows you. Remember, you basically interrogated her family when she went missing for a day. Wait a minute." Grace raised an eyebrow as an idea took shape in her head. "She doesn't know *you*. What if you pretend you're a friend or a brother or something?"

"You're kidding?" Mark looked at her like she'd just told him he couldn't eat another vegetable for the rest of his life.

"Nope." Her eyes scanned his body. "You're perfect. Out of uniform, the right age . . . she won't have to know you're driving a minivan. Just pretend you're an old friend from college or something."

"Who happens to be passing through Bridgeton, Massachusetts? You know they call it Bridgeton because it's literally the bridge to nowhere."

"Okay, so you're a friend in town. Someone she met at the . . . local art fair."

"Was there actually a local art fair?" He challenged her.

"Yep, just two weeks ago. The annual holiday art fair. I'm sure the local art teacher was there." She stared him down, willing him to give in. His eyes slid off her stare, darting anywhere but on her, trying hard to avoid the control she was already starting to have over him.

"Fine." He slammed his hands on the steering wheel. "I need a code though."

"A what?"

"A signal. If something goes haywire in there, I'll need to get access to you."

"Honey, are you afraid a 115 pound teenage girl is going to take you on?" She ran her fingertips through the hair along the side of his head.

"You know what I mean. This girl is obviously crazy. Who knows what she'll do."

"Okay, I tell ya what. If she starts to cast any voodoo spells on you, just call me."

"No, it has to be more discreet. I have an idea. I'll take the keys and press the panic button if things go downhill."

"So, I'm trapped in the car without an option to escape?"

"Are you saying that you'll drive off and leave me stranded with a crazy neurotic perfectionist, if push comes to shove?"

"Noooo . . ." Grace caught herself. "I just feel better with the keys. But come to think of it, I don't think I would be seen driving off in this thing."

"Ass."

"Thank you." She pulled his face to her. "I mean it. Thank you for everything."

"Yeah, yeah." He reached into the backseat, grabbed his Red Sox cap and molded it onto his head.

"Is that supposed to help?"

"I can still be a Sox fan and be a tourist in town."

He slid the keys into his jacket pocket and confidently marched across the street.

"Shit. He looks too much like a cop."

MARK KNEW he was in trouble as soon as Grace told him about her visions. There wasn't a second of doubt about her that trickled into his mind, not an ounce of skepticism in the graphic images that she had presented to him. He was either really open-minded, or he was falling in love with her. Based on what he had committed to do, he was guessing the latter.

He took a deep breath and knocked. Giving a polite amount of time to wait between knocks, he opened the storm door and knocked on the pale yellow door. A wooden sunflower swung side to side on a hook. He thought it was an odd decoration for the middle of winter but he's seen stranger things.

No answer.

He looked over to the minivan. While he could see the outline of Grace's figure, he was comforted in the fact that he couldn't make out who she was. To newcomers, this town appeared to be a shoddier, beach version of Pleasantville, but Mark had witnessed incidents from his youth that were risky enough to make the front page of any big-city newspaper.

He pushed the door open slightly with his boot, the creak that resulted was enough to alert anyone inside the home that someone had entered. There was nothing alarming at first sight, just a typical female kitchen, with pale yellow curtains dancing over the small window above the sink and a basket filled with dried up clementines and browned bananas. A huddle of fruit flies swarmed around the bowl.

Mark heard the sobs coming from the back room; they were deep, breathy sobs that accelerated the closer he got. He pushed the door to the back room open and saw Mackenzie Waterford crumpled in the middle of the floor, hair spilling down her back and shielding the sides of a face that rested in the heels of her hands. She was deep in a fit of tears, her body moving to the rhythm of her struggling breath. Her emotions were so intense, a tornado could've ripped through the house and Mackenzie would still be sitting like a puddle in the middle of the floor, disarray swirling around her.

Mark cleared his throat as he lightly knocked his knuckles on the doorframe one time. The only movement that Mackenzie made was the shuddering that ran through her body, a ripple of emotion creating jerky movements in her thin frame. Mark could see the bumps of her spine through the thin beige sweater that clung to her back.

"Excuse me?" Words finally surfaced, his mouth dry from the sight of such a young girl enduring so much pain. He reminded himself that she was the bad guy here, the suspect in an unlikely case of a missing woman.

The girl dropped her hand from her face and twisted her body toward the door, contorting herself into a pretzel. Her face was mottled with blotches, her eyes rimmed with red, the skin of her lips dry and cracked. In the midst of her meltdown, she still looked beautiful as the browns of her eyes sparkled behind a glaze of tears, real, true emotion cutting through her like a hurricane and leaving her body as the aftermath of the storm. A tiny part of Mark sympathized with the girl; he thought about Rain and how innocent she still was.

"Who are you?" She sniffed and wiped her nose with the back of her hand, which made her look like a toddler.

"I'm a friend of Jenny's. My name is Sam." The name slipped from his lips. "Do you know where she is?" Mark unleashed the question, matter-of-factly, as if they hadn't been searching for the answer to that question for days now. He stepped forward, testing her nerves. "Is everything okay?"

"I've never heard her talk about you, Sam. How does she know you? Let me guess . . . were you another one of her boyfriends? She seemed to have no problem getting around," Mackenzie hissed. She turned her back to him again before using all her effort to push herself up from the floor.

"No, we're just good friends. I met her when she first moved here." He hadn't had enough time to plot out a backstory. "I saw her car in the driveway and thought I'd stop by and say hi . . . check on her art work."

"Fuck her artwork!" She stood, using a thin arm to strike through the painting on the easel. The canvas went flying across the small room, bouncing off a dresser and landing on its back, the eyeball looking straight up to the ceiling.

All Mark could think about was that they caught her at a good time—she was drunk and angry. He had to get what he could out of her.

"Did something happen?"

"Did something happen? She was a lying whore! That's what happened!"

Mark didn't miss the word *was*, skim past her lips.

"I'm sorry, what's your name? Maybe you can tell me what happened. I'm sure we can sort this all out."

THE IMAGE of Jenny's face was imprinted on Mackenzie's mind forever. Just before the woman fell, Mackenzie had recognized something in her eyes, a longing that had seemed to be cured, and a peaceful unity that had bound the two of them together as their eyes connected one last time. She had been angry, furious at Jenny, but she hadn't meant to drive her near the edge of the cliff. It was an accident.

Mackenzie had found something in Jenny that she had longed for her entire life and since she met her, for the first time in her life she felt like she was home. She loved Jenny and felt like she could aspire to be a better person when she was in the presence of the woman. She didn't get that with her own mother and father; she'd never even had a friendship that had bloomed the way theirs had in such a short amount of time, and she couldn't describe it as anything but an undying friendship love. Her own mother never looked at her with the adoration that Jenny looked at her with, even after she excelled in every sport, aced every test and pushed every limit when it came to being the best. Maybe she had been striving for external desires and trying to fill the void in her life all along when Jenny seemed to fill that void instantaneously, like she had flipped a switch.

When they'd reached the top of Donovan Cliff, Mackenzie had been ready to unleash her anger on Jenny. She had gone along with the small talk on the hike up so she could get her alone and get the real story. As painful as she imagined it would sound when the answer hit her ears, she wanted a reason for Jenny's affair with her father. She wanted to hear it from her, and to know exactly why she was willing to break up their friendship and tear her parents apart.

The high peak of the cliff had been closed due to the icy rocks that were deemed too risky for hikers, so they settled on the shorter peak, which still offered a view worthy of painting.

"I want you to see this view. It's beautiful. Totally paint-worthy," Mackenzie said as they maneuvered their boots through the snow-covered branches that led to the top, just steep enough to get their heart rates up, but not quite steep enough to pose any danger.

"How did you find out about this place?" Jenny asked, clutching her art bag across her chest and balancing it on one hip.

"My mom used to take me here. Before Penny was born, she'd take me up here every spring, on the first nice day of the season. It became kind of a tradition of ours."

"That sounds nice. Were you always close to your mom?" Jenny asked, her words sounding sullen. Mackenzie imagined that she was feeling jealous of the woman who was married to the man she was having an affair with.

"Yeah, my mom's the best." She wanted to rub it in her face, push her buttons. "I couldn't imagine having anyone better. She and my dad are so good together, too." She pushed the knife deeper. Instead of responding, Jenny remained silent, the only sound meandering between the two of them was the crunching of snow and crackling of branches.

Mackenzie wondered if Jenny was onto the fact that she knew about the affair, as there was always an ongoing banter between the two of them as they sifted through little life lessons and the future. Jenny had regularly talked about going to Paris to drink coffee in cafes and paint on the plush grass of the cathedral lawns that overlooked the city, while Mackenzie would speak of her dreams of getting into Harvard, hoping to use her education to run a successful business. She didn't know what type of business yet, but she knew that she wanted to be in charge. As opposite as the two of them were, they were like magnets when they were together, balancing out each other's energies.

"Wow, you weren't kidding. This place is beautiful!" Jenny stood there for a moment, taking it all in. The height and panoramic view of the mountains made her feel like a tiny dot on the earth's landscape. A light breeze blew in the wind, a signal that the gray sky was soon ready to bring on a storm.

"It is, isn't it?" Mackenzie sidled up to her, their two figures looking like puzzles pieces clicking together.

"I think I could draw this. I think the coloring is right. This could be my new big piece," Jenny said as she went to work pulling out her sketchpad.

"Of course you can, you can do anything you set your mind to." Mackenzie sat on a rock and faced Jenny, the backdrop of the mountains framing her silhouette. The gray sky, snow-topped trees and rocky hills spotted with dots of white and green complimented her rosy cheeks and deep-brown eyes. "Isn't that what you always told me?"

"That's right, kiddo. You can do whatever you set your mind to," Jenny said as she laid down a tarp and rested the sketchpad on her lap, taking in the setting that she was about to transfer to her paper.

"I guess you took that quite literally when you decided to have an affair with my father," Mackenzie hissed.

Jenny's already colossal eyes grew even wider and rounder, making her look like a blue-eyed owl. She was speechless and cornered. Just the way Mackenzie wanted her.

"Mackenzie . . . it's not like that."

"It's not like what? I *saw* you. I saw you right on school grounds!" She stood, the height of her body towering over Jenny, who looked like she was shrinking into the earth.

"I'm sorry. It's just—"

"It's what, Jenny? What?" She crouched down in front of her, leaning so close that Jenny could breathe in the cold breath that was emitting from Mackenzie's mouth. Jenny started to back off, her eyes darting side to side, suddenly appearing nervous.

"Kenzie, let me explain." She reached for the girl's shoulders, her gloved hands grabbing for the puffy black jacket, her head tilting slightly.

"Don't touch me!" She used both hands to flip Jenny's arms off of her, the force causing Jenny to stumble backwards, catching herself on one of the rocks.

"Mackenzie, you're overreacting. I can explain!"

"There is nothing to explain. You tried to break up my family. How do you think it feels to see your parents get ripped apart by someone you trusted?" She walked toward Jenny, her voice shaking as the words came out chopped.

"I know I know. But, I-I was doing it for a reason."

The two were dancing, Mackenzie in the lead as they moved closer to the edge of the cliff. Mackenzie saw the look on Jenny's face as the realization hit. She saw her eyebrows crumple into two messy caterpillars, her forehead crease into multiple lines closing in on her hairline. She watched as Jenny reached for the silver tree necklace, a nervous tick she had.

Jenny's boot crunched on the cracked pieces of ice, then moved onto a polished slab as she slipped and reached forward, her body hitting the snow that curved off the edge of the cliff. For one instant, her hands grasped for the edge, but the chunk of the snow gave way and with it, her body descended several feet toward the rocky, ice-covered ground.

JUST AS MACKENZIE's emotions were starting to simmer down, Mark's phone vibrated in his pocket.

"Sorry, I'll be quick. It's probably my son," he said to Mackenzie, as if he had to explain himself. He stepped out into the hallway, his boot crunching on something. Cat kibble.

"What the heck is going on in there!" Grace's voice punctured the speaker on the phone.

"I just got her to start talking. Hold tight. Remember the code."

"But, what was she doing in there?"

"Crying."

"Crying? What the—"

"That's what I'm trying to figure out. So, before she gets antsy and decides to run off, let me get back to work. I'll keep you posted."

He heard Grace let out a frustrated growl as he hung up.

CHAPTER TWENTY-FOUR

Anthony Waterford looked both ways before he crossed Main Street. He watched as a green pickup truck swerved from side to side as it pulled out of a side street and onto the road, surpassing the speed limit by a long shot. He clutched his bag close to his body and walked with his head down, eyes peeking out from underneath a Patriot's hat he had just purchased at the convenience store. Nobody would recognize him, especially in this hat. A true-blue born and raised Bridgeton boy and he'd never gotten into the sports teams that New Englanders worshipped. Except for the occasional game of racquetball at the club, the only games that he watched were Mackenzie's soccer matches.

Alebury Avenue hadn't changed much since he was a kid. The fire chief still lived at the top of the street, with the most decorated hydrant in town just outside his house, clearly marked and shoveled out in the winter months. The smell of the ocean stretched across the street and permeated onto Alebury, an added bonus for those who resided on the street. Miss Streeter still lived in the small white house that was set far back on the land, an unusual blueprint for a town that had very few yards. Rumor had it that Miss Streeter's house was a country club back in the day.

As he saw a car pulling into the driveway next to Jenny's, he tucked his head even lower, increased his step and clutched the bag tight to his side. He had to get rid of the sketchpad burning a hole in his pocket. Detective McKenna had already gotten her hands on it, and appeared oddly curious. He couldn't risk anyone else seeing it. He was hoping that Jenny wouldn't be home and he could just wedge the pad between the doors and leave, ridding himself of the mistake that he had made, the can of worms that he'd opened. But her car was there; he would be stuck getting into a conversation he didn't want to get into.

"Geez, Jenny," he said as he trudged through the snow that was piled far too high in the driveway. She needed to either find a real man or invest in a snow blower. He looked down at the fresh tire marks.

"Excuse me, sir?" The voice broke into his thoughts, startling him. He tried to keep walking, pretending he hadn't heard it. "Sir?" The voice got closer. The neighbor was walking toward him. He could either run or fake like he was deaf. He didn't have the heart to do either.

"Yes?" He looked up at the man. He was bundled in one of those long peacoats like his own father used to wear, clutching a bag from the Bridgeton Marketplace.

"Pardon my interruption, but I was just curious. Do you know the young lady who lives next door?" He tipped the rim of his hat up a tad, revealing a set of kind brown eyes.

"Well, not really. I'm just dropping something off to her. This is thirteen Alebury, right?" Anthony looked toward the mailbox, playing dumb.

"Yes, you certainly have the right address. I hadn't seen the young lady in a few days, so I was a bit worried. I was going to shovel her driveway, but my wife frowns upon that because of my heart condition." He motioned toward the car with his free hand. "But, I see that she has returned." He adjusted his hat again before turning on a heel, leaving behind a kind smile. "Well, I better get this ice cream inside to my wife before it melts." He let out a boisterous laugh, his eyes creasing into two slits.

"She may have been on vacation. I believe she's a teacher," Anthony said as the man walked up his freshly shoveled walkway. He let out a deep breath and walked up the steps.

He looked in the window; the house was dark except for the pool of light that spilled out from the back room. He remembered how Jenny called it her "inspiration room" and the way she came to life when she sat at that easel. He hoped she was sitting in front of the easel now, moving on with her life and painting images that inspired her. That's all he had wanted for her. If they'd met in another lifetime, maybe they would've had a chance to travel together and follow those dreams he had lost so many years ago. She still had a chance to do the things she wanted in life, to paint massive murals that would draw crowds; she was still young enough to start a family of her own, to find a man who loved her for her quirky vision of the world. She'd had a brief hold on him, but he knew that he could never leave Beth, or his girls. It had been a short chapter in his life that made him appreciate what he had at home.

He had contemplated setting the sketchpad between the doors quietly and leaving, hoping Jenny was so caught up in her project that she wouldn't hear the creak of the old door. But, he knew he had to make an honest exit out of her life; it was only fair. After three knocks, Anthony made his way in. It wasn't unusual for Jenny to be caught in the midst of a painting, serenaded by some new age music blasting through the house.

"Jenny? Jen? I just wanted to drop something off, I understand if you don't want to talk to me," he said as he eased his way down the hallway, waiting for her overly friendly cat to jump out from somewhere and demand rubs. "I'll just hand this over and leave." He slid the sketchpad out of his messenger bag and pushed open the door to Jenny's inspiration room.

A few loose sheets of paper slid out as his hand went limp and the sketchpad hit the floor.

CHAPTER TWENTY-FIVE

GRACE CLENCHED HER FISTS AND PRESSED HER FEET ONTO THE FLOOR OF the van, sliding the mat forward. "Ugh! Okay, now I really can't take it!"

After she saw a man walk into Jenny's house, she had given up on what little patience had been restraining her in the car. Aside from being a control freak, she didn't want anything to happen to Mark on his mission to help her. It was her vision that had led to the tangle they were now trying to unravel. No way in hell was she letting Mark go down for this.

She pulled the door handle and heard the locks click. "What the fuck!" She banged her elbow into the door. "Damn child fucking safety locks." She manually pulled the lock up and watched it slide up and down one more time like a turtle's head poking out of its shell. She finally left it alone long enough to allow it to stay up, then opened the door so fast she nearly fell into the street.

Knowing she had no time to spare, Grace marched her way up the stairs and into the house. It hadn't taken her long to memorize the layout of the house, and she knew from the light in the window that the art room was where the action was happening. *Wouldn't that be fitting*, she thought to herself. *A crazy teenager goes rogue and murders three, leaving splatters of blood on the paintings that decorated the space.* She scolded herself for letting her imagination get the best of her once again. When she pushed the door open, she saw three sets of eyes staring at her: Mackenzie's brown eyes rimmed with red, Anthony's blue eyes brimming with confusion, and Mark's hazel eyes filling with a mixture of warning and appreciation.

"Detective McKenna?" Anthony turned toward her, papers scattered at his feet.

"Hi, Anthony. Mackenzie." She nodded to both of them.

"Dad, what are you doing here? And, you're that detective that came to our house." Mackenzie looked like she'd seen a ghost.

"Well, I think we all need to explain why we are here," Mark said, throwing himself in the middle of traffic.

"Who the hell are you?" Anthony shot him a seething look.

"Chill out, Dad, he's a friend of Jenny's. He just came by to see her."

"Well, I guess I'll point out the obvious." Grace walked farther into the room. Her presence made Mackenzie shrink, sinking deeper into the sloppy couch she was sitting on. "Mackenzie, why are you at your art teacher's house in the middle of the night? That's a bit odd."

"But—"

"I'm not finished." Grace cut her off, the volume of her words escalating.

"Anthony, you're here—at your daughter's art teacher's house—with . . ." She picked up the fallen sheets of paper at his feet as he stood frozen like a statue. "A sketch that coincidently matches the one on the floor over there. I have to say . . ." She held the sketch of the eye up to Anthony's profile. "These eyes look a lot like yours." He dropped his head. "But why on earth would Mackenzie's art teacher be drawing a picture of you?" She analyzed the photo. "It's a pretty good one, too. I imagine a lot of time was put into these sketches."

"It's because he was having an affair with my teacher." Mackenzie spit the answer out, force and disgust pushing the words forward.

"Mackenzie, let me explain." Anthony looked around the room. "Really, though, this is a family matter. Can we please have some privacy?" Anthony's eyes darted from Grace to Mark.

"Technically, Anthony, you're breaking and entering on private property, so—"

"Grace, don't." Mark interrupted. Grace glared at him.

"Wait, you two know each other?" Anthony asked.

"You know what? I'm sick and tired of people having to *explain* things to me!" Mackenzie rocketed herself up off the couch and for once Grace was grateful for the girl's diversion.

"Mackenzie, listen! Sit down, now!" Anthony's voice boomeranged off the walls.

Angst dripped from Mackenzie's face. She backed up slowly and sunk into the corner of the couch, pulling her knees into her chest, her body retiring into an upright fetal position. "Jenny isn't who you think she is."

Anthony took a deep breath, pulled the wooden stool away from the easel and sat down, resting his feet on the crossbars below.

"Your mother didn't want you to know. I shouldn't be telling you this." He dropped his head in his hands, using his fingertips to massage his forehead.

"What, Dad? Just tell me. Did the letter from Harvard come? I didn't get in, did I? But what does that have to do with Jenny. Were you having an affair with her so she'd write me a good recommendation?"

Grace leaned against the wall and Mark sat on the edge of the couch, braced for the drama that was unfolding before them.

"No, no, honey . . . that's not it." He took another deep breath, then took her hands in his, the nerves evident in the shaking of his grip. "Mackenzie, I'm sorry. I don't know how to say this." He paused. "Jenny Silva is your biological mother."

Mackenzie froze with shock, her frame erect and unmoving, her mouth agape and her eyes searching. She tried to speak, opening her mouth slightly, then hearing the echo of her father's words in her head she closed her mouth again. And then, as realization struck, her face crumpled into a series of different emotions, her brown eyes fluttering and welling with tears as she gasped for breath and fell to the floor in a heap.

"No! No! No!" The one syllable was all she was capable of saying.

"Honey, we were going to tell you when you were eighteen. I'm sorry. Beth is still your mother and she always will be, I promise you that. She loves you and I love you, and I'm sure Jenny can still be a part of your life."

"No, No!" Mackenzie continued to gasp, on the verge of hyperventilating.

Anthony slipped off the stool and kneeled before her, using a hand to rub her back. Remembering that he had an audience, he looked behind at Grace and Mark pleading with them to give them a moment alone.

"WELL, that's not how I expected this evening to turn out," Grace said as she breathed in the cold air on the small back patio.

"Yeah, you can say that again," Mark said, taking in the disarray of flowerpots that were scattered around, some tipped over and others covered so high in snow that they looked like a sculpture. "We're not done, though—you know that, right?"

"Of course." Grace jammed her hands deep into her pockets. "We have a body to find."

"I have another question." Mark's face was flushed from the cold air. "Where was Jenny's car this whole time?" He stabbed his hands into his pockets. "I mean, this is a small town. How many people do you know who drive VW Bugs?"

"No clue. But we're about to find out."

"Do you think we should leave for a while, give them time alone?" Mark asked.

"Absolutely not." Grace turned to him. "I know what you're thinking. I can imagine how heartbreaking it would be to get the news that Mackenzie just did, but you have to remember—she's a suspect. Whatever happened to Jenny Silva was Mackenzie's doing. If we leave now, the girl may run. We can't risk that."

~

THERE WERE SO many emotions surging through Mackenzie at one time that she wasn't sure if she could speak or move properly. She imagined this was what it felt like to be paraplegic, unable to control any mobility. It had been ten minutes since her father had told her the news and she still couldn't manage to sort out any type of sense in her brain. Her entire life she had been told that she was just like her father; she had his natural tendencies, even the way they walked was similar. It didn't make sense.

"But why, why would you adopt me?" Mackenzie had asked, remembering the days when her mother walked around with her pregnant belly, glowing with the anticipation of Penny coming into the world.

"We thought your mother couldn't conceive," Anthony told her. "All the doctors had said the odds were against us. So, we did the research and we found the most beautiful baby in the world—you." He pushed a piece of hair behind her ear. "Penny was a miracle, an added bonus to the beautiful life we already had with you, Mackenzie. We never for a moment loved her any more than we loved you."

He told Mackenzie the story of her arrival into their lives, how they flew to California, eager to meet their new baby girl and take her home. He told her about how Beth documented every moment on camera, not wanting to miss a beat of any of her first moments. Mackenzie had only been two days old when her parents met with the adoption agent and signed the paperwork. Her biological mother, Jenny Silva, had opted for a closed adoption, not revealing any of the detail of her conception. The only thing they knew was that she was very young. Too young to take on the role of motherhood. "Mackenzie, it was just the three of us for all those years, and we were happy. So happy. And then your mother miraculously got pregnant with Penny and—"

"But, I thought . . . I always thought I had mom's eyes and your mannerisms," Mackenzie said, suddenly sounding like a little girl trying hard to fit in.

"Honey, you do. You are just like me!" He got excited for a moment, squeezing her hands harder. "And you happen to have the same wide-set brown eyes as your mother. Science is one thing, true family is another. You are a hell of a lot smarter than any of us." He paused, letting the joke make its way to Mackenzie, spreading a smile across her face. "And you *are* our family. You always will be. I don't care who you turn out to be, you will always be our family. If you don't get into Harvard—which is highly unlikely—you will still be our family."

The question that had been in the back of Mackenzie's mind rose to the surface. "But, why Jenny, Dad? Why did you cheat on Mom with Jenny?"

"Honey, there is no logical explanation for it. I guess a part of me wanted to feel young again. Jenny did that for me. And more than anything, I loved how much of an interest she took in your life. If it weren't for her being at your soccer game with her bag full of paintings and supporting you the way she did, I'd have never even spoken to her." He swiped a hand through his hair and took a breath before continuing. "I didn't know she was your biological mother. I should've guessed, by the way she brought out this other side in you. And then, things just spiraled out of control. She told me that if I didn't leave Beth and become a family with you and her, then she would cause damage to our family. I was afraid that she would hurt you, or come after your mother," he said. "She threatened to tell you she was your biological mother. I had hoped she'd calm down, forget about it all and just be happy to remain being your mentor, maybe set up a date in the future where we sat you down and told you the truth. I knew Beth would have been hesitant at first, maybe feeling a little intimidated by your biological mother entering the picture, but I thought I could work on her and she'd come around. But Jenny just kept getting more and more crazy, and the threats escalated. I'm sorry, Mackenzie, this didn't turn out good for anyone. God knows what she's going to do now. She's probably plotting some scheme somewhere. I'm so afraid that one night she is going to break in with a gun or something and hurt our family."

CHAPTER TWENTY-SIX

THE CALL CAME THE DAY BEFORE CHRISTMAS, ONLY A DAY AFTER Mackenzie found out that Jenny was her biological mother. A body had been found at the bottom of Donovan's Peak by two daredevil hikers with the proper cold weather gear to keep them warm in the low temperature. The victim had been described as a young, light-haired female wearing a red hat and gloves. In addition to the body, a few pieces of paper had been found damp and runny from the snow they'd been sitting in for days.

"Hey, Grace, didn't you have me run a report on a Silva recently?" Joe had asked as she headed out the door to respond to the call. Grace was caught off guard.

"Yeah, I was doing a bit of follow-up on some traffic violations," she said.

"Hmmm . . . okay, kid," Joe crossed his arms and leaned back in his chair, a knowing smile spreading across his face.

Just hours before they got wind of the discovered body, Mackenzie had told Anthony, Mark and Grace the story from start to finish, surrounded by Jenny Silva's artwork in the tiny little room where she found her inspiration. She admitted her anger toward Jenny, admitted to starting a fight, but she'd had no intention of Jenny falling back-

210

ward off the cliff. She had been scared, frightened to tell the police, not wanting to ruin her chances of getting into Harvard. "It was an accident," were the words that she repeated over and over again as she hid her face in her hands. "I never meant to hurt her, I swear."

"Well, unfortunately, Mackenzie, you are going to need to come down to the station. Technically, you witnessed the death of someone and you didn't call the police. The fact that you were driving Jenny's car is a whole other story."

"Wait, you were driving Jenny's car?" Anthony interjected.

"I just took it to the party. I brought it right back here."

"But where has the car been since that day on the cliff? It certainly wasn't parked in our driveway," said Anthony, suddenly suspicious of his daughter's intentions.

"I-I was scared. So, I parked it in a lot over in Greensdale. At the Price Chopper."

"And you decided to take it out for a spin tonight?" Anthony's voice took on the role of scolding father again.

"I didn't know what to do. Her keys were in her bag on the cliff."

Mackenzie was no longer the confident young girl bathed in perfection. She was stuttering and faltering under pressure. She had taken on an entirely different persona. She was a weak little bird and for the first time, Grace felt like she was human.

THE CAR RIDE home was silent, except for the sound of freezing rain bouncing off the windshield of Anthony's Subaru. When they pulled into the driveway, Mackenzie's heart dropped, creating an unrelenting heat in her stomach.

Anthony looked straight ahead at the home that he shared with his wife and two daughters. "We're going to have to tell your mother the whole story, there's no way around it."

Before Mackenzie could respond, Penny opened the door and stood on the front porch, shielded from the sleet that was coming down in sheets. She jumped up and down, motioning for them to come into the house. A big grin was spread across her face, a hint of mystery in her eyes as if she had a big secret she was about to unleash.

"What about Penny?" Mackenzie said softly.

"Penny is your little sister and she always will be. Nothing will change."

"But does she know that I'm not her *real* sister?"

"Don't even say that, Mackenzie. And no, she doesn't know."

The two walked slowly to the door in spite of the hard rain that pelted them, like a punishment that they deserved.

"Kenzie! Daddy! Come quick, come quick!" Penny yelled, the excitement bubbling out of her as she jumped up and down.

For the first time in days, Mackenzie offered up a bittersweet smile. She had seen the little girl grow up, had been there for all of her firsts; she'd seen more of a little girl who wasn't biologically her sister than her own biological mother had seen of her.

"What's all the excitement about?" Anthony asked as Penny tugged on his hand and Mackenzie's, pulling them into the house. Beth stood in the doorway, hands on her hips and a smile sprawled across her face.

"We were gonna wait, but this little girl has trouble keeping secrets," Beth said, as she tousled Penny's hair. Mackenzie and Anthony looked at each other, a silent gesture symbolizing the secret they shared.

Penny led the four of them through the house.

"Okay, close your eyes!" Beth said before they entered the doorway to the kitchen. Anthony and Mackenzie obliged, still feeling the aftershock of the truth they'd just exchanged.

"SURPRISE!" Penny yelled as she held the envelope out in front of her like a sign. A cloud of crimson colored balloons floated behind her, tied to a chair. Anthony and Mackenzie slowly opened their eyes, hesitance fluttering in their lids.

"Wha-what is it?" Mackenzie asked.

"It's from HARVARD, silly!" Penny pushed the envelope into Mackenzie's hands before pressing herself between Anthony and Beth. Anthony grabbed Beth's hand, his eyes expanding wide, in clear shock that she put on this dog and pony show before Mackenzie found out the results of her application. What if she didn't get in? Beth just smiled back at him, as calm as can be, her brown eyes greeting his with pride and self-confidence. Mackenzie noticed that something inside her mother had changed; she seemed to stand taller, filling out her clothing better. As of late, she had been smiling more and worrying less.

Mackenzie began to tear open the envelope, her eyes sealed on Anthony's and a half-smile spread across her lips. She slid the packet out, scanned it and appeared to be absorbing the words on the paper. The three of them gripped hands and watched intently, for what seemed like hours. Mackenzie flipped to the back page, then the front again, before making eye contact with each of them, one by one.

"I . . . I. . ." Tears began to well up in her eyes, making them look like two glossy brown marbles. "I got in." Her words lacked the expected shine, before it really sunk in. "I got into Harvard!" Tears flooded her eyes, seeping into the open lips of her smile.

Her family gathered her in their arms forming one big ball that jumped and cried tears of joy and laughter. It was the most joyous moment of her life.

CHAPTER TWENTY-SEVEN

"GEEZ, WHY WOULD ANYONE WANT TO COME OUT HERE IN THE MIDDLE of winter?" Grace asked Mark as they trudged through the snow. A layer of ice and rain had formed on top like icing on a cake. Each time she attempted to take another step, she struggled to get her boot back up, her sole catching on the sharp-edged layers.

"Die-hard hikers," Mark said, crunching through the snow beside her. "And apparently, women who get into fights with their biological children and get backed off a cliff."

"Funny. Hey, maybe you should walk in front of me so you can create the path. You know, make it a little easier for me." Grace held the flashlight in the direction the hikers had designated as their location.

"Anything for you." Mark took the lead. "So, what do you think is going to happen to Mackenzie? I mean, if she admitted the story. Technically, she didn't push Jenny off the cliff—it was an accident. But I'm just a trainer and an officer, I don't know how death accusations work. My job ends at the traffic violation," Mark said, taking cover under the trees to avoid the sleet. It was finally starting to slow down, simmering down to a light sprinkle.

"That depends on what we find at the scene. Speaking of . . . there they are." She didn't hold back from directing the spotlight at the two hikers, who were now huddled under a tree, clearly bored.

"Thank you for waiting around. Officer Connelly will get your statement while I get to work assessing the body," Grace said, entrusting part of her job to Mark. He had been as much a part of the case as she had and as much as Grace didn't want to admit it, the two of them worked well together. They miraculously had that ability to talk shop and everyday life in the same conversation. It was still new, though. She wasn't ready to let go and free herself of the early-relationship worries just yet.

While she was a trained detective, it wasn't often that Grace came so close to lifeless bodies. She could count on one hand the number of times when she'd had to assess a situation like this one. Typically, it was car accidents, and of course there was the case from a few years back when a two-year-old had washed up on shore. It was one of the hardest summers of Grace's life, working twenty-four hours a day to piece together the horrifying crime that had been inflicted on an innocent child. She still had to block the images out of her head every day.

Grace stood over the body, trying to pinpoint anything that was obvious from a distance. Much to her dismay, the inclement weather didn't pause for anyone. Jenny's body was covered in a layer of snow and ice; only a foot and an outstretched arm were evident, and the blonde tips of her hair escaping from a red hat. Grace could see where the hikers had cleared away some of the snow to confirm that what they were seeing really was the dead body of a young woman. She was lucky the hikers were out there, otherwise the body probably wouldn't have been spotted until spring, after the warmth of the sun melted away all the snow. She used a hand to clear off as much snow as she could, without altering the positioning of Jenny's body.

The fact that Grace had learned so much about the woman in such a short time made it more personal, harder to separate from her own life. Jenny Silva wasn't much younger than Grace, her life still ahead of her. When Grace looked at the gloved hand that reached out to the side, all she could think about were Jenny's paintings of sunflowers.

When she saw the tree charm that dangled from Jenny's neck, beneath layers of clothing, she thought about the woman's dedication to the practice of yoga. It was the necklace that she'd seen in her first vision.

Grace started with the head, taking her time to scrutinize every feature, scrape and birthmark. A shimmer of dark-gray eyeshadow was still evident on Jenny's closed lids. She looked peaceful, like she had fallen into a deep slumber. Her body was rigid from the combination of the low temperatures and rigor mortis. One side of her face was pressed into the snow, as if snuggled up against a soft feathery pillow.

Grace could hear Mark's footsteps behind her, could feel his presence. He knew when to keep quiet and let her do her thing, and he knew when to give her the space she needed. They were so good together that even in the midst of inspecting a dead body, that conclusion floated through her mind. She pulled a small square tarp out of her bag and laid it in front of the body. Kneeling in front of Jenny's upper body, she used two hands to peel the woman's head off the snow to check out the appearance of the other side of her face.

"Shit," Grace said as she saw the deep gash crusted with dried blood and dirt, a swirl of red and browns running from the top of Jenny's cheekbone up to the side of her temple. "Mark, can you hand me my camera?" She dropped Jenny's head so it fell to the other side.

"Is that from hitting the side of the cliff?" Mark asked, handing over the small digital camera. The station didn't have the means to hire a professional forensic photographer, so Grace was stuck being her own. She took a few photos, standing at various angles.

"Doesn't look like it," she said, looking up at the cliff overhead. The top of the cliff, where Jenny had presumably fallen from, was about twenty feet up, but there were no signs of protruding, jagged rocks. The rocks were curvy and smooth, spotted with chunks of earth growing between them. "If Jenny Silva fell off that cliff backwards, as Mackenzie was yelling at her, she'd be falling in the air with her back most likely angled outwards or toward the ground. There is no way her head would've collided with the cliff, and there has been at least a layer of snow on the ground for the past week."

"What are you saying, Grace?"

"I'm saying that by the looks of this injury, Jenny Silva took a blow to the head *after* she fell."

"With what, though?"

"My guess would be one of those nice jagged rocks that fall from the cliff every now and then. Easy to conceal . . . look around." Grace turned and looked out at the view at the vast rocky mountainside. "Think we have a chance at finding a rock with blood on it—one that matches the impression in Jenny's head?" She lifted the woman's head again, angling it toward Mark, dried clusters of blood and dirt raised above a background of black and blue.

"Are you saying she wasn't dead on impact?"

Grace looked up at the cliff that was twenty feet above. "I'm saying that she struggled after the fall, but no, I don't think she was dead."

CHAPTER TWENTY-EIGHT

BETH

Surprisingly, I wasn't as nervous as one would expect to be when driving to the police department to confess to a crime. I guess when you murder someone in cold blood, your mind travels elsewhere. By that point, I'd surpassed the normalcy that made a person want so badly to be found innocent. Maybe I'm not normal. Or maybe I'm a woman who is so dedicated to her family, having been born and raised in the South with strict family values. From the time I was very little, my mother implanted the notion that my role as mother and wife was the most important role in my life and I was to do anything and everything to make my family happy, even if it meant sacrificing my own well-being and joy. It started with jealousy and escalated into an anger that boiled within me. Then, it transformed into that need to be mother and wife. I had turned into a fanatical security guard for my own family, a cutthroat sniper who was only interested in maintaining family values, shooting off anyone who interfered with our foursome.

Having taken Mackenzie to Donovan Cliff from the time she was very little, I knew the landscape well, so when I followed Jenny and Mackenzie up there that day, I knew all the places where my presence could be concealed. I tiptoed in a set of man-sized footprints that had already lined the pathway up the hill, then I took a detour. Instead of going to the cliff where they were, I went to the landing, at the bottom of the rocky terrain, where teenagers went to make out and the occasional homeless person took shelter. Certain trees that had been there for years served as the perfect hiding place and I knew that if I sat at the bottom of the cliff, I could hear the voices above and I could gain some insight into their relationship.

I was jealous that Mackenzie was taking this woman to the spot that I had taken her to so many times. The very spot where I had taught her about birds and nature and the simple things in life, something I could claim ownership over. When I heard them arguing, I left. I couldn't take witnessing my daughter's heart breaking any longer, and I didn't want to risk her seeing me there. It was the look on her face when she came home after she went missing that clued me into something. While Mackenzie came off cool and collected in front of the detective, I picked up on a small stutter and a slight trip over her words. The things that only a mother can detect. She was nervous. I knew something had happened with Jenny on Donovan Cliff. A mother can sense these things. So, I went back and did what my own mother would've done for her family: I cleaned up my daughter's mess.

As soon as the detective walked out the front door, I slipped out the back. I hadn't expected Mackenzie to confront Jenny about her father, let alone drive her to the edge of the cliff. When I first saw Jenny's body, flailing on the ground, I considered calling the police and getting her help. But all these thoughts of Mackenzie being locked up in jail flashed before me. I couldn't bear seeing her lose everything she'd worked so hard for. I did what I had to do . . . what any good mother would've done. I dug through a pile of snow until I found a rock that was loose enough to extract from the cold ground. And just as she tried to ask me for help, I turned her face to look the other way. It wasn't fair that she had to see the weapon that would drive her to her death, and I didn't want to be the last face she saw before she left this world. I took a deep breath and thought of my mother's words as I crushed her skull and watched the life slip out of her. After I was sure she had taken her last breath, I threw the rock down the second cliff and walked back in the pre-made footprints.

I decided to drive along the beach route to the station, knowing that this may be the last time that I see the vast, everlasting body of water that marries the edge of Bridgeton Beach. Soon enough, my family will be back to normal. Anthony will find himself another wife, probably someone younger. Maybe *even artsy, like Jenny Silva was. Penny will grow into herself, her precocious personality guiding her through life. And Mackenzie, well, she will go off to Harvard and be a successful doctor or lawyer or business owner. I'm sure the guilt of driving her biological mother off the cliff will silhouette her through life, but knowing that she wasn't the ultimate cause of her mother's death will hopefully appease some of that guilt, freeing her to go on with her own life. She will do big things in this world and maybe, just maybe, she will write to me or send me a video of her graduating from Harvard. Until then, I will watch from behind bars and cheer her on through life, the way a mother and wife is supposed to do.*

EPILOGUE

GRACE HAD NEVER HEARD HER HOUSE SO LOUD WITH ACTIVITY. HER mother was frantically stirring some type of herbal soup on the stove, as her friend Beverly went to work rolling decorative napkins for the Christmas dinner. Grace was putting the finishing touches on the vegetarian casserole that she was about to pop into the oven.

"I should roll eight napkins, right?" Beverly looked up from her project at the table.

"I've got Bill from my pottery class, James and Sheila from yoga, and Connie and Dana from book club. And us three. Yep, that makes eight," Ellen said, the bones in her wrist protruding as she continued to stir the pot.

"Wait, one more. Can you make nine rolls?" Grace asked nonchalantly, sliding the casserole pan into the oven and wiping her hand on the apron that matched her mother's, a wardrobe demand Ellen made every year.

"Oh for Pete's sake, Grace Hope McKenna, Brody is *not* getting a seat at the table this year. I think Connie is allergic to dogs, anyway." Ellen went to work defending the random friends who were joining them for Christmas dinner. For a free-spirited hippy, she had her reservations about animals.

"No, eh . . . actually, I have a friend joining us," Grace said as both women looked up from their tasks, silence hovering around the sentence that just spilled out of her mouth. Grace's social life had always been as active as a sloth hanging from a tree.

"Okay, I'll grab another card for the name tag." Bev got up from her seat and rummaged through the box of crafts that Ellen brought over. "Ahhh, here we go. What's her name?"

"Mark Connolly." Grace had prepared herself for the bomb that she had just dropped. She was well aware that a scene was going to be made.

Ellen dropped the wooden spoon in the pot, her rampant stirs pulling the spoon into a whirlpool. "Grace Hope McKenna—"

"Mom, enough with the middle name."

"My baby has a boyfriend! Did you hear that Bev, my baby has a *boyfriend*!" Ellen's small frame leaped across the kitchen, transforming her body into some type of hippy dance as she circled around Grace, flailing her arms in the air.

"Good job, Grace." Bev continued to focus on writing Mark's name out in cursive scrawl, never the one to show much enthusiasm about anything. That was one of the things that Grace loved about Bev. You always knew she meant what she said because the only time she spoke was when she had something really important to say, unlike all those other people who throw around words uselessly, wasting everyone's energy.

"He's not really a boyfriend. I mean we don't have a label. We just—"

"So, who is he? What does he do? Is he an architect? Maybe he can work on tearing down that wall in the living room that you've always talked about. Or is he . . . ? Hmmm . . . I could really see you with a professor. Someone smart and fancy—"

"He's a cop."

Again, silence hugged her words. "Come on, you're kidding right? But you always said—"

"I know what I always said, Mom."

"Can't always control those things, Ell." Bev threw the words out, clearly hearing the conversation and trying to only put in her two cents when absolutely needed.

"I'm just shocked. You always said you'd never date another cop!"

"Yeah, well, I guess I'm married to my job, so why not date my co-workers," Grace joked, finally feeling okay with the commitment she was forming with Mark. And as if there were a higher power looking out for her, the doorbell rang.

"Saved by the bell," Grace said as she walked toward the door, Ellen following closely behind and Brody sauntering over from his spot in the kitchen, giving up the food smells for a chance to get pets from strangers. Grace was hoping that her mother's hodgepodge of friends showed up before Mark, so Ellen would be distracted by them instead of sniffing around her and Mark's relationship. Instead, they all seemed to arrive at the same time. Mark entered first, a bottle of Cabernet in his hand. He held the door open for the others who had just parked and were making their way to the door, gifts and casserole dishes in tow.

"Mom, this is Mark," Grace said to Ellen, who was standing right behind her, awaiting her introduction.

"It's a pleasure meeting you, Mrs. McKenna." Mark leaned in for a handshake but instead, Ellen reached her outstretched arms around him, pulling him into a tight hug.

"Ellen, please call me Ellen," she said, before looking ahead to greet her other guests. Bill from pottery class and James and Sheila from yoga walked through the threshold, hugging Ellen in greeting and looking at Mark and Grace for introductions.

"You must be the infamous Bill from my mom's pottery class," Grace said as she extended a hand out to the thin man with sandy-brown hair and a pair of black-rimmed glasses.

"It's a pleasure meeting you . . . Grace, is it?" Bill gripped her hand, holding a bottle of bourbon in the other.

In an instant, all of Grace's Christmas spirit melted away as a vision of a girl presented itself the moment their eyes met. Black curls outline the girl's pale face, like tiny corkscrews protruding from her bloodied head. Her eyes were a pale blue outlined in dark wet lashes with smudges of gray eyeliner. They held onto Grace, pulling her into a world of fright and pain. A streak of blood ran from the girl's deeply lined red lips onto a patch of white snow. The man's face also looked familiar to Grace. He looked rough beneath the surface of his smart clothing and glasses, but there was a familiarity in his eyes.

"I, uh, gotta check on the food." Grace dropped his hand and crashed into Mark as she turned away.

"Grace, what's wrong?" Mark pulled her aside, his arms steadying her shaking shoulders. She didn't need to answer; he could see it in her eyes and the way they darted back and forth, the result of an unwanted vision before her. He pulled her into a comforting hug and looked over her head at Bill, who seemed to be in a deep conversation with Ellen, his hands resting on her forearms as he looked at her intently while she talked excitedly about something. Van Gogh rubbed up against her legs and let out a loud meow.

"Do you remember the guy that Officer Jeffries brought into the station last week? The one with the botched rearview who works at Price Chopper?"

"Yeah, why? Jeffries was just on another one of his power trips," Mark said, but he realized that Grace was in a state of shock, angst apparent in her quivering lips as she looked straight ahead at the man.

"Mark, do me a favor? Check the driveway and see what cars are out there."

"Of course."

He peeked out the glass alongside the door as she leaned into his side.

A shaggy green pickup truck was parked behind her Jeep, one of the rearview mirrors dangling off the driver's side.

WANT MORE OF DETECTIVE GRACE MCKENNA?

Find the rest of the series on Amazon today!

Sign up for my newsletter for freebies and updates on new releases.

Up Next:
Buried Secrets

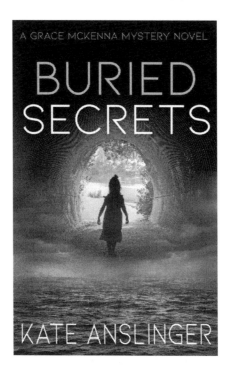

In Buried Secrets, Grace welcomes you back into her world as she tries to piece together another crime in Bridgeton, Massachusetts. When Grace responds to a routine call, she meets Miriam Caverly, an older woman with a past that is less than mundane. Alongside her boyfriend and ex-cop, Mark Connolly, Grace is thrown into a tangle of town secrets that force her to step outside the town's boundaries for answers that she is scared to face. A town drunk with a bitter past, a well-intentioned family strapped with the burden of a tragedy, and a lineup of memorable characters, make Buried Secrets an intense page-turner that follows The Gift in a perfectly aligned chain of events.

IF YOU ENJOYED THIS BOOK...

I would greatly appreciate it if you would leave a review on Amazon, so other readers can discover my work.

Thank you!

ACKNOWLEDGMENTS

This book was really a stretch for me, but much in the same way that Grace McKenna had visions, I had a gut feeling that told me to write it. First and foremost, I'd like to thank those who are always cheering me on. Thank you Rex, for your undying marketing efforts and never being too shy to boast about "your daughter...the author." Love you more. Mom, thanks for being my backbone and always being there for plot and character advice. These twists are for you. Thank you to my husband, "Slinger," who just so happened to walk in the room to offer me a piece of peanut butter fudge. Slinger, your timing is impeccable and your support is appreciated. Thank you Emily June for letting "mommy work" and for always greeting me with the biggest smiles and warmest hugs. I love you to the moon and the stars and the sky. Thanks to my fab editor, Christina Lepre. Your honesty and attention to detail allowed this book to move forward. Maria Aiello, thank you for your expertise and professionalism with the cover design. I told you what I envisioned and you created an exact replica.

A special thank you goes to the police officers that helped me with facts and those tiny little details that make a big difference...Brian Allaire, Dawne Armitstead, and Paul DeLeo. Thanks to the Winthrop Police Department for letting me hangout with you for the day. Jeremy Neas, thanks for your skydiving expertise. Thank you Leahanna Neas for always being my cheerleader and simply being proud...even if I get four traffic violations in one day. Thanks to Christie Conlee for being an avid reader and for bringing me up when I'm down. I eat my olives.

A very special thank you goes to my manager, Kristina Caverly...after thirty years of friendship, you are still my best source of honesty. I love you.

As always, a special thanks goes to my pals at the Winthrop Book Depot, where my imagination comes to life on the page. Harriet Lundberg...thanks for your help with names and Susan and Suzanne Martucci...thanks for being you.

Made in the USA
Middletown, DE
22 September 2023

39052140R10142